Praise for Warren Adler's Fiction

"Warren Adler writes with skill and a sense of scene."
— *The New York Times Book Review* on
The War of the Roses

"Engrossing, gripping, absorbing... written by a superb
storyteller. Adler's pen uses brisk, descriptive strokes that
are enviable and masterful."
— *West Coast Review of Books* on *Trans-Siberian Express*

"A fast-paced suspense story... only a seasoned
newspaperman could have written with such inside
skills."
— *The Washington Star* on *The Henderson Equation*

"High-tension political intrigue with excellent
dramatization of the worlds of good and evil."
— *Calgary Herald* on *The Casanova Embrace*

"A man who willingly rips the veil from political
intrigue."
— *Bethesda Tribune* on *Undertow*

Warren Adler's political thrillers are...

Praise for Warren Adler's Fiona Fitzgerald Mystery Series

"High-class suspense."
— *The New York Times* on *American Quartet*

"Adler's a dandy plot-weaver, a real tale-teller."
— *Los Angeles Times* on *American Sextet*

"Adler's depiction of Washington—its geography, social whirl, political intrigue—rings true."
— *Booklist* on *Senator Love*

"A wildly kaleidoscopic look at the scandals and political life of Washington D.C."
— *Los Angeles Times* on *Death of a Washington Madame*

"Both the public and the private story in Adler's second book about intrepid sergeant Fitzgerald make good reading, capturing the political scene and the passionate duplicity of those who would wield power."
— *Publishers Weekly* on *Immaculate Deception*

THE DAVID EMBRACE

by Warren Adler

STONEHOUSE PRODUCTIONS

Produced by Stonehouse Productions

Published Stonehouse Productions
www.warrenadler.com

Cover design by David Ter-Avanesyan/TER33 Design

Cover image, *"'David' by Michelangelo"*, by *Jörg
Bittner Unna*, used under *CC BY 3.0*, with changes made
to the original image's tone, contrast and cropping.

For Sunny

Contents

Chapter 1

The man stood on the escarpment overlooking the little bay at Cap Ferrat, binoculars to his eyes, braced against the gnarled and stunted tree. He studied the boat, its bright work ablaze like a necklace of glistening diamonds as it captured the fire of the late afternoon sun.

The passport in his pocket with Her Majesty's Government coat of arms read John Champion, not his own name but one taken from his grab bag of aliases and forged documents of various nationalities. The picture on the passport as he looked now in real life showed his hair blond, dyed for the occasion. Age on the document was given as thirty-seven, two years shy of the truth. Eyes were shown as blue. Close enough. His were paler, more like Wedgwood.

He marveled at the boat's more-than-a-hundred feet of sleek beauty, its streamlined profile low on the water, the broad beam and yards of afterdeck. But aesthetics were not the issue here.

For the umpteenth time, he studied the area abaft the wheelhouse, a sheltered oasis for sunbathers, knowing that this, hopefully, could be his target area, the place to where Max Hamilton escaped when the cabin heat penetrated his walrus body and became intolerable for his bulk. He was, Champion had learned, allergic to air-conditioning, a fortuitous fact. It was August, blazing hot, the perfect environment for his plan.

For the past week, he had observed Hamilton in the still-hot wee hours, eschewing the air-conditioned cabin below. He had advertised in interviews that the cold air wreaked hell on his sinuses. Odd, Champion thought, how people signed their death warrants.

Hamilton lay supine on the cushioned bench along the rail, his big naked belly rising like an airbag berm over his khaki shorts, inflating and deflating as he sucked in and expelled the hot, moist, herb-scented air. Above him in the bridge house with no line of sight to the sunbathing area, the captain and mate spelled each other on the watch while the two deckhands presumably slumbered below decks in a forward compartment.

In the five months he had been researching and stalking Hamilton from continent to continent, this was the venue that offered the greatest opportunity for accidental death. The sea was nature's perfect killing instrument. He had studied the yacht's lines and construction, imaging on his computer the configuration of its cabins and the bowels of its engine room.

He had concluded finally that he had a single viable option: to board the boat as it cruised, do the deed, and disappear. This was the kind of challenge that excited him. In his business, planning and logistics were everything. His life depended on them.

He had been painstaking in his effort to devise a method that was quick, simple, soundless, and above all, would leave no trace of intrusion. The challenge totally mobilized his imagination, and finally a plan had emerged. The plan, by his computation, had only a forty percent risk rate, which illustrated, once again, why he was so highly compensated and prized by Parker.

"You are our star," Parker had assured him. He distrusted the compliment. Parker, the broker of death, wore ten faces, none real.

A mountain-climbing school in Zurich provided the only real boarding instrument, a power gun that could send up a hook to wrap around an outcropping on the deck or the deck rail itself, having strength to hold his weight for the climb to the deck. He had the metal hook wrapped in a rubber coating so as to leave no telltale signs along the chrome deck rail. In these two elements were the highest percentages of the margin of error.

For weeks he practiced the hooking method on deserted buildings and moored yachts in deserted marinas. Finding a moving target unobserved proved almost daunting, although he took practice shots at slow-moving freight trains that rolled through rural areas in England and France.

Wearing a wet suit, he conditioned himself for long-distance swimming. By now, he was as ready as he ever would be. He was satisfied that, within the realm of the doable, forty percent was left to chance.

But even that percentage was less than reliable. Chance was a whore. It could never be trusted.

Chapter 2

As Angela drove north on the long lonely drive toward the French Riviera, memories of her stay in Florence offered a delicious way to hasten the time, a private entertainment, a tale of bonding, exhilarating conversation, and, above all, the startling and perhaps life-changing "incident."

It had occurred on the fourth and last day of her Florence visit with her irrepressible Aunt Emma. There was Emma in her sensible low-heeled, laced shoes, her hip-hugging white slacks and silk print blouse suitably festooned with necklaces of gold and the accompanying bands of bracelets. Around her neck, she wore a solid persimmon-red flowing scarf, a ploy to take the emphasis off the crinkles marring her skin, looking like reflattened, rumpled paper.

And she, Angela, in her longish crepe skirt, open sandals, and cotton blouse unfastened to a third button showing the upper rounds of good breasts, her raven hair brushed off her face and done in a braided knot, and a short ponytail held in place by a black ribbon.

It wasn't as if they had saved for last the Galleria dell'Accademia to see the Michelangelos, but each time that they made the attempt to enter, the long line outside exposed to the hot sun had daunted them, and they had retreated.

Now, of course, they had little choice. You couldn't possibly leave Florence without seeing Michelangelo's David, the real thing, not the replicas, not the miniatures sold in almost every tourist knickknack shop in the town, or the one shamelessly displayed in the shopping mall of Caesar's Palace in Las Vegas.

They had been two very ordinary looking tourists, the distinguished older lady, her indomitable and favorite aunt, Emma, who had already buried two husbands and was on the verge of acquiring a third—and that did not include reputedly numerous lovers, most still living and some now dead.

And herself, Angela Ford, more than a quarter century her junior—mother of two, wife of wildly successful and wealthy Tom Ford, senior vice president of the Oyster Bay Garden Club, board member of the Long Island Community Benefit League and chairman emeritus of the Junior League, ex-president of the Oyster Bay Library Association, recipient of the Credit to Community Award—on a typical sightseeing holiday, soaking up the great Renaissance culture of Florence.

Emma had been there before, but that was in the sixties, she said, and most of her time then was devoted to romance. Emma, by her own admission, had devoted her entire life to romance, replete with all the fleshly pleasures.

They had dutifully read the guidebooks, researched the remarkable wonders of DaVinci, Botticelli, Bellini, Raphael, Titian, and others whose names they would never dare to pronounce to a Florentine. They had trudged through the cathedrals, piazzas, and museums, bought gold trinkets on the Ponte Vecchio and, pleasurably exhausted with effort and the heat, reposed in the deliciously air-conditioned splendor of their two-bedroom suite at the Grand Hotel with a wonderful view of the gently flowing Arno.

Being with her father's only sister was always a special time for Angela. Lately, they had been separated by distance and Emma's busy other life, which meant that their intercourse was limited to telephone conversations, which greatly inhibited intimacy. Besides, Emma was not a zealous correspondent. At last Angela had the legendary Emma all to herself.

Even at her aunt's advanced age, the middle sixties, her beauty still endured miraculously, and it was well known that she could still throw off the scent that had the capacity to ignite men's lust and set their hearts aflame. This was not secondhand knowledge. Startled and with unsuspecting envy, Angela had confirmed this effect with her own eyes. Being with her exuberant and outrageously enticing Aunt Emma, Angela knew, would be as memorable and exciting as anything Florence had to offer. And it was.

"What possible interest can men still have in this decrepit carcass?" Emma had sighed on their very first night in Florence, standing nude in front of the full-length antique oval standing mirror in Angela's hotel bedroom.

Her curvy tight body, seen from the rear, looked twenty years younger than her chronological age, maybe more, the buttocks still high where the hard rounds met the thighs on which were no trace of cellulite, the waist tight and narrow from that angle, and the back unblemished, the vertebrae faint and straight.

"There stands Auntie fishing for compliments," Angela had remarked, embarrassed by the older woman's daring and trying hard not to show it. Out of respect, she did not offer a rebuke.

But that did not foreclose on Angela's more than casual inspection of her aunt's body as she proceeded to observe the frontal view in the reflection. The narrow waist showed a slight bulge that exercise could not remove, but the breasts still hung with heavy-melon roundness, only slightly dropped from what must have been spectacular youthful orbs, with nipples that continued to look pugnacious in their pink, not brown, areolas.

Between these still-shapely breasts, which Angela suspected might have benefited from the surgeon's knife, although there were no visible scars, Emma wore a jeweled cross. "You wouldn't be displaying yourself if you weren't proud of your body."

"It's my character and experience they're after," Emma said with self-effacing hyperbole, continuing to pose, her hands lightly outlining her body, then coming to rest on the underside of either breast, raising them like an offering. She winked at Angela's image in the mirror. "It baffles me."

If one concentrated on cause and effect, Emma's talk, in those moments when they lay physically exhausted and up to their eyeballs in visual and historical nourishment, one might make a strong case for Emma as the catalyst for the "incident."

They had established this routine after the first day of touring. Shedding their practical sightseeing garments, they had showered the sweat off their bodies in their respective bathrooms, donned terry-cloth robes supplied by the hotel, then munched on the light repast room service had efficiently provided, smoked salmon, caviar with all the trimmings, and a bottle of chilled vintage champagne to split between them.

"And another bottle of the same for additional fortification, just in case," Emma had interrupted as Angela spoke to the room service people on the phone.

"Make that two bottles," Angela said obediently.

A fawning waiter arrived and set up their table, adorned with damask tablecloth, expensive plates, silver and crystal with two red roses in a slender vase. Popping the cork, he poured the first in the older woman's glass and then waited for Emma's decision on its quality.

Emma reached into her robe, lifted the cross from between her breasts, the mounds of which did not fail to catch the attention of the waiter, and proceeded to use the vertical part as a swizzle stick.

Somewhat startled, Angela watched the fizzy bubbles dance over the surface of the liquid as Emma sipped, smacked, and swallowed.

"Bene," she said, smiling upward toward the waiter in what Emma noted was, for her, a perfectly natural seductively languorous movement. The gesture was not lost on the waiter, who showed a slight tremor of the hand as he poured Angela's glass, replaced the bottle, and bowed out of the room.

"You are something, Aunt Emma," Angela marveled

as they picked their way through the food and washed it down with champagne.

Satisfied, and comfortably buzzed by the champagne, they lay side by side on the queen-sized bed in Angela's room. Emma had suggested separate bedrooms instead of sharing, actually insisted, in her remarkably persuasive way.

It was not a question of price. For Emma apparently it had never been a question of price. Angela had just gotten used to having money, although Tom had assured her that they were comfortably fixed years ago.

"I'm too nocturnal, darling," Emma told her, as if to assuage any unintended insult about the private bedrooms. "Getting through the night is the hardest part at my age."

Yet most of their waking nontouring hours were spent in Angela's bedroom.

"Don't you just love this?" Emma asked. "Two girls together, like a slumber party. Isn't it delicious?"

It was indeed and made Angela wonder if she had ever experienced "delicious" in quite the way Aunt Emma had meant it. In Emma's sense, "delicious" had the connotation of forbidden, secret, words that bespoke a world that Angela had rarely glimpsed, perhaps never.

Looking too far inward was something Angela worked hard to avoid. When she had made some attempt at these side excursions and had expressed to Tom the results of such introspection, he had always countered with the idea that "overanalysis" could be dangerous to equilibrium.

Equilibrium had become for Angela the overriding consideration of her life. It meant balance and safety. Not that she had ever felt endangered. So far her life had been lived in a protective cocoon, not exactly sheltered, but far from adventurous. She wondered if she should be disturbed by such an implication. Vaguely, she admitted to herself, she might be missing out on something, but she had not allowed herself to dwell on such a possibility.

Perhaps she had deliberately persuaded her aunt to take this travel jaunt for other reasons besides simple companionship. There she was being overanalytical. Nevertheless, this close proximity to Aunt Emma had the air of some beginning adventure, something… well, something… delicious.

Chapter 3

"It must pass muster," Parker had insisted to Champion through thick, moist lips, the words wrapped in the vapors of his lager breath, as they sat across the table in the seedy little pub in Chelsea on a chilly day in March.

Parker conducted his killing business here, reaching out to his nefarious world from a battered pay-phone booth that housed a telephone that had seen better days. When it rang, it coughed out a scratchy sound unique in the annals of telecommunications. In his business one never used cell phones. The digital world was too dangerous, too transparent. The landline was a neglected communications tool, hardly a blip on law enforcement's high-tech menu.

The pub regulars were so used to its ring's grating cacophony that they paid it little attention, nor did they care. On more than one occasion, Parker would, for whatever reason, refuse to take the call, and the sound would become just another decibel in the background clatter to be ignored.

When he chose to answer, Parker simply waddled back and forth, closing the booth's squeaky-hinged door, spoke for a moment or two, rarely longer, then waddled back to his table to dip his beak in the black stout he favored. His office, by law, kept regular pub hours, open at eleven, shut down for the night at eleven. The people who called knew the schedule.

Considering the murderous reach of the line, it never ceased to amaze Champion how clever Parker had been in setting up his working office on this site. It was as secure as the most secure red phone in any government intelligence office. Who among the authorities would think to bother with a wretched, barely used pay phone in a foul lager-smelling pub?

Of course, Parker had, unbeknownst to the proprietor, installed a tap indicator in the connection, and all operatives communicated with him only via public phones and never mobiles. In all the years of its operation, the tap indicator had, miraculously, never barked. If it had, of course, it would have meant the end of the game.

Parker was a puffy weasel of a man in his fifties, his mousy little eyes hidden behind Coke-bottle lenses. On the table in front of them was Parker's pint of regular, while in reach of Champion's hand was a split of good champagne, his own drink of choice.

With his soiled trench coat open to reveal a tie askew over a wrinkled white shirt with the top button missing and a chalk-striped suit, the lapels polished by wear, Parker did not look like a prime prospect from central casting to play the villainous matchmaker between interested parties and, whatever the euphemism one preferred, a professional kill er.

"Above all, we must keep to the standard. That is essential."

Parker always spoke in deep-throated elliptical sentences, making the information imparted seem profound, as if they were engaging in work crucial to the benefit of mankind. There was prissiness in it as well. From the beginning of his association, Parker had struck Champion as a cartoon character in a comic strip with a very dark story line.

"Without the slightest effluvia of suicide," Parker said, lifting his pint and taking a deep sip, leaving a foamy mustache above his thick lips. "It mustn't look as if he skipped out on things. The clarions will ring."

Champion had heard Parker's reasoning on this point ad infinitum. The message was burned into his mind along with his entire lecture on the subject of assassination.

"It is an honorable profession," Parker intoned each time he met Champion face to face. It was part of a longstanding ritual, as if their job needed perpetual justification.

"Happens every day somewhere, everywhere. Humans persist in finding ways to eliminate their fellow man for a variety of reasons, but mostly because they are obstacles to some imagined goal. Most of these eliminations happen under the radar screen of officialdom. They are disguised as natural deaths by drugs or some such foreign element, simple accidents and other traumas that seem perfectly logical and happenstance. These methods are our expertise, which we sell to those who need our service like any other business."

He looked about the pub, a third-class establishment by any criterion, with a red-faced barman half hidden behind upturned glasses and a clot of badly dressed men perched like ruffled crows around the bar. There were a few tables nearby populated by elderly regulars silent in their solitude behind their pints of dark liquid.

Champion had long ceased to question the incongruity of the location and the circumstances for these meetings. Parker never seemed to fear being overheard. They could have been trading in ties, condoms, or cigars for all it mattered to Parker and, presumably, to the people within earshot.

"I am merely a middle man," Parker had told him at the very beginning of their association. "We've both come out of the same stinking swamp. Freelancers now. No more grunting over slop at the public trough. Whatever were they to do with us anyway? No future in official elimination anymore. Slim pickings these days. The game has moved too far east. Language and cultural difficulties abound. They have their own sinister ways out there in the oily slime. Our niche has shifted somewhat from government to commerce. For the present."

Champion had no idea how these assignments came about, although some, he suspected, were policy hits, some government sponsored, but most, these days, were for private motives of greed or personal animosity, all deliberately arranged below the surveillance-prone radar screen of high tech. One quick glance around Parker's pubby office told that story.

"Private entrepreneurship, my boy. Higher multiples in that," Parker pointed out with a throaty gleeful chuckle. There was no reason for Champion to pursue Parker's sources. He characterized himself as a kind of "temp" employee, a secretary, chef, or computer expert rented by the day. The pay, of course, was extraordinary.

Parker, Champion knew, kept each of his operatives separate, which was no problem, since, by definition, they were loners, people like himself, who owned heart-dead emotional circuits. Conscience, guilt, remorse, compassion, attachment, love, sympathy, and related moral inhibitions had somehow been mysteriously suppressed in his human circuitry much in the same way that retroviruses suppressed immune systems. He had often wondered whether DNA would confirm this.

The objectives in these assignments were "eliminations" in a manner that was perceived as an accident or, in special cases, suicide. Crude devices such as firearms, explosives, sharp instruments, and poisons were to be utilized only in extremis. The game, always, was to keep the authorities at bay. Such devices were, by Parker's standards, strictly for movie thugs.

Which did not mean that Champion was ignorant of their uses. In fact, he had on two occasions had to use an explosive device to accomplish an assignment, invariably a risk. He had managed to confer blame on the IRA, although it meant that a few civilian innocents had to meet their maker along with the designated target.

Usually, Parker was able to extract a bonus from the "sponsor" for a "clean" elimination, which meant an official verdict that ruled out foul play. So far, his own record in this regard was perfect.

Payment followed a byzantine but high-tech movement of monies in numerous accounts in various countries throughout the world. Parker apparently had a firm grasp of such machinations and kept a sharp eye on that end of the business, allocating all "fees" in a timely and efficient manner. When it came to money, cyberspace was the game of choice. Champion did not question Parker's skill in this regard, and it had, thus far, worked.

But although the pay was extraordinary, the rules of employment were rigid, unchanging, and absolute. There were no golden parachutes in this operation.

It was, as Parker had reiterated many times, "a cradle-to-the-grave operation." There were no resignations or retirement opportunities. In for a penny, in for a pound, the saying goes. Once in, however, there was no way out, except to oblivion. Death was the only option for a quitter or, for that matter, anyone who endangered the operation, including a client. The operation had a zero-tolerance code of conduct. It was a marriage where "until death do you part" had no provisions for divorce. None.

Parker also knew Champion's true identity, not that it mattered, since errant bytes had already been officially purged from all electronic nooks and crannies, courtesy of his government employment.

Champion's real name was Adam Haynes, an American, Minnesota born, orphaned early, no siblings, brought up in foster homes, state-college educated, a self-contained loner by choice and inclination.

No Adam Haynes existed anymore. Birth certificate obliterated. Fingerprint records gone. No social security possible for Adam Haynes. It didn't matter. He had no emotional tie to this old identity and had deliberately flatlined it in his mind, ruthlessly tamping down memory. The government's secret gurus had seen him as the perfect candidate for their special needs. It took no leap on his part to go private.

He was everyman or no man now, a series of random identities, with false documents obtained through Parker's secure channels. Champion had been somewhat surprised to discover how easily the usual standards of morality dissolved with the scuttling of one's original identity.

Parker upended his pint and signaled for the barman to pour another. Then he raised himself from the table and waddled to the bar to pick up the pint.

"Our little darling is Max Hamilton," he said, settling back into his seat. Hamilton was a mogul who controlled vast holdings on a global scale. "They say he's a bit of a bastard." Parker took another deep sip and wiped away the residue on the back of his hand. He giggled like a blushing girl. "You'll be striking a blow for mankind."

A brief pause and suddenly, like a swiftly moving dark squall, all lightness in Parker's demeanor disappeared.

"In the matter of a high-profile man like Hamilton, investigators will leave no stone unturned," Parker had warned. "There is too much at stake here. If there is the slightest hint of foul play or suicide…" The words trailed off and Parker seemed briefly distracted. "Bells will clang everywhere, insurance companies, intelligence agencies, Interpol, police of numerous countries. Could be a balls-up donnybrook. The only way the impending cacophony can be muted is if his nudge into oblivion appears accidental."

Champion noted Parker's anxieties but did not react.

"The fat bastard has more enemies than there are maggots on a rotting carcass." Parker's haunches moved under his trench coat as he reached for his lager, then he held the glass in midair, shook his head, clicked his tongue, and chuckled. "My kind of bloke."

"To the world, you see," he continued, "the murder motive will seem quite logical. And, as stated, there should be no hint of suicide, although that could be an intrinsic difficulty. What we have been told about him is that he is utterly without guile and, therefore, suicide would hardly be in character. He is, after all, a greedy ruthless pig of a man. He has destroyed legions. Legions. Without an iota of remorse." As quickly as he had become serious, he reverted to the comical. "Pot calls the kettle." He giggled again and moved his hand with the glass.

The lager continued its journey to Parker's thick lips and he swallowed sloppily, then licked the residual foam from his mouth with a pink darting tongue.

"The applause from the gallery will be deafening. If you were visible, women would throw you their panties." Another little chuckle bubbled up from his chest. "Tracking him down will take some doing. He's a manic jetsetter, dashes around the world in his airplane, his yacht, his private train. Fortunately he is a media sweetheart. You'll find data files galore. Just plug in and zoom away."

Computers were an essential part of the trade, a requirement actually, despite the low-tech communication system

Parker employed for his operatives.

Once every month was the usual contact schedule between mother and her killing kittens. In an emergency Parker could reach them by calling up an Internet password on a computer he worked God knew where, but only as a signal, never for transmission. The pay phone was their system of choice, the only safe bet. Champion knew none of the others.

"Any deadline?"

"Within six months would be lovely," Parker said, downing his pint. He banged the glass on the table, a gesture that attracted no attention from the other habituates.

"Our client," Parker continued, "is more interested in surety than speed. You see the logic, of course?"

He lifted a hand to signal the barman for a refill then turned back to him. "But accidental death. Bloody marvelous! And our clients, it is hinted, have much to gain. We do this well, there are excellent incentives. I love incentives. Isn't it wonderful, working for beasts to eliminate beasts? Makes it all worthwhile, don't you think?" Parker chuckled deeply.

Champion wished that Parker would spare him the commentary. A name was all that was needed, a simple label for the human organism targeted for elimination. And that had already been proffered. By then, Champion was impatient to get on with it.

Parker had merely iterated what was well known. Hamilton controlled all kinds of businesses throughout the world. Brash and brutal in his dealings, he lived on notoriety and reveled in ruthlessness. So what, Champion thought. Hamilton could also have been the soil of goodness for all Champion cared about the human element. Character wasn't his concern.

It was Hamilton's itinerary that counted. He would have to be stalked, run to ground zero. That was the part that would fill his mind, trigger his imagination, and, as a subtext to all this, placate the aloneness he must live with.

"This one meets the Robin Hood criteria hands down," Parker said with a squeal of delight, hiccupping strongly, sending a blast of lager stink in Champion's direction. "Our man is thoroughly monstrous and without any saving graces. Think of his demise as eliminating rubbish. If we owned a moral compass, his death would point to true north."

Champion shrugged an acknowledgment, amused by Parker's Robin Hood reference, which was a staple of their conversations. Robin Hood was hardly their role model. Their work was decidedly unheroic, or not designed for the greater good, and Champion couldn't care less if his target was a monster or a saint.

Since joining Parker, he had been employed fourteen times. All had been flawless hits, hence Parker's confidence.

The elimination of human obstacles was inherent in the species behavior. Besides, he had the talent for it. This was the ultimate rationalization for anyone involved in the business of assassination. Champion had embraced this persuasive abstraction, embellishing it with his own observation of the existing culture and his reading of the past. It also paid well, very well.

Killing to resolve differences was a genetically programmed, inherently human response to conflict. So-called civilized societies, to prevent chaos, had organized acceptable rules to regulate this instinctive response.

It was inevitable that such a powerful drive should attract innovative entrepreneurs like Parker and assassination experts like Champion, who understood that the essential ingredient of this line of work was not the killing part but what followed. The true creative talent, highly valued in monetary terms, was in the skill of evasion. A clean kill with a minimum of "residue" meant a spotless getaway.

Champion had no illusion about how Parker had found him. Beached intelligence operatives, their special skills currently in reduced official demand, were traceable through a labyrinth of mysterious connections. This wasn't serendipity. Somewhere, Champion was convinced, there was a cosmic magnet.

Actually, it had worked out surprisingly well, despite Parker's eccentric, and disgusting, demeanor. In business, especially in the financial arrangements, Parker had been impeccable. Great sums had passed between them.

Champion used the funds to live well, mostly in private clubs or luxurious hotels, using a roster of names, suitably documented. Bogus documentation, he had discovered, was the world's least-discussed cottage industry.

Even when he had performed an allegedly quasi-official mission, a CIA or MI5 hit, he managed to tell himself that he was merely soldiering. But the more he did this, the less he confronted any larger moral question. It became merely an exercise in method, the efficiency of the kill, and the matter of successful evasion. Nothing loftier. Just business.

Champion stood up and prepared to leave, looking down at the seated Parker, who was squinting upward through his Coke bottles.

"Nothing more to be said until this is all behind us," Parker said. "Unless, of course, we have a dustup." He shrugged. "In that case, I'll see you in the afterlife." Parker chuckled at his little joke.

"There isn't any," Champion said.

"I hope you're right. I hate intense heat."

Champion strode out of the pub into the chill March evening.

Chapter 4

The trip through Italy had been trancelike as she sped through the superhighway toward France recalling the events of her stay in Florence.

To Angela, Aunt Emma had always been more legend than reality, her lifestyle providing grist for gossipy tidbits and innuendo, and there were times when her parents were, as they put it, reluctant to discuss her. She knew that her father adored his sister, which was good enough for Angela, who adored her father.

In her thirty-odd years of conscious memory about Aunt Emma, Angela had seen her make appearances and disappearances. She was always telephoning from odd places, sending gifts, appearing at family gatherings, always with another man. Between her two dead husbands, and before and after, there was always someone who needed an introduction, a man invariably handsome. Emma would describe them in her antiquated way as her new "beaus," and always their principal virtues were "gallantry," which seemed a mysterious attribute, and "generosity," which was more easily defined.

Angela had always been intrigued by her colorful aunt and had eagerly sought her company when she visited. She had always been described as Emma's favorite niece, notwithstanding the fact that she was Emma's only niece.

Emma never had children nor did she appear to regret it. Angela's father had hinted that offspring would have inhibited his sister's hyperactive love life, of which he obviously did not approve.

With her father dead of a heart attack less than a year ago, Angela made a concerted effort to establish a strong relationship with Aunt Emma, who, after the death of her latest husband, lived lavishly in Santa Fe in what she described as an "adobe hut."

Angela had never been there, although she and Tom had been invited numerous times. Nevertheless, reaching out to Aunt Emma seemed a priority after her father's death, as if she were a surrogate for her lost and beloved dad.

Angela had noted something alien emerge in herself after her father's death. This alien thing was a powerful but vague curiosity about matters secret and hidden and not quite defined. Overanalysis, Tom would have told her. But then, confiding in Tom was no longer a priority. There seemed less and less to consult with him about, especially now that the children were older and pursuing their own agendas in faraway places.

She knew in her soul that she loved her father, although they had carefully edited themselves in offering confidences to each other. Now that he was gone, she terribly regretted the repression. What had gone on inside him, beyond the bland and loving exterior? Perhaps this was yet another reason she had reached out to Aunt Emma.

She felt no such regret in the case of her mother, who had died a few years before. Rigidly traditional, her mother had chosen the well-trodden path of the dutiful wife-mother, unmarred by the winds of political change.

The apple, Angela had noted, as far as her own life was concerned, had not fallen far from the tree. Even the frequent absences of her husband, busy pursuing his own ambitions, did not prod her out of rejecting the role he had fashioned for her, the good mother, devoted wife, good citizen. With the children gone and Tom's absences increasing, she was taking a harder look at what her life was all about, if anything.

She was beginning to feel a strong blip on what had always been an unruffled horizon, as if she were somehow squandering her freedom. Perhaps, too, she began to think, she had traded too much of her youth for mere tranquility.

As always, she resisted overanalyzing this noticeable change, attributing it to various generalized conditions, described ad infinitum in the media, whose concentration on demographics was now focusing briefly on the cusp-of-forty age group, her own, attributing angst and uncertainty of both genders to the approaching menopause in women and the classic midlife crisis in men. They weren't boomers, and they weren't the X generation. They were floaters, somewhere in between, nameless, perhaps anonymous.

Angela tried earnestly to be above such clichés, although she sensed that they weren't far off the mark. She had made conventional choices, married at nineteen to a clearly ambitious and very handsome go-getter who provided her with a living standard far in excess of anything she might have imagined.

Hadn't she chosen the role of devoted mother to her two children, Sandra and Peter, now pursuing their own fledgling agendas? Sandra studying animal husbandry in Argentina and Peter, who had whizzed through college by nineteen, working for an investment banking firm in Beijing.

"But why so far?" she had wondered aloud.

"It's a global village now," Tom had said, underlining and approving their career choices. She had agreed, of course. How could she disagree with the proven wisdom of her respected husband who drew his inspiration from the bigger-than-life role model of Max Hamilton, in whose service he had grown and prospered? And yet, she still questioned the sheer distance of the separation, as if it might be attributed to something in her children that had escaped her notice. Or in her or Tom.

Yet how could she complain? Tom had broken the mold for his peers. He had been one of those focused whiz-kid Harvard lawyers who started high and shot up the ladder with the speed of lightning.

One might say that his success had been "instant." She too had done her part, providing him with an "instant" family. The children were born a year apart with the older one, Peter, actually emerging just shy of her twentieth birthday.

Before he was thirty, largely due to his having Max Hamilton as his principal client, Tom's income had reached well above the seven-figure line, which, she knew, was a report card of "fulfillment" for him. And it did give her the luxury of a mansion in Oyster Bay, complete with household help, expensive private schools for their children, an apartment in Manhattan, and all the other gewgaws that qualified them both as champion sprinters in the race toward whatever qualified as the finish line.

Such largesse required compromises, of course. Or as Tom put it often: no gain without pain. Part of that pain was his frequent and growing absences, which were no longer hurtful. But the sting was still as painful as ever in the command performances demanded of her when Tom needed to entertain and be entertained with or on behalf of Max Hamilton. She had been ever the obedient helpmate, although she had never fully resigned herself to the process.

But she considered that rendering unto Caesar what was his. Hadn't they their private lives, their children, their sense of family, their health? Tom, by the evidence of time spent, loved his work, and she seemed to get a great deal of satisfaction from her various good works. Didn't she?

It was true that Tom was gone frequently, but she kept herself busy enough with her community work not to fret over these absences. They were one of the conditions of the marriage bargain. Weren't they?

Although he spent most weeknights in Manhattan, Tom gave her no reason to doubt his familial devotion, despite diminished sexual contact between them, which she attributed largely to his sacrificing his libido to the bitch goddess of ambition.

Occasionally, it crossed her mind that Tom was humping one or another from the pack of female sycophants, colleagues, paralegals, or secretaries who filled his life. This, too, might have accounted for his declining libido, but she never could affirm to herself that she felt threatened. Besides, there were other personal ways to satisfy an occasional lustful fantasy, none of which featured Tom nor coincided with his weekend visitations. When it did happen between them, it seemed pallid, swift, and obligatory, and she took no joy in it.

Once upon a time, in her teens and early twenties, sex had seemed to be part of the accepted ritual of her relationship with Tom. They made love—she could never say fucked—two or three times a week, always without her attaining orgasm.

Even her resort to faking enthusiasm was less than believable, especially to herself. To compensate, she developed certain skills to induce him to quickly climax. She supposed it satisfied him. Thankfully, it was never a topic of discussion between them.

But she became less and less concerned about any potential unfaithfulness on his part as the issue of sexual harassment and the danger of AIDS grew in importance. Tom would never be foolish enough to put himself in harm's way on either score. He had too much to lose.

She was more concerned with the power wielded by Tom's assistant, Cynthia Bilton. Her plainness might rule out any sexual involvement, but Angela sensed that she had long ago become an indispensable part of Tom's life.

"My business life only," Tom assured her, explaining that a man in his position needed an administrator to assume the ancillary burdens of his overwhelmingly heavy schedule. To Angela, Cynthia was possessive and imperious, superior and arrogant, treating her like an irrelevant necessary evil in her husband's life.

When she complained, Tom promised to talk to Cynthia and for a while her attitude changed, then reverted back to form. It was not uncommon for wives to be jealous of their husband's administrative assistants, Tom had pointed out. Eventually, she had stopped complaining, accepting Cynthia Bilton as a fact of life.

Besides, Tom, having reached critical financial mass, was, thanks to Max's affection and sponsorship, building up their exchequer at an astounding rate. Having come from modest circumstances, she was determined not to lift her nose at the idea of having money, lots of money.

There were, of course, social emoluments and ego satisfactions, especially for Tom, who liked the high profile of prestige. Arts foundations were putting them on boards. They were mentioned in the social columns. They contributed to everything. Wall space in their Oyster Bay house was devoted to expensive paintings mostly by contemporary name artists. She supposed it symbolized that they were somehow ahead of the pack in taste and sensibility.

Wasn't all that the good life? The good, good life? She admitted to herself that she was never going to be the kind of woman who trashed her blessings on the grounds of vague discontent. Nor did she surrender to any self-criticism on the basis of political agendas that opined that women who were merely wives and mothers and not careerists were somehow lesser than those who braved the rat race.

"Are we really successful, Tom?" she had often asked her husband. It was a question posed in different permutations, as if she were never quite sure that they had arrived at such a place.

"Don't belabor the obvious," he had replied with some annoyance. Tom sometimes seemed as if he were a missionary for the cult of success and made it clear that his drive for fulfillment, which apparently meant different things to him than to her, was far from over.

With the children gone, she was well aware that she was going through another common adjustment, dubbed the empty-nest syndrome. But adjustment, she assured herself, did not inevitably lead to depression, a condition she was witnessing in others going through the same phase.

Lately Tom seemed increasingly obsessed with the idea that there was more, lots more, to squeeze from the grapefruit of fulfillment. He spent more time away from home, hinting at some gargantuan deal in the offing, a deal of deals, that would be the culmination of his striving and make him "King of the Hill," an appellation he was actually using with great frequency.

King of what hill? she had wondered. The reality for her was that the more successful he became, the less it mattered to her.

Chapter 5

She passed through the Italian-French border, surprised that it was open, with the barricades down and no need to show her passport. She was beginning to feel the fatigue of the long day, but the prospect of a nice drink and a pleasant dinner at the Bel Air in Saint-Jean-Cap-Ferrat revitalized her.

Perhaps it was because she was leaving Italy behind that she felt a sudden surge of longing to be with Aunt Emma again, and she was transported back in time to what had become the four most memorable days of her life. She giggled to herself when she realized how time had transfused itself in her memory. She was, after all, recalling events that could be measured in hours.

She had been lying stretched out on the queen-size bed in Florence, the River Arno flowing relentlessly and unchanging outside the hotel window. With Aunt Emma propped on pillows beside her, assiduously swizzling her champagne with the vertical side of her jeweled cross, Angela's agenda was on the verge of a radical epiphany.

At the time, of course, she was barely aware of it, perhaps totally unaware. This was in retrospect, after the "incident" had occurred, and she was milking images and voices so recent they had barely time to "cure" in her mind.

They had been pleasantly inebriated, with tongues loosened and their minds floating, drifting away from their customary moorings. Even in recall, their alertness had to be intense, since the memories were so textured, so real, that their senses could not have been dull or unawakened at the time.

"Odd," Angela remembered saying, which seemed even then like the starting point of the journey. "Despite the fact that our lives touched infrequently, I've always been in awe of you, Aunt Emma. I've always loved being with you. Of course, Dad was not stingy in describing what he knew about your exploits. What a portrait he painted of his adventuresome sister!"

Angela had actually edited her father's remark. He had characterized her conduct more as wild and willful than adventuresome. But his real meaning, she knew, was that he was proud of her for taking risks and following her own path wherever it had taken her.

"Portrait of me?" Emma asked.

Angela shrugged and held out her glass to be swizzled by the cross.

"What did he mean, Angela, darling? Was I portrayed as a selfish bitch? A woolly romantic, a man-eating whore, a what?"

"Not a whore," Angela corrected, sipping the champagne.

"Why not? I loved… making love. I still adore it, the wonder of it. Nature's pleasure train, long delicious waves of pleasure." She lifted a finger. "Both in the giving and the taking. The male body, that wonderful swordlike part, so endearing—the penis is the most beautiful object on earth."

"Aunt Emma!" Angela exclaimed, giggling.

"I'm sixty-five years old. I can say anything I wish, even that which is feministically incorrect. To many women the penis is an object of scorn and a symbol of enslavement. To me, it's the glorious wand of love." She turned toward her niece. "I do believe you're blushing."

Angela felt her face, feeling the heat.

"God, I feel as if I'm eleven years old and have just discovered—"

"Discovered what?"

"My… you know."

"Is that what you still call it? Your 'you know'? How old is this woman? Thirty-eight?"

"Nine."

"The best ten years of a woman's life, and you still call it your 'you know'? Let me tell you, my darling, that 'you know' is where the soul of a woman reposes. Not the heart, mind you. The soul."

"I don't believe this," Angela said, giggling again.

"I'm talking of love, my dear. Remember love?"

"Vaguely," Angela sighed.

"There you see, there is the problem. Vaguely? Such an imprint must be on you always, etched deep in your heart. Vaguely. You poor dear deprived thing."

"Problem? Deprived?" Angela snapped, stirring, her giggles stifled, suddenly defensive and reacting to Emma's suddenly obtrusive observation.

"Getting too close to the bone, am I?"

"Not really," Angela lied.

"Really, see? Like vaguely. Too tentative, I'd say."

Angela withheld comment. She's deliberately trying to upset my equilibrium, Angela thought, taking a deep sip of champagne for fortification.

"No one can give it to you. You have to find it in yourself."

"Find what?"

"Your erotic center."

Where was she taking her? Angela wondered.

Her aunt slipped into a brief reverie, than roused herself.

"Not just the physical thing," Emma sighed. "Not simply the connection, the strong arms wrapped around you, the flesh touching, the feel of the man inside you, vanquishing, joining, the pleasure, the joy, the wonder of it. And yet. Not only that." She turned toward her niece and stroked her arm. "How I wish..." Her voice trailed off and she sipped her champagne again, still touching Angela's arm.

A sudden fear seized her. She considered moving her arm, but the implication was too disturbing to contemplate. She let it lie there, wondering if her aunt's fingers would begin to stroke her. Was this the beginning of a seduction? She could actually envision herself in her aunt's arms, feeling the comfort of her sexual caress.

"Do you know the most amazing thing, Angela?" Emma said. Again she had slipped into a brief reverie and come back, her fingers stroking now, but absently.

Angela felt her fear dissipate. The caress, she assured herself, was motherly. "I can sometimes, not always, actually remember all my lovers. Isn't that odd? I'm not sure if it's the flesh remembering or the memory of sight or sound, but at times, I can see them marching in my mind, like soldiers, naked soldiers in lockstep."

"You make it sound as if there were battalions of them," Angela said, relieved to note that the spotlight was now turned in her aunt's direction.

"How many in a battalion?" Emma asked, patting Angela's arm in a friendly rebuke.

"Many," Angela replied, stealing a glance at her aunt, who returned it, her eyes shining like hot coals in the declining light. With shadows deepening, smoothing the lines of her face, she looked younger, girlish.

"I never have toted them up. I suppose putting a number on them would diminish them somehow."

"Do you maintain contact with any of them?" Angela asked. It seemed a logical response.

"I do get calls now and then," Emma replied vaguely, setting up boundaries, "but you must remember that I am not dead yet. There are still men in my life."

"Plural, Aunt Emma?"

Emma sat up and poured herself another glass of champagne.

"It seems so odd having a woman for a confidante," she said.

"I'm your niece, Aunt Emma," Angela said, sensing the beginning of an alcoholic slur on her tongue. "Bound by blood."

"Aunt Emma. Auntie," Emma chirped.

"Down to cases, please," Angela pressed. "Aunt Emma is now the subject for the rest of the evening."

Better this way, Angela decided. Earlier her equilibrium had been compromised, her balance upset. Must not overanalyze, she warned herself, hearing Tom's voice, an unwelcome intrusion which she quickly shooed out of her mind.

"My present loves… yes, that was under discussion, I believe. Three: a young one for sport, an older one for comfort, and yet another for… for adventure."

"Incredible," Angela said, not quite knowing how to react. Emma caught the ambivalence of her reaction and lifted herself on her elbow and looked into Angela's face.

"Why incredible? I know, the age factor. You can't picture this aging carcass in flagrante delicto. Somehow it's unbecoming in dear old auntie, making love at her age. Is that it?"

"Maybe that," Angela said honestly, once she had determined that there was no anger in her aunt's voice.

"Or is it the idea of three?"

"That, too, I suppose," Angela replied, determined to maintain the integrity of this new relationship with absolute candor.

"Perhaps the risk factor as well," Emma pressed, dipping the cross into the champagne and swizzling, then sipping. "Are you going to ask me if I practice safe sex?"

"It crossed my mind, yes."

"I don't," Emma said emphatically. Angela repressed any urge to respond. It seemed ludicrous to lecture a sixty-five-year-old woman on the dangers of risky sex.

She was talking of health risks but thinking of other kinds of risks, life's risks, psychic risks that she had somehow always associated with Aunt Emma and her behavior, as reported by her father, usually before or after Emma came to visit. These reports, like bulletins from far-off places, built this legend about Aunt Emma.

She heard her father's words echo in her mind. They were judgmental. "Like all self-centered people, Emma is outside the orbit of ordinary morality. She is always loving but never remorseful, selfish but never contrite. She takes risks but for her own purposes, willing to accept the consequences but never bothering about the consequences to others. She hears only her own drummer."

This, boiled down, was always the theme of his musings about his sister, her history marked by widowhood, restless moving around the country, new beaus, and other colorful Aunt Emma adventures. These factual meanderings came to Angela in brief sound bites that seemed like a whispered Greek chorus when Emma was visiting or the object of discussion.

"All right," Angela said, trying to relate these reports to Aunt Emma in the flesh, the reality of the legend. "I surrender to experience."

"Wrong. You surrender to endurance. Endurance counts for a great deal in this life. And I have certainly done amazingly well in that category."

Emma lay back on the pillow and looked up at the ceiling. She laughed throatily, with only the slightest hint of inebriation.

"I am incredible, aren't I, Angela?" Emma said reaching out again and touching her niece's arm.

"Very."

"I have been making love, real love, since I was thirteen years old, my darling. It's a way of life with me. It's what I do." She giggled. "It's my only marketable skill." Then she laughed uproariously until tears came into her eyes, and she began a coughing fit, gripping Angela's arm for stability.

"I can't imagine what's going through your mind about your dear old auntie," Emma said.

"I'm trying to imagine you as a hooker."

"Why is that so difficult, darling?" Emma said, restraining her laughter. "I have always profited through loving. I am a multimillionaire through loving." Her cheeks puffed and her laughter came out with a rasping sound on a blast of repressed breath. No reply seemed necessary as Angela waited for her aunt's laughing fit to taper off.

She had seen her father enjoy himself like that, remembering with sudden sadness his capacity for humor and joy. It was good remembering, observing the inclination of her genes. Yet it was a component that she feared had evaded her like a faulty or missing part of her DNA. Another thread of memory suddenly intruded. "Emma never hurts for moolah," her father had said, validating Aunt Emma's assertion. Men had always showered her with gifts.

"But never by design," Emma said, as if reading her niece's mind, which seemed even then to be following some inevitable path. "I follow my heart. Always." As if to say there was incidental material profit in that, but more importantly vast psychic riches.

The room was darkening, the shadows disappearing. A tender breeze billowed the light fabric that covered the windows and lifted the moist air of the river into their space. Even in the darkness, Emma's eyes sparkled, greedily catching the last remnants of natural light.

"You loved them all?" Angela asked, like some naive prepubescent.

Emma shrugged, tapped her teeth with the cross, used it to swizzle the champagne, and then upended her glass.

"The evidence seems clear," she said after swallowing, winking.

"The battalions?"

"Of course. Without love, love in a thousand incarnations, we confront the void."

"We do?"

She felt her guard slipping again, her balance faltering.

"Angela, darling. That is the first rule of life."

Her aunt seemed to be observing her with pity, as if she had misspelled a simple word.

"I must be missing something," Angela responded honestly. There it was again, but hardly tentative. An admission. Yes, she was missing something, had missed something. Ahead she could see only an infinity of missing somethings. "Maybe if you explained—" Angela began after a short pause, exposing her ignorance.

"Explaining means diminishment, darling. It loses its real truth in the translation," Emma said. It seemed a rebuke, but Angela wasn't sure.

She seemed to Angela to be turning deeply serious suddenly, the mood changing. She hoped the alcohol would not make Aunt Emma contentious.

"Dad said you were a romantic," Angela said, conscious of an effort to alter the sudden mood change.

"Absolutely. A dyed-in-the-wool unreconstructed romantic. Romance is the salt of life. Recognizing that makes me a realist as well."

She seemed to withdraw for a moment to contemplate the idea.

"As I have said, follow your heart, darling," Emma sighed. "It will take you directly to bliss, and that is everything."

"Everything?"

"I am talking now of the true passion, the one true passion. If it happens to you, and it could happen in the blink of an eye with the speed of light, you will think you are the luckiest woman on earth. And you will be."

"You've lost me," Angela said, somewhat ingenuously, suddenly fearful of the idea of being lost in this way. It was unnerving, tantalizing, in fact. Had Aunt Emma found a path to life's buried treasure while she, Angela, had found only buried rubbish? She felt herself becoming both resentful and bereft.

"It is difficult to convey. It is all-consuming, magical, obsessive, wonderful, joyous. Also, there is no escape from it. You must play it out to the end. Give up everything for it."

"It?"

"We are not talking here of… well… this will sound awfully crude to you, Angela. Cock fever. Not that, which is a different obsession entirely. A counterfeit. Believe me, I have been in the grip of that obsession many times. It is fleeting, and, in the end, merely a pleasantly lustful diversion. The true passion includes sexual ecstasy. Yes, ecstasy. Not only repetitive orgasmic explosions that take over the body, but a total consummation, mental, physical, spiritual."

"I've never experienced anything like that," Angela blurted. By then, equilibrium had disappeared. "You make it sound so… cosmic."

"And so it is. The true passion, it rules. It must be obeyed."

"To the exclusion of everything?"

"Of course. It can't be evaded or dismissed. It is the central issue of the life force. To deny it is a form of death."

Angela watched her aunt's face, the eyes shining with memory. She fell silent. What was there to say?

"In its grip," Emma continued, "you do things that you never thought you were capable of doing. All the boundaries you have lived within fall. Nothing is as it was. Consequences mean nothing. You are set free, floating on a magic carpet."

"Floating to where?" Angela asked, seeking some counterweight to her aunt's hyperbole, hoping to find some barrier to her own sense of deprivation.

"To where?" Emma leveled her eyes at her niece. "To the only place that matters." Angela watched as she once again turned her eyes away and seemed to fade into a reverie of memory.

"You make it sound... so one-sided," Angela said, still seeking the counterweight.

Emma nodded.

"Yes, I suppose it could be... well... like slavery. No, I'm not talking of one-sided, unrequited love. I am talking here of mutuality, perfect pairing, lovers, the truest passion. Without mutuality, where are we?"

Angela turned the idea over in her mind. Was Aunt Emma creating a romantic myth out of simple biology? she wondered.

"It came to me once," Emma said. "In midlife. I was prepared to give up everything for that one moment."

"And did you?"

"Of course. Everything. I was married, you see. But all consequences were meaningless against being with him. It was as if I was lost until I met him, and through my love for him found myself. Became complete. It was exactly that way for him as well. It had to be. We ran away together. Jettisoned all the baggage we had accumulated. Erased our histories. Everything for love."

To Angela it was as if her aunt were talking in a foreign language, full of obscure and elusive symbols. Yet, she found herself striving to understand.

"What was he like?"

"He was beautiful. He grows lovelier every time I recall him. Exquisite. In his arms I came to know the meaning of myself as a woman. Beyond that, words always fail me. We coupled ourselves into elation and exhaustion. It was ecstasy. Our bodies created a kind of human fireworks. Sometimes I think I actually invented him, created him out of my own reflection and desire." She smiled. "Do you know he told me that was exactly what he believed had happened to him? And he, too, confessed that he had found in himself what it meant to be a man. You see. Mutuality."

"But…" Angela searched for a response that might trigger some understanding and comprehension in herself. "I mean… it can't be all physicality and blind emotion. What about… well… character? There is more to a person than just… just those aspects."

"Character?" Emma shrugged, her eyes drifting away from Angela's face, as if confronting another dimension. "We are talking here of entering a dream of passion that transcends everything, that sweeps away reason, morality, judgments, conditions, appraisals, that defies analysis. Character? He could have been anything. The worst sinner, a moral nightmare or the most lily-white saint, of any race, religion, a beggar or a billionaire, stout or slender, tall or short, of any age beyond puberty." Emma chuckled and winked. "It wouldn't have mattered." She paused and looked at Angela archly. "Am I heading into confusing territory?"

"Yes, a dream of passion. Really, Aunt Emma."

"That's the problem with relating experience, dear. It loses much in translation."

"And did this man enter with you into this so-called dream of passion, ignoring all consequences?" Angela asked.

"Of course. Everything becomes secondary, meaningless." She sighed. "He left a wife of twenty years. He was a rising star in a great business enterprise. He walked away from that. And he had two young children, of which he was the sole support."

"You let him do that?"

"Let him? There are no choices here. Once in its clutches, there is no way to stop such a power." She shook her head and turned back to observe Angela, her eyes incandescent. "We were beyond judgment, and we had no regrets."

"How long were you together?"

"When we were together, time dissolved, became meaningless. But if you need a measurement, perhaps a year, no more." She paused, bit her lip, her eyes glistening with moisture. "He died. We were in New York. He was hit by a car. Fini. Over like a flash. But never here. Never here." She tapped her heart and her temple. She fought further tears and breathed deeply to recover. "For years I thought that destiny had played a cruel trick on us, taking him like that. Then it occurred to me that perhaps destiny was very crafty. It preserved him forever in the apogee of our ecstasy. It could never have gotten better than it was. The cup of joy was already full to the brim."

"I must say, Aunt Emma, you express yourself in such a vivid way."

"Why not? This was the defining period of my life," Emma said. It could have been the light, or an illusion, but the years seemed to disappear from her face. "And in memory it still is."

"I can't conceive of it," Angela said, thinking of her ordinary life. She had known only one man in a sexual way. Only Tom. Passion? Ecstasy? Meaningless words. Another word popped into her mind from their earlier exchange. Deprived. She felt hollow and inert.

"Unless it happens to you."

"Me? Hardly."

"Perhaps," Aunt Emma said observing her with what seemed like pity again.

Emma appeared to be getting drowsy now, as if the excitement of her explanation had drained her. She yawned, and Angela yawned sympathetically.

"This body needs sleep," Angela said looking at Aunt Emma, who smiled and petted Angela's hair. She got up from the bed and, starting toward the door between their bedrooms, turned.

"I hope I haven't disturbed you, dear," she said.

Angela refrained from answering. There was no point to it. Aunt Emma already knew the answer.

Chapter 6

Observation alone was useful, but never complete. More had been needed if the act was going to, as Parker had put it, pass muster. The actual killing part was a mere detail. If that were the only issue, a high-powered rifle with a night scope would serve nicely.

Passing muster, on the other hand, required research, resourcefulness, stealth, and, above all, imagination. Champion had fixed his mind on a soundless fall into the briny deep, to be carried out while the boat was underway, motors humming to mask the splash, and no marks or future forensic revelations of foul play. It was a tall order, of course, but not professionally impossible.

Two days earlier, on Wednesday, he had noted that two of the crew had made for the shore in the boat's dinghy. By the time they reached the quay, Champion was on the scene, having sped there in his Jaguar, reaching it just in time to see the men roll off in a cab. He followed them to a bar in the nether world of Nice and planted himself at a table to listen and observe.

With professional patience, dedicated intelligence gathering, and luck, he managed to piece together Hamilton's short-range cruising plans.

In two days, on Friday, they were to cruise forty miles southwestward along the coast heading for Cap Camarat, dropping anchor in the bay of Saint-Tropez where Hamilton was to have breakfast and lunch aboard with shore guests.

This was the core bit of intelligence that Champion had waited for. Opportunity had presented itself. It would be a coast-hugging leisurely journey, chart supported with a radar assist to traverse obstacles along the underwater shelf.

He tracked the shoreline over the forty-mile course, exploring every inch of coastal terrain and its relationship with the sea. He consulted official weather sources to ascertain expected sea conditions and temperatures.

The wind, too, was an essential ingredient in the plan. He hoped for a land breeze or no breeze at all. A hot humid evening, even with the boat underway, would bring Hamilton to the afterdeck.

He drew various potential cruising courses on computerized nautical maps summoned up on his laptop. He also calculated distance and speed and how a swimming man could vector in on a moving boat.

There was one spot shown on the charts where a little peninsula jutted out to sea, forming a thirty-foot promontory that fell sheer into a suitable depth for a safe dive. It was well away from the underwater shelf and was the course of choice to skippers sailing up the coast to Saint-Tropez.

He had established himself as the fictitious John Champion, a Brit from Brighton. Early on he had discovered a talent for accents and imagined he could sound as English as it was possible for an American to affect. He had American, Irish, and Australian passports as well, but he was less proficient with a brogue, although almost authentic as an Aussie.

He had checked into the posh Bel Air on the tip of Cap Ferrat, one of the most exclusive hotels on the Riviera. For the benefit of the concierge and service people, he fitted himself with a schedule that was, more or less, unvarying during the two weeks he had been in residence.

For two hours before a late breakfast, he worked out in the hotel gym on weights and a treadmill. It was a daily routine wherever he was. He respected his body and kept it in tip-top shape.

In midafternoon, he called for his car and proceeded on his ritual of surveillance, rarely returning before two or three in the morning. He hoped that his perceived lifestyle might suggest that he was a rich playboy, an image he was bent on fostering.

At times, he deliberately varied his routine, eating lunch or even an early dinner in his room. But the things he ordered, the edibles and beverages, were the most exotic and luxurious that money could buy: vintage Dom Pérignon, beluga caviar, pâté de foie gras, and items of similar expense.

Such victuals were not uncommon in the hotels and clubs he frequented. Besides, he enjoyed them, both the sensory pleasure they gave his palate and the idea of them. His profession had made him reasonably comfortable financially, and what good was money if the glories of having it were not observed? He knew he was the cliché of a poverty-stricken youth. He didn't care.

His stay at the Bel Air offered an interesting irony. He appreciated irony. It lapped at the edge of his theory of oblivion, suggesting forces at work where the logic was not apparent. Like seeing Max Hamilton playing the fatherly patron to his group at dinner in the Bel Air dining room. Apparently the hotel was one of his regular places to entertain when the troupe of entertainees exceeded the capacity of his yacht's dining room and sleeping quarters. He had overheard one of the hotel staff remarking on the ebb and flow of Hamilton retainers moving in and out of the hotel, their movements subject to their master's bidding.

He had watched Max from a vantage on the terrace hidden in the soft darkness: Max the consummate host, cajoling, persuading those from whom he wanted something, while his circle of sycophants and fellow plunderers and lackeys of his private claque fawned and toadied to their master's wishes. He held court, pushing the vintage champagne, pâté de fois gras, and beluga down the gullets of the party, although he seemed the most prolific imbiber.

It occurred to Champion that death by indulgence was equally as imminent as his own projected effort, suggesting that his was a race against time and natural causes. At one point in his surveillance, he imagined that Hamilton had seen him through the thin veil of darkness, their eyes meeting, his glowing like red coals, as they exchanged final confirmation of Max's appointment in Samara with him, Champion, as guide to that destination.

That exchange was the very heart of the irony, and he hoped that Hamilton would interpret what he saw of

Champion in the darkness as none other than the Angel of Death himself.

There was Max Hamilton, his bulk encased in a massive blazer and polka-dot self-tied bow tie, casually askew, his chins shivering like jelly as he moved through the ritual of playing the center of interest, always, Champion assumed happily, for the purpose of aggrandizement and plunder.

Sop up your fill, he remarked to himself. Glut yourself. Fatten. The fish below are awaiting their feast.

Driving his rented black Vanden Plas eight-cylinder Jaguar with stolen Parisian plates, he volunteered an explanation to those among the service people charged with cars that this was a female friend's Jag and that he would be joined by the same sometime in the third week of his stay.

Creating identities and backstories was one of his special skills. In an odd way, it assuaged aloneness, the necessary condition of the life he had chosen.

Aloneness was the abiding reality of his life. His only memory of any loving relationships was the one he had with his parents. He had lost his mother to disease when he was three years old.

For the next three years, he had gone on a wild, bizarre hegira with his father. It was a relationship not without love but with profound consequences. No other relationship, loving or otherwise, with male or female, had intruded on his journey from oblivion to oblivion in the thirty-three years since.

He was not sure if living this way was his preference or his destiny. He had abandoned his identity, not just in name and documentation but also in his inner world. Since he was no longer who he was, he had no human ties to anything. This helped him nullify any feelings he might have toward others and gave him permission to dispatch them with impunity. Who was he really? Did it matter? He viewed himself as the man from nowhere.

Because he was nobody, he developed a gift for mimicry and invention. By observing others, he found he could copy them in speech and style. And he had acquired the ability of creating and remembering personal histories, which he often took as his own. He had become a human chameleon.

When he needed sexual relief, he bought it from women, transient identities with mindless bodies with which to slake a sometimes-unbearable lust. Especially after a mission, it often took days, even weeks, to satisfy. He supposed such raging desire validated his humanity, at least in a biological sense.

He liked clubs and hotels largely because he was not conspicuous eating alone in them, and room service was always available. Also, in these institutions, eccentricities were tolerated, and the staff offered a semblance of protection.

When he was not planning and plotting, he went to elaborate lengths creating and recreating himself, researching new identities, studying maps of cities where this new person might reside, familiarizing himself with the landmarks, customs, and geography that might provide him with just enough information for a credible performance.

Some identities stayed for a longer period in the safety

zone. He monitored them frequently. When they moved into a zone of possible danger, he killed them off.

As John Champion, he had established his pattern for the benefit of his audience, the supernumeraries who serviced the Bel Air. In the trunk of the Jaguar was everything he would need for his mission.

At times, he knew, certain risks were unavoidable, no matter what precautions he took. He would be taking a huge risk with his current assignment, a calculation already made. If something went awry, he could be transported to oblivion, an oblivion that he did not fear.

As a blip of random information, his termination meant that he would simply vanish, and eventually his many personas and identities would evaporate from all human memory and confound those who might venture by chance into the mysteries of his computerized fictions.

What he really feared most was the prospect of stultifying incarceration, although he was somewhat mollified by the fact that he could always put a stop to it and enter oblivion at will through numerous lethal means, including simple resignation, a surefire method to raise the ire of Parker and Company and provide a swift demise.

On Friday evening, he had observed the Hamilton yacht depart the little bay and head southward at a leisurely pace pretty much within the range of his calculations. It took him a little over an hour to drive to the site where he intended to put himself into the sea. A gravel road led to within fifty yards of the point.

Moving the car into a copse he had reconnoitered earlier,

he changed into his wet suit and cap, smeared waterproof blacking on his face, and then put on black rubber gloves and checked his equipment—the power gun, an expandable float with built-in inflator, and a knife with a serrated edge.

He had determined that this was going to be a bare-bones operation with only two pieces of operational equipment that could go wrong, his power gun and the float, the reliability of which he had tested again and again.

There were worries, of course, mishaps or circumstances that were beyond his control for which there were no contingencies. Witnesses could pop up unexpectedly. Someone could be observing him at this very moment. The area was a perfect spot for a lovers' tryst.

Or someone might see him in the water. A curious sight at that late hour, it could trigger panic in some worried observer or linger in the mind and provide investigators with some titillating grist for their mill.

These items were, however, worries after the fact. As for the main event, he cut off all contemplation of the myriad things that might go wrong.

He dove into the water at the time he had estimated that Hamilton's boat would be within range. Swimming steadily and easily, his power gun and float strapped to his back, he moved through the surprisingly warm and calm waters, pausing occasionally to peer northward for any sign of the Hamilton yacht's running lights.

Other boats floated far in the distance. About a mile from shore he stopped, inflated his float, and rested comfortably as he waited in the stillness, the only sound the lapping of the water against his float. Minutes passed, and then a half hour had gone by. He wondered if the boat had put in elsewhere.

If his information was incorrect, he would simply wait for another opportunity. He was under no time pressure. He had met with Parker in March. It was August. Occasionally, he put his head below the water's surface hoping to pick up an echo of the boat's motors. Nothing.

An hour passed before he detected the first sounds of oncoming propellers. They hummed in a way that indicated that the boat's movement was leisurely. Looking north, he saw the configuration of Hamilton's yacht's lights and determined that he had accurately plotted the ship's course.

His major problem would be dealing with the turbulence of the yacht's wake so that he could get enough purchase on the power gun to send the rubber hook to its target. Holding on to the float for support until he could get a good reading on the ship's bearings, he waited for what he calculated was precisely the right moment to puncture it with the point of his knife.

When he did so, it collapsed quickly with a steady hiss. Gathering the float's remains, he folded them and attached them to a D clamp on his wet suit. Then he quickly adjusted his relationship to the boat so as to stay away from the prow as it cut through the water.

It was moving toward him now at a gentle speed, less than he had estimated, which accounted for the delay. He unlatched the power gun, finding himself on the starboard side of the oncoming ship bearing down on him now with steady and mindless resolve.

He fired when the boat was just about to clear him broadside, aiming for a clear shot at the stern rail. Holding on to the gun with both hands, he needed a few seconds after the shot to steady himself in the turbulence of the boat's wake, and it was a few moments before he could assess the effectiveness of his shot.

Suddenly the slack in the line disappeared, and he knew he had found his target. The rubber hook had latched on to the stern rail, and soon he found himself slicing through the water, bracing against its drag.

He held on to the power gun with both hands as the line pulled him along through the water. The hook had bonded with the rail and now carried him along as if he were waterskiing. Finding his balance, he started up the line. Hand over hand he moved upward along the line until he was out of the water and no longer struggling with its drag.

Using the boat's skin as leverage, he shimmied up the line with silent precision until he reached the rail. From his vantage at the boat's stern, he could see the captain and mate in the wheelhouse peering ahead in the direction in which the boat was running.

He had only a few seconds to pass out of their line of sight. Darkness was on his side, the quarter moon offering little boost to visibility.

He was pleased to see that the hook had not made a mark on the chrome of the rail. Leaving it attached, he hopped smoothly over the rail onto the deck.

Stealthily, in a crouching position, he crept toward the sunbathing area where the warm night had done its work. Hamilton lay on his back locked in a deep sleep, his jellied bulk moving with the rhythm of his snoring breath.

Removing his knife from its sheath, Champion sprang like a stalking coyote toward the supine figure and poked Hamilton awake. The eyes opened lethargically, then wider with fright and confusion.

He put the knife close to Hamilton's neck, whispering an order to rise and get on his knees facing the deck rail. It was made of wood at that point, and owing to the height of the rubber mattress used by Hamilton, there was less than a foot's clearance from the mattress to the top of the rail.

"Hands in the air," Champion whispered, an order quickly obeyed. In the split second of their eye contact, Champion again imagined a sense of recognition between them, as if Hamilton had retained it in their silent exchange at the Bel Air.

I've come, Champion wanted to say. Did Hamilton's eyes acknowledge a welcome, as if he had been waiting for this moment?

"Please—" Hamilton began, a plea quickly aborted by a strong push along the shoulder blades, toppling him over the rail and into the rippling blackness of the Mediterranean Sea. In a quick reflex action, Champion moved swiftly across the stern deck, removed the rubber hook, and jumped into the ship's wake. It was all over in a matter of seconds.

Treading water, he watched the ship cut smoothly and

obliviously through the sea, its rear lights disappearing into the darkness, the sound of its motors fading. Where Hamilton had fallen, he saw agitation on the shiny surface and heard what he supposed were the squeals and struggles of the drowning man.

He debated briefly with himself on the value of helping the process, deciding finally that it was forensically safer to let nature take its course. Gathering the line, he rolled it up, and attached it and the power gun to the D clamp on his wet suit, and started swimming leisurely toward shore, pausing occasionally to listen for any further sounds from the struggling man. Not a human voice broke the silence of the natural order.

To pass the time as he swam, he relived his effort moment to moment, checking his memory for any mistakes he might have made. His rubber gloves foreclosed on any possibility of fingerprints, not on file anywhere, and he was determined to keep them anonymous. The air would dry any signs of wetness on the deck. Except for the pressure on the man's shoulder blades, he had not touched the body. No alarm had been sounded.

Had he achieved a foolproof accidental death? The short distance between the top of the mattress and the deck rail could provide the alibi of accident. Somehow the man had twisted in his sleep or tried to rise from the wrong side, a fatal error. Only time would tell if such a scenario held water. He chuckled at the irony of such a thought.

The boat had drawn him farther south from the point where he had emerged, which meant he had to swim farther to reach it. It surprised him that he was not tired as he climbed upward along the rocks to the promontory from which he had dived.

Fortunately the area had remained deserted, giving him the leisure to remove his "working" togs and change into the dry clothes he had brought with him wrapped in plastic, a blue blazer, gray slacks, sport shirt, and loafers.

He dismantled the power gun, removed the rubber coating from the hook, and rolled the line into a small bundle. Each of the pieces, including the wet suit, cap, gloves, and the remains of the float, was to be disposed of along the way, all by burial in prearranged places. Nothing would be left to the whore of chance.

It remained to be seen whether all the planning had paid off, although he was confident that he had accomplished his mission without flaw. He did not, of course, search his inner landscape for any jagged outcrops of emotion.

He had noted Hamilton's fear, but only as a detail to be observed, although he could not deny to himself that some mysterious communication had taken place between them. It was merely another blip to be flattened in his mind.

As for the triad of remorse, contrition, and guilt or any other debilitating psychic ripples, he detected no signs in himself, validating once again his conviction that he had long ago excised such tendencies, if any had survived his childhood in the first place.

As he drove, the adrenaline that had energized his bloodstream slowly subsided, giving way to a special kind of restlessness that invariably followed an assignment. It was the moment when sexual tension burst through the bonds of his disciplined repression and demanded to be served.

To deflect this pressing need, he turned his mind to another area of his professional spectrum, his evasion itinerary. His highly specialized modus operandi eschewed immediate movement, which invited suspicion. To that end, he would spend another week at the Bel Air, a playboy in residence.

Chapter 7

Cars whizzed by her as she drove steadily and cautiously on the piage, alert to the fact that she would soon reach the Nice turnoff, her exit of choice to reach Cap Ferrat, although it meant going north again along the coast road.

Surprisingly, she did not feel the ravages of fatigue that might have been expected after such a long drive. Recalling in detail the events of her Florence experiences exhilarated her.

The end of the journey, she realized, would abort the continuity of memory, causing her to redouble her efforts to interpret the full meaning of her encounter with Aunt Emma.

"Did I say something stupid last night?" Emma had asked, as they trekked through the Uffizi on the day before the "incident." Somehow the conversation that day and evening seemed the quintessential moment of the entire encounter with Aunt Emma. It came back to her so vividly that she had the sensation that Aunt Emma was sitting beside her in the car.

Puzzling, oddly challenging, startling, revealing, but not stupid, Angela thought.

"Not that I can remember," she said.

"Good."

They moved from gallery to gallery, Emma commenting

on the paintings.

"But it was delicious," she said. "Two girls confiding. Wasn't it?" Delicious again.

"Yes, it was," Angela said sincerely, reveling in the word. Yes, it had been delicious despite the fact that the revelations were, unfortunately, one-sided. In retrospect, she wished she might have matched her aunt in kind. Their conversations had left her strangely diminished, feeling irrelevant and confused. True passion. Erotic center. Compared to Aunt Emma she might have been a plant, unflowering, with unpromising shoots and shrunken roots.

Emma put her arm around Angela's shoulders.

"We're going to be even greater friends, aren't we, darling?"

Angela nodded. She hoped it would happen, although she was having difficulty coming to grips with her aunt's view of life and the disturbing way it highlighted her own rather pallid existence.

In the light of morning, however, without the stimulus of the champagne, she tried to counter any further sense of deprivation by staking out a judgmental position, assuming a high moral tone. Aunt Emma's life, she told herself, was defined by promiscuity hidden under the amorphous mask of something she called by pretentious names like love, passion, the life force. What did they mean?

Despite Aunt Emma's denials, Angela speculated that pure lust was her aunt's motivating force, her desire triggering a hormonal overflow that created a powerful sexual itch. Actually such an explanation sounded far too clinical and came close to characterizing Aunt Emma as a bit of a nymphomaniac.

She searched her memories. Had her father ever used that term? Hadn't Aunt Emma herself admitted that she had been making love since she was thirteen? Back then when fear of pregnancy made virginity more the norm than the exception? After all, when Aunt Emma was still a teenager, the pill and the resultant sexual revolution were years away. Aunt Emma had taken big risks for sexual pleasure, perhaps one risk too many. Angela wondered whether a botched abortion really was the dark secret of her aunt's infertility.

But had Aunt Emma really confided, or rather provided mere generalities and pontifical philosophies that only seemed profound when accompanied by gobs of champagne?

"Follow your heart." What did that mean? And that nonsense about where the soul resides. There? And yet, Angela admitted, the strangely exotic view of life provided by her aunt had aroused the dormant sexual side of her. Indeed, before she fell asleep her mind had wandered into fantasy, and she had felt a curious reaction "down there," although she was too exhausted to make any physical moves to gratify herself. This reaction baffled her and posed secret questions she had never allowed herself to pose before.

To know more, whatever that meant, grew in importance as the day progressed. To know more what? The truth? About what? And how was this relevant to Angela's world? Why did it suddenly matter so much? The questions proliferated in her mind.

Later, back in their room at the Grand, like a taped rerun they reclined on Angela's bed, again well oiled with champagne, "confiding."

Angela saw in the scene an element of her own orchestration, as if it were she who had manipulated her aunt into the present situation and lulled her into this mode of candor and confidence for her own ends.

"Florence opens one up, don't you think?" Emma said. "Each day of looking at those magnificent works expands the inner eye."

"Well put, Auntie," Angela said.

They lay on propped pillows sipping champagne. Emma's sense of intimacy seemed to have grown, and she was now regularly swizzling Angela's champagne with the cross. In fact, at each fresh pour, Angela was lifting her glass to have it done.

"Think of the jillions of eyes that have seen these sights," Emma said. "Boggles one. What do you think they take away with them?"

"A fresh look at life," Angela said, studying her aunt. "The fact is that of all the sights in Florence, you're the real boggler, Aunt Emma."

"Little me?" Emma giggled.

"And your battalions."

"Who still march on," Emma laughed. "I am the Pied Piper of Amore."

"Was it…?" Angela began, hesitating, trying to frame the question in some precise way. "Is it… what is the word?"

Angela pretended a prolonged search. "Fulfilling?"

Emma burst into laughter.

"Filling, yes. But filling full… obviously not. I am not yet filled with them, and all the oncoming battalions may not fill me."

Giddy with champagne, she lifted her cross again and swizzled both of their glasses. Then she pointed at Angela with the vertical bar of the cross.

"But I'll tell you this. I believe I have been on the right track. The sheer pleasure of the attempt is well worth the candle, I can assure you. Sometimes I feel… well, it's Florence… all that religion around… that I am doing God's work, finding pleasure in the way he made us. Giving as good as I get. I get as much pleasure in the giving as the getting. I love making men squeal with joy. Such a marvelously practical way we were made. Taking our principal pleasure in the act of propagation." Her voice trailed off as she took a deep sip, but before she could begin, Angela interrupted, oddly agitated.

"Aunt Emma… but you haven't propagated." As it came out of her mouth, it seemed an insult. Angela was immediately contrite. Emma brushed it away.

"By design, darling. On my part…" She looked up, embellishing the theme. "I was fastidious in keeping those feisty little spermatozoa at bay." She laughed again. "God bless the technology of birth control." Emma winked. "I simply weighed the issue in terms of time. As George Bernard Shaw said, 'Youth is wasted on the young.' I suppose my decision flew in the face of our female destiny to propagate." She shrugged and sucked in a deep breath. "Your father thought I was a selfish voluptuary. Perhaps he was right."

It had never occurred to Angela to reject childbearing, although, she did not find anything very special or mystical in conception.

Indeed, she could not remember if there was any pleasure in it at all. Or passion. The idea set her on some alien path within herself. Love and passion—this was the way her aunt defined herself.

"There are other things in life, Aunt Emma," Angela said, feeling uncomfortably defensive. After all, the experience of child rearing had been gratifying and, despite her aunt's contrary view, a fulfillment of her gender's destiny.

"Are there?" Emma said raising her eyebrows and cocking her head mischievously, waiting for Angela to cite some profound alternatives.

"Of course," Angela said, groping for ideas and deliberately steering Emma away from the issue of children. "Like appreciation of art, music, literature, flowers, animals… like achieving contentment and self-esteem—"

"That silly hyphenate," Emma interrupted with a huff of dismissal, clicking her tongue. "See how psychobabble has polluted the language."

"You are impossible, Aunt Emma," Angela said hoping she was hiding her irritability.

"Aren't I though?" Emma laughed, reaching over once again to pour the champagne into their glasses. "Emma, the impossible. Actually it is very useful to be considered impossible. People more readily accept your actions, especially if they do not conform to their expectations and ideas of proper conduct."

An edge of seriousness was creeping into her voice.

"The flip side," Angela said suddenly. It was what she had been reaching for, the contention that there was a flip side to her aunt's lifestyle.

One simply could not take one's pleasure whenever one saw an opportunity. There were always other considerations and consequences. Living, like art, was a discipline, requiring restraints. One did not follow one's "heart" like a predatory animal following a scent. Not that Aunt Emma could be considered predatory. Self-indulgent certainly. Angela could not deny a shiver of envy.

"Flip side?" Emma said, obviously baffled.

"I mean…" Angela sucked in a deep breath. "I don't know how to put this…"

"When you're in that mode, I'd suggest a deep draught of the old giggly as a first step." The cross came out from between her breasts and swizzled their glasses. Angela felt her aunt watching her with mischievous eyes as she gulped a mouthful. "There now… try again."

"What I knew about you, Aunt Emma, is only what I learned from you on your brief visits and all that anecdotal stuff from Dad and my own… well… imagination."

"Ah yes, I knew my brother's characterization. To him I was the wild nymph, his implications quite clear?"

Angela nodded.

"A bee that flits from flower to flower, sucking up nectar?"

"Well put, Auntie."

She was happy to see the conversation proceeding sweetly.

"Thinking only of herself. A heartbreaker and a home wrecker?"

"More or less."

"An insatiable bitch?"

It seemed a discordant note, but Angela challenged the accusation.

"Now you're fishing for compliments."

There was a long pause. Suddenly Emma put down her glass on the night table beside the bed and sat up. Then she turned and looked down at her reclining niece. Angela felt the heat of her glance as it bore down at her, laser-like. The mood had definitely changed. Gaiety vanished. A profound moment seemed gathering.

"I'm fishing for you, my darling."

"Me?"

Angela was startled. She had assumed that Aunt Emma was the subject under scrutiny. She had been wrong.

"Can you say, Angela, that you are very pleased with your life?"

Angela waited, assembling her thoughts. It needed to be put into words. Aunt Emma represented something that might have been in vogue years ago, generations ago. The quaint enslaving idea of the passionate romantic female, that only through love, meaning with the male counterpart, the phallic magnet of the life force, was there real fulfillment. And only that kind of love could induce real passion.

Oh, Aunt Emma was charming, endearing, witty, and, of course, wonderfully unorthodox, the so-called rebellious spirit, more an amusement than a serious contender for a present-day role model. Angela wanted to say so but in a way that would not wound.

"Pleased? I have two children, a very successful husband. I live well. I'm quite rich. I devote much of my life to helping others. I have a modicum of freedom. I'm here with you, for example."

It occurred to her suddenly that she was presenting a rather meager case. But she persisted gamely.

"I don't measure my fulfillment by the power or frequency of my orgasms or the magnetism of my attraction to men. This idea of the so-called grand passion that sweeps through you like a hurricane… well,… I'm not sure it's possible to divorce yourself from your reason to that extent. And, Aunt Emma… I adore you. I really do, and I hope you're not taking this unkindly or think I'm deliberately spoiling our time together, but really, I do not believe that a woman's soul resides in the—"

"The you know," Aunt Emma said smiling broadly, apparently not the slightest bit intimidated by her niece's eloquence.

"My…" Angela cleared her throat, "…cunt is not the center of my universe," she blurted with sudden exasperation, while still trying to maintain some semblance of good humor, although her equilibrium was totally out of whack, and she knew it.

Emma put a hand over her mouth in mock surprise.

"The C word." She clapped her hands. "Angela dear, young ladies of certain upbringing do not say such words."

"And not everything is defined by…" Again she cleared her throat. "…dicks."

"Oh my God. I must get the soap."

"And…" Her throat went dry. "Fucking isn't everything."

Despite herself, Angela burst into laughter. She must be drunk. This was ludicrous. Wasn't she trying to make some profound statement? It had deteriorated into an orgy of slang, and they both were loving it. They lay back on the bed doubled up with uncontrolled laughter, quieting finally in diminishing spasms.

"You were wonderful," Emma said, embracing her niece. They clung together on the bed. "So old-fashioned."

"Old-fashioned?" Angela stopped laughing abruptly. "I'm old-fashioned? Because I'm not one of those career women out there competing toe to toe with men? In control, as they say, of my own destiny? Wouldn't most of them just love to change places with me?" Angela paused for a moment, hoping her next remark wouldn't be too hurtful. "You're not exactly the epitome of the modern woman either, Aunt Emma. The way you talk, one would think that your principal career was carried out on your back."

"And on my knees, elbows, and stomach," Emma said, showing no sign of offense. "But what has that got to do with anything. Being a woman isn't just an attitude. It's a biological and psychological miracle. It has nothing to do with ambition or greed or competing with men or anything material."

"What then?"

Emma raised herself on her elbow and swizzled her glass again, but did not bring it to her lips.

"I told you. Find your erotic center, and you'll know."

Emma swung her legs over the side of the bed and stood up. Then she looked down at Angela, who lay sprawled on the quilt, her robe askew.

"You're quite beautiful, Angela," Emma said. It was another one of her mysterious implications.

She watched as Aunt Emma upended her glass. The gesture unwrinkled her neck flesh. In that attitude her neck looked much younger, swanlike. In fact, her whole image looked younger in the declining light. The wild nymph!

"Big day tomorrow, darling," Emma said. "David or bust."

Her aunt bent over the bed and planted a cool kiss on Angela's cheek. Emma's breath smelled sweet with the champagne, and Angela breathed in her aunt's fragrance. For some reason, she reached out and held her as tightly as the position made possible.

"I know, sweetheart," Emma whispered. "I know."

What did Aunt Emma know? Angela asked herself after her aunt had disengaged and gone off to her own room. She lay in her bed for a long time, wrestling with an uncommon sense of anxiety.

What is going on here? she demanded of herself, searching for some inner spigot that might shut off such disturbing feelings. It was as if some unseen force was trying to tear her from her moorings.

She found it increasingly difficult to chase such feelings, and her agitation accelerated. Picking up the phone, she decided to call Tom. Hearing his voice, she decided, might reconnect her again with her more familiar self.

"He's in conference, Mrs. Ford," the smoothly efficient voice of Tom's administrative assistant, Cynthia Bilton, said. Tom Ford's business affairs were the woman's life. A ball buster, Tom had admitted, citing his need to apportion time and energies. Angela had finally surrendered the point.

"It's really pressing, Cynthia," Angela said, deliberately flaunting her position as wife. "Very."

She could almost hear the computer in Cynthia's mind evaluating the priorities.

"Nothing gone wrong in Florence?"

"Nothing gone wrong anywhere, Cynthia. Just put me through please."

"Anything I can do?" the woman persisted.

"Put me through, please."

There was a moment's hesitation.

"Of course."

The silence was palpable as she waited for the connection. It was morning in Manhattan, a working day. Tom was elaborately connected to his various minions with cutting-edge technology, they and Angela never knowing quite where he was. For all she knew, he could be anywhere.

"Angela!"

His voice was familiar enough for reassurance.

"I bring greetings from Florence," Angela said cheerily, wondering why his voice had not calmed her agitation.

"That it?"

"My Aunt Emma is a pistol —" she began.

"But you're having a good time?" he interrupted. His attention seemed otherwise engaged, but he was too smooth to make it appear that he was trying to deflect her, cut her short.

It struck her how good he was at compartmentalizing. His world was like a vast bank of safety-deposit boxes that he could open and close at will, never mixing their contents. Had she thought about this before? Was it her skill as well? Why was she thinking these thoughts?

"I know I'm calling at a bad time," she said.

"Is there something wrong?"

"No. Everything is fine. I just needed to…" her voice trailed off.

"It's okay," he said.

"Have you heard from the children?" she asked, hesitating, remembering suddenly that she had not given them the name of her hotel. Compared to what he was doing, this must seem to him like trivia, she thought. But since she had opened the domestic box, he was not going to mix contents. Perhaps he had many boxes open at this moment.

"Peter called from China," he said. "He says you cannot believe what's happening there. Says it's the land of opportunity."

"Wonderful. And Sandra?"

"Somewhere in the Argentine north on a ranch. She's probably out of touch."

His voice seemed more impersonal than usual. She expected that he was sitting in his conference room, that people were watching him as he spoke.

"How's the weather in Florence?"

"Hot."

"Hot everywhere it seems. Max said it's stifling on the Riviera."

"Dear old Max," she sighed.

She was not looking forward to Max's four-day extravaganza. They were booked at the Bel Air until Max's yacht returned from Saint-Tropez, which would be sometime during the weekend, probably Sunday. Max used it as a kind of floating hotel for his business associates and their wives or significant others. It was a stultifying prospect, being trapped and manipulated in Max's dog and pony show.

She detested the man, his bulk and his overbearing ways, but this was one of those command performances. The bonus, of course, was the Florence trip with Aunt Emma.

"Are you enjoying Aunt Emma?" Tom asked. He had little knowledge of or emotional ties to her.

"Enjoying?" she asked aloud. "Yes, it's an experience."

"See you soon. Should get in early Sunday morning," he said.

She felt the box being closed, smoothly, as if on a well-oiled hinge. It struck her that the need for this conversation had vanished completely. Had she believed it would be comforting, chase anxiety, repress uncertainty? It hadn't.

She wished that her father were alive. His was the only voice that could ever soothe her.

"Dad," she said aloud, to the dark and empty room.

At this moment the sound of his voice would have been enough. Perhaps, she thought, she should have recorded it and had it available to her as needed. The way he said it, "Angela."

"I need you, Daddy," she said to the empty space, not quite knowing why.

Lying alone in her bed, she felt oddly desolate. Getting up, she paced the room, looked out the window, watched the moon's glow shimmer on the softly moving Arno.

Nothing seemed to placate her anxiety. She put on her nightgown, creamed her face, and slipped between the sheets. Within moments, she realized that she would never get to sleep. Getting up again, she went to the door of her aunt's room and opened it.

"Aunt Emma," she whispered, moving closer to the bed, feeling like a frightened child.

"Angela?" Her aunt's voice was drenched with sleep.

"I can't seem to…"

She saw the cover rise and her aunt's body move to one side of the bed.

"Crawl in, darling." Emma beckoned.

She moved under the covers beside her aunt, her back turning to Emma. Then her aunt moved closer and held her as if they were two spoons. She felt the comfort of their flesh touching, the transfer of its soothing warmth. She hadn't realized how cold she was.

Her aunt pressed closer, an arm swung around, moved under her breast, cupping it. Only then, did her anxiety disappear, and after a while she fell asleep.

Chapter 8

Tom Ford put the phone back in its cradle and removed his long legs from the antique stool he kept beside the chair in his private office exactly for that purpose. He liked to think of this little office just off the big conference room, from which he had been summoned by Cynthia Bilton, as his most personal domain, reserved for that compartment of his life that represented stability, tradition, values.

He loved the concept of values, that pure place, away from the filth and grit of business.

This little office, representing the centrality of his family compartment, was a shrine to those values. On his antique desk were pictures of Angela and the children in silver frames of various sizes. There were also pictures on the wall, signposts marking the trail of his family life, the children as babies, the children doing their various sports, Angela's progression from a young bride to mature matron, them as newlyweds on their honeymoon in Hawaii, all smiling, their faces a living emblem of their happiness.

Tom really looked at these pictures often, studied them. They reassured him, he told himself, rationalized his reasons for doing what he was doing. The fact was, he needed reasons, needed them badly. They gave moral heft to his machinations to vastly increase his wealth, depersonalized what might be seen as pure greed or thirst for power. Above all, it excused him from spending so much time away from them. After all, wasn't he pursuing their interests as well as his own?

Yet it troubled him when both children decided to rush to other parts of the globe. Was it because of something that he and Angela had done, or not done? Fortunately, he was too busy to dwell on such thoughts.

He did make certain that he was available to them at all times, wherever he was in the world. The same went for Angela, within reason, of course. His life, that part of it that he reserved for them, was arranged so that neither they nor the so-called outside world would ever have a moment's doubt about his dedication to the values of the family hearth.

No, he would protest to himself at certain vulnerable moments, as if he had been debating it strenuously in his subconscious. They were his armor against any accusation, internal or external, that he was a venal, greedy, unfeeling bastard, a clone of his mentor.

To keep up appearances, he had vowed never to give Angela any idea that he was less than the devoted husband and father, and he had carefully schooled Cynthia Bilton in adopting this caveat. Nothing must stand in the way of that. Nothing. If his appearance was important for Angela's agenda, Cynthia, who structured his schedule must give it his highest priority.

"Angela and the children must be made to feel that they have first call on me," he had told Cynthia often. Above all, she must never be made to feel insecure about Cynthia's role in his life.

Cynthia complied with practiced diplomacy. She was, after all, his expediter, his gatekeeper, his confidante, his instrument… and his fucktress.

Before he had ever laid eyes on her, he had designed her in his mind. Above all, she must have a nonthreatening appearance, an ordinary forgettable face, a hard body that could be well disguised in practical business clothing.

Where she had erred in presenting herself, he had already imagined the corrections. No cosmetic enhancements, hair ordinary, dress gray without the embellishments of color, her shoes practical. Her face was bony, thin, with sharp angles, and a slightly hooked nose that barely separated close-set eyes, the color deep brown, almost black, the lips tight and thin. She had the predatory look of a bird fixed on a visible kill.

Under the deliberately unattractive clothing, he sensed instinctively the hard flat stomach, the shapely upturned breasts, small but rounded, like her buttocks. Her body, he was surprised to learn, was supple, elastic. She could assume sexual positions of enormous variety, enhancing muscular skills in her genitals that he could not imagine in a grown woman.

Above all, she had to project a persona of unflappable efficiency, cleverly disguised under a patina of carefully practiced charm. She had to be articulate and knowledge-able, an expert in all computerized communications proce-dures and skills, alert, brilliant, and quick thinking.

Above all else, she had to be willing to put herself—body,

soul, heart, and mind—exclusively at the service of Tom Ford. Full time. This was not a job. This was a life, a calling. This was an entrée into another compartment of his life, the one in which he kept the truth of himself, his yearnings, his ambition, his secret heart.

No outside considerations were permissible. No parents, siblings, husband, children, and absolutely no lovers. None. There was also a great deal of dissimulation required. Her primary deception was that she had to pretend that she actually pursued a life outside of the immediate orbit of Tom Ford.

A great deal of testing had been required to fill this role. Cynthia had not been the first candidate. A number had been rejected, one after nearly six months of service, although she had not yet received full initiation. It had cost him a pretty penny.

Although he could construct an impenetrable corporate web, interlocking networks leading to dead ends and innumerable obstacles to surveillance by nosy international investigators, which was exactly what he had done for Max Hamilton, he could not guarantee no betrayal by his most trusted lieutenant, which meant that she would have to perpetually prove her loyalty and absolute devotion.

Naturally, there had been an element of paranoia about their relationship, which gradually subsided as Cynthia, more and more, passed every test Tom had thrown in her path. However you looked at it though, it was a devil's bargain.

In its way, it was not any different from the bargain he

had struck with Max Hamilton. He had given up all clients and devoted himself exclusively to Max's world, a world filled with deceptions and manipulation, some legal, some illegal. On Max's behalf, he was perpetually on call. Nothing had greater priority.

His first glimpse of Max was of a giant ape-man, his bulging hirsute body, skimpily covered around the waist with a towel as he sat on a Chippendale copy in his suite at the Waldorf Astoria blithely eating a watermelon and spitting the seeds indiscriminately over the expensive Oriental rug.

The intimidation was not only in the act of watermelon eating itself and the display of flesh in front of the crisply dressed young Harvard lawyer, but in the wait which had been interminable as what seemed like hundreds were called to the audience before him. He was then a lowly junior in an old-line Wall Street firm assigned to the man on a minor contract matter, largely because none of the senior partners were, that day, prepared to suffer the humiliations administered by their largest client.

The sagacious and brutish Hamilton, understanding the reluctance of the partners to attend him that day, apparently made the snap decision to use the young Tom Ford as an instrument to intimidate the firm and its key vested senior partners.

Even Tom would acknowledge that much of what he knew about greed, chicanery, double-dealing, deception, betrayal, and thievery he had learned in that one-day crash course as the watermelon seeds rained down on the carpet like a hailstorm from the man's moist, greedy maw.

"Does it bother you to fuck people over, son?" Hamilton asked snappishly.

Tom remembered how he had struggled to come up with answers that would ingratiate. He had been smart enough to know that this man could thickly butter the bread of an ambitious young lawyer.

"Yes, it might bother me," Tom had answered. "But it won't inhibit me."

Hamilton laughed, his big belly shaking.

"Business is winning. Fucking people over is a time-honored instrument in the service of that cause. Do you agree?"

Tom was shocked by the comment, but showed no reaction. He wanted this assignment and, even then, foresaw the possibilities of gain. After all, it was Hamilton who wielded the power here, not Tom. Perhaps it was at that moment that Tom received his epiphany. Better to give orders than take them.

"Bluntly speaking, probably, Mr. Hamilton. But it is, I suppose, only one arrow in the quiver."

"Arrow in the quiver," Hamilton roared, his eyes filling with tears and his body shaking in a paroxysm of coughing. "What a bullshitter you are, Ford."

Tom wasn't certain how to respond. But he could see that he was making a favorable impression. The "arrow in the quiver" reference had jumped into his mind. It implied aggressiveness and lethal intention.

"The question is, are you a good lawyer?" Hamilton barked.

"Damned good," Tom said without hesitation.

"Can you put zingers into contracts?"

"Zingers?"

"A sentence or two so subtle and twisting that it totally negates the meaning to favor our side over theirs. That's what a good lawyer is. Someone who can create a paper trail that keeps the other side on the ropes. You get my drift?"

"More or less."

"That's a stupid answer, Ford. A good lawyer is a man who can rationalize and protect a thief. I'm a thief. I steal companies. I strip them clean and buy more companies with the strippings. I borrow up to the eyeballs to force the banks to be my partners. That's the real road to success. Get the money, boys, and handcuff their balls to your fists. When you move, they have no choice. I have no ethics and can lie with impunity. In fact, I love to lie. Am I shocking you?"

Tom shrugged.

"Of course, I am." He undid the towel from his waist and threw it on the floor. "Here I am sitting balls-ass-naked and lecturing to a snot-nose lawyer from… I'll bet… Yale."

"Harvard."

"Better. I like to buy a good façade. A good façade is an absolute necessity when you are in the business of fucking people over and stealing businesses. I have a family façade, a church façade, a social façade. I have a yacht, a jet, limousines, country houses, the whole enchilada. With a good façade people are never certain you are as big a bastard as you really are. I like manipulating people. I am a cheat and a fraud. But put me in a good suit with clean linen and a polka-dot bow tie, and I can charm the pants off anyone. I get what I want. Don't I have a great sense of the dramatic?"

"I couldn't argue with that."

Tom was startled by the man's bluster and candor. His body was a mess, the flesh rolling down the front of him like melted wax. But despite Hamilton's weirdness and eccentricity, Tom was mesmerized. No, charmed was the right word. This was one of the most important business tycoons in the world, a man who made thousands quake with fear, and here he was, a mass of overstuffed naked flesh, offering up a nightmare of lunatic control fantasies.

"I make instant decisions about people. They are almost always wrong, and I have to self-correct quickly. I hound people, fire them, cheat them, browbeat them. I am a cocksucker of the first order. I trust nobody. I also overpay. I believe in overpaying. I overpay for everything, to buy companies, to employees for services rendered. I keep your firm and other law firms all over the world busy with lawsuits. Lawyers love me. Everything I do is actionable. One day either the whole fucking façade might crumble, or I'll die richer than Croesus. Either way it won't matter."

"Why not?"

"Because I'll be dead, asshole. That's when the fun will really begin." He finished the watermelon and threw the rinds on the floor.

"Pretty disgusting, eh? I know manners, believe me. I have dined with kings and potentates. Did you know I fucked Margaret Thatcher?"

Tom felt his throat constrict. He had begun to perspire. He searched his mind for comment and found none to offer.

"Cold bitch. I wouldn't fuck her with your dick. I lied. Do I seem certifiable?"

Tom shrugged.

"Don't answer that. Howard Hughes was certifiable. But he had money. That protected him." He slapped his naked thighs. "Here's the game plan. I'll probably regret it. You're to be my principal contact in the firm. Everything clears through you. You write a contract that backfires, your ass is grass. But I may fire you long before that. You tell those shits to triple your salary. If they don't, call me. They'll do it though. Triple their fees as well. Anybody has in mind to fuck me over in that firm, you tell me. Got it?"

Things seemed to be going too fast. Again Tom was at a loss for words.

"Don't think you've impressed me. You haven't. You're only an instrument. In the end, you'll probably fuck me."

For Tom it was too vivid a memory to ever be forgotten. It set up a strange chemistry between them, both miraculous and poisonous. Fate. Destiny. He could never understand it, except that it established the ground rules between them and began Tom's burrowing into the very entrails of Max Hamilton.

It was not an apt simile, Tom knew, but he had, through clever dealings of his own, actually fattened Max's enterprises, not with blubber but with muscle. Since he had made the decision to one day take control of the Hamilton enterprises, he had no interest in taking over an empire headed for collapse. He let Max play the hunter, while he made certain that the vanquished prey was edible.

But where Max was a greedy philanderer, a womanizer of enormous appetites with an assortment of sexual tastes, Tom considered such careless conduct a dangerous lapse of business security, a threat to his own future.

It also alienated Max's much-put-upon wife and daughters, who sided with the mother and bristled at her perpetual humiliation.

Such conduct required Tom to use his considerable persuasive skills to keep the family in line, both in an emotional and a legal way. He had been assiduous in keeping up a running and sympathetic hand-holding dialogue with Mrs. Hamilton over the years to which she had been responsive. Unfortunately, Max's two daughters were too bitter about their father's neglect to enter into any relationship with anyone associated with him, especially his lawyer.

Tom was well aware that the Hamilton marriage bond, especially one of long standing entered into without the thought of prenuptial agreements, could engender troubling circumstances, especially in the event of Max's death. He was hoping that money alone would solve the problem with the wife and daughters and had made provisions that, he hoped, were of such magnitude that they couldn't be refused.

But his principal energies were applied to fulfilling his own agenda, which was to eventually take over complete control of the Hamilton business empire. Instead of worrying about the trust of numerous whores who could and had been costly and potentially damaging, he had confined his confidences to a single individual, Cynthia Bilton.

Because of their close business and personal relationship, it was impossible to hide from her the paper concoction that he had devised to eventually take over control of the Hamilton empire. He could only hope there would not be a suggestive lesson in it for Cynthia, which was another reason he had required her absolute fealty and her conducting herself in a manner that would not trigger his paranoia.

Embedded in all the complicated legalese and tangle of contracts as well as the people relationships which he had helped forge for Max, there was the unalterable single-minded and ambitious living fingerprint of Tom Ford.

As in the case of Tom and Max, the present bargain between Cynthia and Tom did have its very substantial material rewards: a salary of two million dollars a year with a half-million-dollar bonus every year, stepped up to three million by the third year, eventually by the sixth year rising to five million a year, suitably protected offshore, wherever possible. And numerous ongoing perks: an apartment in Manhattan, limousine transportation, whatever was required materially for the luxurious life.

Tom understood, of course, that the key question in that kind of relationship was the balance between money and betrayal. Or, put another way, could money in the end buy total loyalty? He had strong doubts, which meant that Cynthia Bilton would never, under any circumstances, ever secure her freedom from his closest observation… even if she wanted to.

Yet she did have the key to most, but not all, of his psychic compartments. Unfortunately, there was no way for him to cover all eventualities. The human animal being what it is, with its unreliable record of certainty, would always be prey to some emotional aberration that could wreck their arrangement or, worse, destroy his ability to play the game. Like Max, he would always be at risk.

Risk, he had learned, was inherent in everything. Although he had vetted Cynthia with thoroughness, gray areas could not be avoided.

Born in Cleveland, Ohio, a child of strict Irish Catholic parents who were killed in a train wreck, she had been educated in convent schools and had graduated from Ohio State University with a degree in business. Of course, he had learned these facts through his own investigations prior to his meeting her. He was not a man to enter into any new situation unprepared.

An older brother, Patrick, had gone off to live and work in London for an American bank. Cynthia had followed him after graduation from Ohio State and had worked for a year for an American export firm on Bond Street. She had an apartment near her brother in Kensington. The brother was drowned in a boating accident off the Dover coast. Tom had, of course, considered the tragedy, like that of her parents, fortuitous and an obvious point in Cynthia's favor.

There was, however, one element of disharmony. At their initial interview, she had failed to mention that she had a brother, alive or dead.

Back in the states she took a job as an assistant to the

vice president of a Cleveland bank and had worked her way up to a vice presidency. She had apparently proved far more than a female token, becoming expert in international banking methods far exceeding the needs of a midsized regional bank. A headhunter had brought her to Tom's attention, and by the time of their very first interview, he had concluded that, except for the business of her brother, she met almost all the criteria he had designed.

A significant part of the lure, aside from her impeccable qualifications, was the absence of close relatives or friends, and she had adamantly stated that she was not the least bit interested in any romantic involvements. Her own experience with family, she had told him, the horror and misery of the loss of her parents, had filled her with a determination to avoid such commitments at any cost.

Tom had made certain that she had been forewarned that the interview would be penetrating and incisive, and, to foreclose on future complications, he had made her sign an affidavit that she was fully aware of the impending intimacy of the questions on the grounds of corporate security considerations. He realized, of course, that there might be legal inhibitions on such an arrangement, but, nevertheless, he took the risk. He needed to know everything he could about a person chosen to be his most intimate associate.

Although she had told him of the death of her parents, the evasion of the fact that she had a male sibling had set off warning bells in his mind. The odd cover-up of this information was a sticking point in her being hired.

In her favor was the fact that she had not denied the information. She had simply not mentioned it, merely confirming that she had no living relatives or emotional ties to anyone.

Aside from that, she had passed every test of his judgment. Finally, during their third interview, he asked her:

"Are you certain, Miss Bilton, that you've told me everything?"

He was, of course, deliberately intimidating, borrowing an attitude he had learned from Max Hamilton. To her credit, she understood immediately what he was referring to, and it seemed to trigger an epiphany in her, as if she had finally realized both the extent of his reach and the true nature of the job.

"I had a brother who died in an accident," she told him.

"Was there any reason you kept this hidden?"

She hesitated, but only for a moment. It was obvious that she knew this was her last hurdle and she seemed determined to face it directly.

"I did not want the fact that I had lost my entire family through accident to color your opinion of me. Perhaps you might think me a bad-luck charm. The fact that you've inquired makes me believe you knew all along. Did you discover, too, that he was with the CIA?"

Tom Ford was genuinely surprised at this assertion and showed it.

"Now there is a revelation," he said. "My information had him as a representative of an American bank in London. Our intelligence sources must be slipping. We'll have to correct that. CIA, you say?"

"Very, very sensitive CIA," Cynthia told him, lowering her voice. In an odd gesture she looked from side to side as if others might be present, an unnecessary reflex since they were alone in his office. She bit her lip and then began to speak. He did not interrupt her.

"The bank was a CIA front. He was covert, part of the CIA's dirty deeds department."

"He told you that?"

"I was with him in London during his final days, and I'm also the executor of his estate. Not much in money, but he did leave information. He seemed to sense that his usefulness was coming to the end. The CIA was very neat in those days. There was no career future in assassination. No future, although…" she paused, "…considering the current world situation, it might soon be making a comeback." It was, Tom thought, a throwaway line, and then she continued with a shrug. "In the end, he never used it as insurance. But he wanted me to know his involvement. A matter of conscience, he told me. He was only thirty-three."

"The report said he drowned in a boating accident."

"The police said it was an accident. There was no autopsy, partly my fault. I bought the explanation and had him cremated. It was only later, when I heard the tape he had secretly left, that I knew. He suspected that they would eliminate him."

"That's a heavy-duty explanation," Tom said, fascinated by the revelation. This woman knows intrigue and conspiracy, he told himself. In his mind, it clinched his choice. She was it.

"You cannot imagine what goes on. It's a filthy business. Criminal acts in the name of defense and security. He admitted that he loved the excitement of it, although as a good Catholic boy, he was beginning to have moral reservations. The tape was also a confession. It was extremely well documented. He named names, contacts, murders. It was a primer for assassination."

"My God!"

"You wanted complete candor."

"Where is the tape?"

"I destroyed it."

"Did they know he left it?"

"Aside from myself. No one knows." She paused. "Now you. It is a dangerous piece of information, especially for me. If it were known, I would be immediately dispatched to oblivion."

"How do you know you can trust me?"

"I don't. But I want this job badly enough to risk my life for it."

"How can one argue with such trust? How can I not hire you?"

"I was hoping you would see my true value."

He had intuited correctly.

Months later, she had confessed that she had memorized everything on the tape. The information had been put to good use.

***

So far everything between Tom and Cynthia had held a steady course, although he suspected that there were natural resentments, sometimes bubbling briefly to the surface, such as a tendency during intimate moments to reveal signs of discomfort about his guarded family compartment.

He could also sense a certain growing greediness about her own sexual needs, a reversal of sorts, since it had been her job to cater to his demands, although her reactions were a factor in his stimulation. What disturbed him most was, of all things, her eagerness to dedicate herself to him in that way, a paradox since that was the condition of the job.

From the beginning it was a tricky balance, although he had explained what was required of her. He had been deliberately crude, wanting to shock her with the sheer outrageousness of his demand.

"In addition to everything else, I want you to be completely at my beck and call. Utterly. I must become your number-one priority in every aspect. Do you read me?"

"Considering the number you put out there, I would expect nothing less. I am ready."

"Every aspect," he repeated. "You will have no other life."

"Try me."

"No second chances. Zero tolerance. Do you understand?"

He was intentionally monstrous, although it had taken nearly a year for him to make the demand, on the eve of her entitlement to her first million-dollar bonus. He was not above intimidation and understood its timing well.

"I'm surprised you didn't put it in the job description earlier."

Considering that she was to have no outside life anyway, it seemed in some ways a logical reaction. He had expected some resistance, and her quick positive response surprised him.

"Ready when you are," she said. "I'm sick of masturbation."

She had even raised her skirt to show that all she had on underneath was a garter belt, no panties.

"You see," she said. "I've been ready all along. I've always wanted to be your whore."

Of course, he would not have made the proposal unless he was dead certain of her consent, but her reaction was strangely perplexing. This was the kind of chemistry that could not be ordered from a menu and when put into action proved an embarrassment of riches. Although his enjoyment was her principal mission, she seemed to know that her pleasure and abandonment also enhanced his. Her erotic appetites were a lot more than he expected. His only caveat: we must leave a little, very little, for Angela.

Yet, he did not think of himself as a monster for creating this job requirement for Cynthia Bilton. He thought of it more as a strategy of containment and control, keeping it all manageable. By this arrangement, he could eliminate any outside complications, the kind that mixed up compartments and brought unhappy results.

Of course it was a deception, a necessary one, in which, of all people, Angela, trusting, naive, innocent Angela, was an unwitting participant. His life, he told her often, was made up of many compartments, the most important of which was reserved for her and the family. He had no doubt that she had absolute faith in his rectitude, commitment, and faithfulness.

It would, he was certain, be beyond her comprehension to see Cynthia Bilton as anything more than a loyal lackey, however she might secretly resent her role in his business life. Besides, it was inconceivable that Angela could possibly believe that Cynthia was his private whore.

She was more than that, of course, although the sexual aspect was a good indicator of the way she performed her duties as his trusted lieutenant in all categories of his other lives, the lives tucked secretly away in various compartments.

In the realm of pleasure, she had paid attention to the minutest of details, not only of his sexual preferences but the pleasures of the palate and his eye as well, far surpassing his wife in indulgence and efficiency. He liked Ketel One vodka, for example, and truffles from Fortnum & Mason, steaks charred and pink, certain Thai foods, coffee with an almond taste, and the sight of the color blue in various manifestations.

She apparently kept a mental catalogue of these special delights, although he carefully monitored her actions in this regard to prevent himself from being lulled into a state of uncritical acceptance. Above all, his guarded self had to be perpetually maintained. His life depended on it.

Under Tom's scrutiny, Cynthia kept her outside persona—her image, her dress, her hair, her face—free of any hint of femininity and attractiveness. He was quite pleased with this masquerade, proud of her ability to hide the truth behind the façade, the enormous sexual energy and expertise.

The real thrill, he had concluded after much puzzling reflection, was the game itself, reveling in the manipulation of people, as if they were as bloodless as chess pieces. In moving them around the board, he had little regard for their humanity, following no agenda but his own. He had learned to love winning for the sake of winning.

Had he always felt that? He doubted it and had, to explain such an endless game, come to believe that he had been infected with the virus from a prime carrier, Max Hamilton, who exhibited the most virulent of symptoms.

The point of the game, as Tom and all those afflicted well knew, was to keep the game going at all costs. To be a serious player, which meant achieving total control of the entire board and keeping it, also meant understanding that the rules were that there were no rules.

Virtue, and all its complementary attributes, was suspended forever. Morality was nonexistent. Fairness was extinct. Ruthlessness, deception, disloyalty, betrayal, chicanery, and intimidation were the weapons of choice. Rule makers, corporate competitors, governments, and people who stood in the way were obstacles to be vanquished. The fun of it was in its marvelous nastiness, its fantastic greediness, and all its delights in terms of money, power, and the ultimate joy of manipulating others. Above all, he was especially proud of the fidelity of his insight into himself.

He had often reflected on how this attitude and drive had evolved in him. Did it have its roots in his father's failure, a man with enormous creative instincts and ideas, who had been shunted aside by more powerful forces? He had inherited a small daily newspaper in Winterset, a town of twelve thousand in central Ohio, which he had parlayed into a three-town chain.

Although his business was small by any standards, his father nevertheless had a strong sense of place in this narrow orbit, which had once encompassed Tom Ford's entire world. There was reflected glory in it as well, and Tom enjoyed basking in his father's respect and prestige. His mother, too, reveled in the cachet of her husband's reputation, which stressed his wisdom and sense of justice, qualities that permeated the editorials he wrote.

Unfortunately, his father's business acumen did not match his vaunted integrity, and he was forced to sell the papers to a larger chain at the very moment when Tom had graduated with honors from Harvard Law School and had brought to town his new bride.

The new owners let his father stay on in a lesser role, but his power was swiftly eroded, which forever demonstrated to Tom that taking away a man's power was a particularly vicious form of psychic castration.

From there, like the proverbial pebble in the pond, the ripple effect was a disaster for the family. His once-beloved father died on the shoals of depression, and his mother lived her life in an upscale Florida retirement community in a perpetual alcoholic haze. His sister, Madeline, apparently found her need for a reconstituted family satisfied by her membership in a Montana religious cult. He hadn't heard from her in years.

All this historical angst created the logic of his present mindset, which was based on the twin fears of power loss and family wreckage. Such fears, he had learned, easily justified any act that kept such catastrophes at bay. As a man who was convinced he understood the origins of his actions, Tom Ford had found he could be comfortable in any act that put distance between himself and potential disaster.

Everything he did, however it strayed from mainstream morality or violated society's norms, was fully justified. And all his energies were put at the service of reducing risk and consequences to the two ruling passions of his life.

At the family's collapse, Tom brought his new wife to Manhattan and joined a prestigious law firm, the principal client of which was Max Hamilton.

The rest, as they say, is history.

Chapter 9

Throughout the long drive, the "incident" lay tucked away on the membrane of her subconscious, ready to be recalled again and again as she pondered the completely unprecedented and explosive reaction. There was no question in her mind that Aunt Emma's conversation had primed her mind and body for the experience.

Still, she searched for some touchstone, some logic for its occurrence. Did it portend something that she was still unaware of? Did it herald some strange crack in the hard shell of her sexuality? It was baffling yet remarkable in the intensity and ecstasy of its orgasmic rush.

They waited in line along the old stone wall of the Accademia. Aunt Emma looked suspiciously at the sun's slant, remarking that it would be a close race between being admitted and having to brave the unforgiving rays of the August sun.

Fortunately, the line hadn't been as long as it had been on the three previous days, and there was a hope that they could be admitted just in time to avoid the sun's fury.

Angela, although apologetic for making them late, felt considerably refreshed after a dreamless dead sleep, surprised to find herself in Aunt Emma's bed when she awoke. Aunt Emma was already dressed, sipping her coffee, and reading the Herald Tribune.

"My God!" Angela had exclaimed, rushing into her own bathroom for her morning ablutions. In less than a half hour she was finished, and they were on their way to the Accademia.

"Thanks for getting me through the night, Aunt Emma," Angela said as they waited in line.

"I did nothing but occupy space."

"You were there to comfort me."

"Was I?" Emma said, modestly trying to dismiss her importance to Angela's well-being. "It happens," she shrugged.

"Withdrawal from one's regular routine," Angela said. "Not to mention the champagne." These had been among the various rationalizations for last night's condition.

"Ah, yes, the champagne. We certainly did lap up a great deal of that liquid. You must condition your body for it."

"I'll remember that next time we get together."

"Which I hope will be soon."

She put her arm through her niece's and squeezed it.

"Does it ever happen to you, Aunt Emma?"

Emma looked thoughtful.

"I never let it get that far. And, of course, I can always summon the comfort of a man. I have found a man to be an excellent cure for that sort of condition."

There it was again, Angela thought, summoning a sense of magnanimity. There was also an air of sadness about the morning. Later, Aunt Emma would be flying home, and she would be off to Cap Ferrat.

"I'm going to miss you, Aunt Emma," Angela said. "I

loved being with you."

"I'm so glad. Wasn't it fun… you know, talking?"

"And drinking."

"And drinking."

Emma laughed.

"And you'll be tooling around the Riviera in the Hamilton yacht. Not exactly a shabby prospect."

"With you there it wouldn't be, Aunt Emma. The truth is that it's a terrible bore. Max holds court. He has you trapped at sea. They talk deals all day long—deals, takeovers, manipulations."

"And Tom?"

"He's very much a part of it. Long ago I learned to shut my ears to it. I go through the motions."

With the exception of last night, she had managed to put the cruise on Max's yacht out of her mind. It was an exercise she had grown quite good at it, putting things out of her mind.

"You're still going to drive?" Emma asked.

She nodded. What was her rush? She'd get to the Bel Air in time for bed. The line moved and they followed in tandem, moving through the elaborate door.

In the near distance, she saw the statue of David, standing, towering, at the far end of the corridor, his alabaster marble skin glowing in the brightness of the elaborate skylight, a dominating presence.

Along the corridor leading to the David, there were other sculptures by Michelangelo, unfinished by the master, half emerging from the stone that held them. Hadn't she read somewhere that the great sculptor had said that he could see the figure in the block of marble, and all he had to do was to eliminate the excess? But that one, David, commanded the space, vanquishing all forms in its view.

In the David's presence, as she moved toward it, the human species seemed to diminish. The crowd of spectators became amorphous, molten fluid puddling harmlessly on the floor at the feet of the colossus. She was mesmerized, pulled toward it by the force of its creation, a compelling maleness emerging victorious from its prison of marble.

As she circled the statue, she felt the centrality of its power, filling her, beckoning her, seducing her. She was totally unprepared for its massive effect.

The white body, courageously positioned in perfect arrogant relaxation, the right shoulder slightly lowered, the right muscled arm holding the bunched handle of the sling, which slid down over the top cheek of his shapely buttock. His left hand raised to chin level held the other end of the sling, leading the eye to observe the shapely face, a wide oval with perfect contemplative lips, over a chin that cried out for a cleft, and a nose sloping from a frowning noble forehead topped with a curled mass, as the large almond-shaped eyes studied the seemingly impregnable Goliath, searching for the giant's vulnerability.

As she moved around it, Angela's eyes hungrily searched for every detail, taking in the magnificent body, the magnificent perfection of the buttocks rising from the supple, perfect, youthful back, the erect nipples poking out of the deep chest, and moved downward over the muscled hips and stomach, down to the patch of pubic hair and below — a penis, full of sensual promise resting on its bed of seemingly soft testicles, proudly hung between the graceful tapering thighs, which themselves led downward to strong perfect legs and massive feet.

It… he… was a living, pulsing presence, every vein visible in the alabaster flesh, blood-filled and alive. Here was the essence of manhood, the power and the glory of its raging sexuality.

"My God!" Aunt Emma whispered, her breath hot on Angela's skin. "That is what I call a man. I could die for his embrace."

Angela could not tear her eyes from the infinite body, roaming and repeating the journey over from the tousled crown, the young and vigorous face, the broad shoulders, the massive muscular arms, the strong oversized hands, the torso, lingering on the rounded moons of his buttocks.

"Don't you just feel the force of it?" Aunt Emma asked.

Angela's eyes, like a moist searching tongue, greedily caressed the figure, the buttocks, the nipples, the chest, the stomach, and moved downward to the massive phallus, uncut, the bulb ready to emerge from its sheath, beginning, she was certain, to pump with life, ready to rise, the huge testicles boiling, heavy and full, like massive ripe fruit.

Angela felt this force taking hold of her, something bubbling deep inside her, a hot moist powerful wave gathering, foam-tipped, rolling relentlessly toward her.

Inside herself, she felt the fluids charging, the moisture oozing out of her, soaking the crotch of her panties. Her heart raced as the inner wave gathered strength rolling toward her.

She could not remove her glance from the mesmerizing presence of this giant male, alive now in her mind, inflaming her body, as she imagined that it was moving forward to embrace her, engulf her with his giant arms, the hands and fingers caressing, exploring as she spread her legs to receive the giant veined and alabaster phallus.

Her breath came in gasps and she had to back up to the wall for support.

"What is it, Angela?"

She heard Emma's voice, but it came from a long way off. Backed up against the wall, she could feel the giant male's embrace, the sheer power of it, plunging into her body, pumping, stroking. Every pore opened and oozed and that center part of her swelled and gushed, the hot fluids sliding down her thighs.

She felt herself letting go, the wave slapping the edges of her essence, exploding inside, the massive phallus erupting as the wave broke. She bit her lip to keep herself from screaming as the orgasm came, thundering through her, burning her with pleasure. She felt powerless, in the grip of this gargantuan explosion, bleeding with moisture.

"Are you all right?" Emma asked.

She had lost all sense of space and time, her only benchmark being the unbearable pleasure of the experience, the "incident" as it would forever be labeled in her mind.

At that moment, she could only sense what effect it was about to have on her life, this aftershock of floodgates smashed open. Yet she dared not carry her thoughts beyond the moment, fearing them, knowing only that something profound had changed inside her.

When she was fully conscious again of her surroundings, she inspected the scene carefully. It seemed ordinary now, people looking upward at the massive statue, ignoring her presence. She surmised that, oddly, she had not become a spectacle for public consumption. What had happened had occurred inside her. Only Aunt Emma had observed an outward reaction. Their eyes met now.

"Better?" Emma asked, inspecting her face.

Angela nodded without explanation, fighting to regain her composure. Then, miming a gesture that indicated she was off to the ladies room, she hurried back down the corridor where she could see the sign.

Inside the ladies room, she ducked into an empty booth and sat down on the lidded toilet. She was still agitated, the physical residue of her experience very obvious. She removed her panties, which were soaked through.

The experience was, in the light of reflection, incomprehensible. She could make no sense out of such a reaction to what was, after all, an inanimate object. It could be defined clinically she supposed as a massive multiple orgasm, something she had never in her life experienced. It had seized her like a giant earthquake.

Perhaps, she speculated, such a reaction was not uncommon, although never publicly discussed. After all, on exhibit here, was a giant figure in all his naked masculine glory. Was her reaction testimony to the masterpiece, a transfer-ence of sexual emotion, handed down through the centuries by the magic hammer and chisel of Michelangelo?

But while her mind groped for understanding, her physical state calmed somewhat. Blotting the moisture on her body with paper, she stepped out of the booth, threw the soaked panties in a trash bin, then washed her face, ran a brush through her hair, and repaired her makeup.

As she watched her face in the mirror, she felt reason and logic returning. Everything in life had to have an explanation, her practical side told her. It was time, she told herself, for her "no nonsense" side to take over. What had happened, given Aunt Emma's conditioning of her mind, could be attributed to the power of suggestion.

Her sessions with Aunt Emma, the nightly infusion of mind-bending intoxication, the emphasis on sexuality, and the images planted by her aunt in her imagination had just welled up in the face of this naked marvel and his giant genitalia and triggered a predictable reaction. That was it. Of course. No need for any metaphysical conundrums or cosmic abstractions.

She debated sharing the experience with Aunt Emma, and it was only when she had left the ladies room and saw her aunt rise from the bench where she had sat waiting for her that Angela decided how to explain what had happened.

"What was it, Angela?" Emma asked.

"I came to Florence, to come in Florence," she trilled, hoping the humor might trivialize the "incident," make it seem less profound. Aunt Emma looked at her puzzled at first, until understanding emerged.

"You didn't?"

"It just happened," Angela said feeling her face flush.

"Lucky you," Aunt Emma said, putting her arm under Angela's as they moved out into the now sun-drenched street in front of the Accademia.

Chapter 10

"Early tonight, Mr. Champion?" the uniformed young man at the hotel entrance said as he opened the door of the Jaguar, preparatory to parking it.

Champion nodded, pleased with the observation. Of all nights, this was the one to be seen arriving earlier than usual. He strode through the elaborate marbled lobby where the night concierge greeted him with a broad smile. Champion had already established his excellent tipping credentials.

In a moment of uncertainty, he considered the possibility of approaching the man to request that he be provided with female companionship—bodies actually, since the exchange would be the intercourse of flesh, nothing more.

He had discovered through practice that experienced concierges in the most luxurious hotels in the world could be trusted for a price to come up with sexual partners of any gender, racial variety, or specialty of the highest proficiency.

But for some reason, he decided not to, although, if an investigation had ensued, the encounter might have further validated his alibi. Depending on the accuracy of the finding of time of death, he was otherwise engaged. In planning his evasions, his mental meanderings led him to imagine every conceivable possibility. This was, of course, the equally challenging part of his hydra-headed profession.

He chose instead to go downstairs to the bar, a lavishly appointed lounge dominated by an aquarium in which exotic fish cavorted in shimmering elegance. The bar was half filled, and a black pianist played vaguely familiar songs. It was a bizarre commercial tribute the writer W. Somerset Maugham, who had maintained a home nearby and was supposed to have arrived at this place, in another incarnation, for his evening cocktail.

He rejected, as he always did, a seat at the bar itself because of the danger of being exposed to the chumminess induced by alcohol and proximity. Although he liked the sensation of the high, he was well aware of the dangers of alcohol as an agent in relaxing discipline and encouraging inadvertency.

He was shown a table for one, actually two, since his back faced the wall, and a chair was placed at the opposite end of the table. From there he was able to observe the people chatting and imbibing in the lounge.

Ordering a bottle of Dom Pérignon vintage, although it was unlikely he would consume more than half, he deliberately let his eyes linger briefly on the various occupants of the place, mostly to fix in their minds an identity and a mood, of being alert and lighthearted, which would counter any suggestion that he had spent the earlier part of the evening on a killing expedition.

And then he felt her presence, before he actually saw her. He had not seen her enter, and by the time he raised his eyes from his champagne glass to observe her, she was sliding into the table next to him, her body angling forward as it moved, the curve of her buttocks, tight and hard in their sheaf of beige skirt, gliding past, her hips swinging gracefully, as her body floated downward into place.

To contemplate the source of the impact her presence had made, he had turned full face toward her. With shutter-speed efficiency, he photographed her permanently in his mind, the naturally jet-black sheen of her hair, falling in soft waves to her shoulders, catching spangles of light, the large puddles of greenish eyes framed in black lashes, absorbing the world over high cheekbones between which jutted a gently curving Roman nose, the lips, the lower one larger than the upper one, sensuous and pouting.

She wore a silk beige blouse, open enough to reveal the beginning of creamy white fullness. His eye searched for and found the telltale impressions of her nipples on the fabric. That same buttermilk whiteness was also in the flesh of her hands. He noted that her fingers were long, tapered, with a diamond wedding ring on the appropriate digit.

Aside from her physical presence, he could smell the intoxicating aroma of her aura, a commingling of perfume that brought to mind white flowers and whatever else emanated from the essence of her. He realized at once that her presence was something unique, a disruption of the activity in his tightly wound self, and he made a conscious effort to obliterate the intrusion. This had never happened to him before. He had never noticed a woman before with such greedy detail and intensity. Immediately, he sensed the danger, but could not find the will to extricate himself.

Sipping his second glass of champagne, he forced himself into a stonewalling mode, willing an imaginary wall around him, keeping his body rigid, and trying to mimic a glazed look, as if he were concentrating on some deeply internal thoughts.

He was only modestly successful, his plan defeated, finally, by the sound of her voice, deep and throaty, a bedroom voice, whispering. She was making an inquiry about a glass of champagne.

"Not as good as that, madame, but more than adequate," the waiter said. He was a young man, blond and imperious in his crisp tuxedo, as he pointed with his chin to the bottle of Dom Pérignon leaning like the tower of Pisa in its silver bucket.

Champion's response was pure reflex, his voice traveling faster than his caution. Even then, he knew he was taking a step forward on thin ice.

"Please pour the lady," Champion said, offering no smile and hoping that his tone did not reveal his interest.

"Oh, no," the woman protested, turning to face him more directly. He felt her scrutiny, which excited him, although he made no outward sign to reveal his unfamiliar and self-threatening emotional response. By then, whatever he was feeling was no longer stoppable. Fool, he admonished himself, his reaction baffling.

"I'll never be able to finish this by myself," he said, despite all the inhibitions boiling in his mind. Their glances touched briefly. Did he turn away first? He wasn't certain. The waiter watched them, alert to whatever decision might be made.

"You're being very generous but I—"

"Not generous… practical. I hate waste," he replied, conscious of his detour, berating himself again for his weakness, adrift and unable to find his mooring.

If this had been a mere physical attraction, he might have been able to resist and quickly crawl back into his shell like a threatened turtle. This though was beyond the physical, more than that, much more. Retreat! He heard the echo of the command in his brain confusing him. This had never happened to him before. Ever.

"So do I," the woman said, recalling him to his remark about waste. He shrugged to the waiter, who took the gesture as a sign of acceptance. The waiter quickly returned to the bar and was back with an empty champagne glass that he placed in front of the woman. Then he removed the bottle from its icy bath, wrapped it in a white napkin, and poured the bubbly liquid into the woman's glass.

In a gesture of acceptance, she slowly raised the glass to her lips offering a broad smile, showing white even teeth. The very act, the delicate way she held the stem of the glass, the sensuous lips curling around the rim, so pedestrian and unnoticed in others, was painfully titillating to Champion, who felt the ache of desire from his eyes to his scrotum.

His fingers actually shook as he lifted his own glass. What is happening here? he asked himself, regretting that he had not taken steps to assuage his sexual tension with the mindless bodies of the concierge's selection. Get up at once, he ordered himself, disobeying. The rebellion against his logic was ominous.

"No substitute for the best," the woman said, returning the glass to the table. He had watched her fingers traveling downward, wishing, imploring them silently to reach out and touch his flesh as they touched the tablecloth. He used her silence to muster his energy for another stab at a retreat. It wasn't to be.

"I've just driven up from Florence," the woman said, a casual remark he told himself, not at all flirtatious. She was, he assumed from the ring she wore, a married woman on a holiday or possibly a recent widow vacationing to forget. It was the kind of deliberate thought meant to inhibit the wild energy that was running through him, fueled by her proximity.

"Did you?" he replied, emptying his own glass. The waiter rushed to the silver bucket, lifted the bottle and deftly refilled the glass. He watched the bubbles jump upward and burst on the surface of the golden liquid, wondering if he was showing convincing disinterest. For some reason, the woman, now that the ice was broken, seemed determined to pursue a dialogue.

"Those tunnels. Engineering miracles. I tried to count them. Gave up at fifty. Ah, but Florence… yes, Florence."

She seemed to lose herself in memory, her sense of place disappearing into herself, which gave him an opportunity to observe her with even more intensity. Studying her only confirmed his special interest. He felt ensnared, a fly caught in the sticky silver threads of the elaborate web she had, perhaps deliberately, spun. It occurred to him suddenly that she might be some special agent, designed especially to seduce and ensnare.

Again, by concentrating his gaze elsewhere, he made a futile effort to disengage, but the hook had bitten too deep.

When he again lifted his eyes, he found himself peering into hers. They locked glances in what felt like an epiphany of recognition, as if she, or he, were someone from a long-ago, far more innocent time, childhood perhaps, and they were both searching each other's face, as if both were determined to place each other in adulthood.

He knew it was time to flee, that he had better go away, vanish. Then reason, or was it rationalization, intervened. This was no mystical experience, merely the manifestation of his adrenaline high, a residue from the tension of his long stalking experience and its culmination, the intoxication of the hunter who has, finally, spilled and imbibed the blood of his kill.

Again he disobeyed his instincts and remained, although it suddenly crossed his mind once more that she might be an investigative plant of some sort. In his business, this was the most treacherous time, the aftermath, the moment of greatest risk.

It occurred to him, too, that this magnetizing attraction might have been induced artificially, something chemically fabricated, a mysterious weapon, judiciously applied. If so, it had certainly worked on him, rendering him powerless in her presence.

"Have you ever been?" she asked.

"Been?"

"To Florence."

"Afraid not, Mrs...." he said, lifting his glass again.

"Ford. Angela Ford."

He noted the alertness of the young waiter who moved like a cat toward their table and lifted the bottle again.

"The lady?" he asked.

"No, really," she said, placing a palm over her empty glass. "The long drive was fatiguing. I did it in one hop. I'm afraid the bubbly will do me in."

Champion nodded to the waiter who acknowledged the refusal, replaced the bottle, and faded away.

"You must go to Florence," she said. "It fills one up. I couldn't bear to leave. Unfortunately duty called."

"Duty?"

She sighed, but offered no explanation. He watched her move as if she were getting ready to leave. The gesture induced a baffling sense of panic. Was she going to leave the fly in the web, trapped, doomed to rot in immobility?

"On business, I suppose?" He wanted the question to seem casual, almost tentative.

"You might call it that," she said, and for the first time he caught a note of resignation in her voice. Of course, he wanted to pursue it further. A part of him hungered to know more about her, to know everything.

At the same time he dreaded the intimacy and braced for questions she might ask about him. He searched his mind for some potential response but drew a blank, as if the slate of his imagination was suddenly bone-dry, empty.

"This hotel, of course, is magnificent," she said. "But then they always are. He would never think of holding a rendezvous anyplace lesser." Her lips turned up offering the hint of an ironic smile.

Did this mean she was already lost to him? All doors closed? All possibilities aborted? He was, after all, merely a stranger, a casual prop, a speck of dust caught briefly in the eye, crossing her consciousness as a tiny inconsequential distraction.

Where had his expectations come from? he wondered, noting odd physical things assaulting him that had never happened to him before. His palms were moist. Trickles of icy perspiration were rolling down his back. He felt something relentless deep inside him, goading him. A pounding erection pushed against the containment of his pants.

An idea flashed across his mind. A solution. He felt the blood coursing through his veins, pounding and urgent. If this bout of madness did not go away, he would have to eliminate the source. He had done it for others. He would have to do it for himself. For the first time in his life, the idea of someone else's death frightened him.

Then he heard his own voice again, a compulsion of sound.

"Why are you here?" he asked, wondering suddenly if any fragment of his real self could be seen. The woman flashed him a strange and puzzled glance.

"Max Hamilton," she said, as if it were the most logical response in the world. Thankfully, she turned back too quickly to see what he was certain was a complexion gone dead white.

Chapter 11

Whereas Tom Ford, by his own admission, divided his life into compartments, Cynthia Bilton had divided her life into chapters. Chapter one had been an idyllic, gentle, very traditional Catholic upbringing. She had had loving parents, a wonderful, caring brother two years older than she, and a life peopled with interesting friends and neighbors.

In memory, this early life had become a fairy-tale existence, an incandescent transient moment. Her father had been a traveling salesman, a man never without a joke or a smile and, for her, always kisses, laughter, and presents.

He was always coming or going with suitcases filled with samples of his wares, which he would call "intimate things for the well-cared-for lady," always accompanied by a wink to her mother, a sweet pink-faced lady, who seemed perpetually scented with sugar and milk.

They lived in a bright and airy apartment in a suburb of Cleveland, and she attended a school taught by nuns who still wore black habits but, even in retrospect, didn't appear as severe and unforgiving as those she met later on in chapter two.

Religion was her mother's most fervent activity, and both Cynthia and her brother were indoctrinated in the teachings of the Church, accepting without question all the rituals and dogma demanded by the priests and nuns.

She remembered that part of her life as comfortable, predictable, and above all, safe. There were dos and don'ts and a clear path laid out for her and her brother to follow. Sin was well defined along the usual lines of the Ten Commandments, although there were some that she never did comprehend.

She understood, of course, about stealing and lying and cheating, also cussing.

In that benign world, devils and angels were separated by a deep chasm and carefully identified. She knew her catechism and was early on introduced to confession, although it was always confusing to her when the priest asked if she touched herself. She had no clear picture of what that meant but quickly learned that there were fewer Hail Marys meted out when she told the priest that she did not touch herself.

Her brother was more rebellious and questioning, but her parents excused that on the grounds of his gender. In that chapter, gender was a defining matter in her relationship with her brother, Timmy. Boys, by their very nature, were different from girls. Boys were tougher, stronger, more pugnacious, which she thought meant meaner and more athletic and, therefore, wilder. Girls were quieter, better mannered, and less aggressive.

In that first chapter everything was in its place. Everybody knew their roles in life and pursued them cheerfully, without complaint. The pervasive attitude was one of optimism. If one did the right thing, then one surely would be rewarded in this life and, more important, in the next.

If there was a dark side, it did not intrude in memory. Perhaps, Cynthia concluded, it was because the next chapter was so brutal, so black, that by comparison, anything would seem brighter.

It began on a bitter-cold day in January when a policeman came to the house and told her brother and her that their parents had been killed at a railroad crossing in a collision with a train. She was nine and her brother was twelve at the time.

The aftermath of this event was still a jumble in her mind. Caring friends and neighbors came forward to help with the funeral, but with the passage of time, they seemed to drift away, their interest declining as the children's bleak condition worsened.

They were destitute. No provisions had been made for them. They were minors without prospects. Their parents carried no insurance. For them, their parents' death was a catastrophe for which they were ill prepared. They found themselves at the mercy of various Catholic charities that shunted them from one church-sponsored orphanage to another.

Unfortunately, they had had the bad luck to land in an orphanage where the benign goodness of the religious life had been severely perverted and replaced by an evil brutality that was totally foreign to their previous existence. A repressive discipline, administered by twisted, cruel, and unforgiving priests and nuns, took over their lives.

At first she had been confused over the harshness of her treatment. For what seemed like no justifying reason,

Cynthia would be summoned to the office of one of the administrators and berated for infractions of rules she had no knowledge of. Her punishment consisted of her being stripped naked and shouted at by the administrator, a nun in civilian clothes who was often joined in the session by a priest.

For a young girl to whom modesty had been taught as a virtue, such treatment was an unimaginable humiliation. When she tried to hide her budding young breasts or the sparse thatch of pubic hairs that were beginning to sprout on her body, the two torturers, one on each side, would seize her arms and berate her for not cooperating in such a cleansing form of rebuke.

On penalty of further punishment, which they assured her was probably beyond her capacity to endure, she was warned never to discuss what went on during these sessions, a caveat that she obeyed out of abject fear. Most times it was impossible to understand why these things were being done to her, only that it was, according to her tormentors, good for her soul.

As months went by and these ministrations became a weekly routine, she assumed that the other girls were also subjected to such activities, and it began to dawn on her that the thing to do to win favor with these authorities was to submit with enthusiasm to whatever she was called upon to do during these sessions.

In observing the reactions of the nun and the priest, she concluded that she was the object of some obscure ritual that demanded not only nakedness but also a kind of performance. She was still totally naive at the time. In her home, sex had never been discussed, and what she learned from her friends was too mysterious to be understood.

Occasionally, she would ask her brother what such and such meant, and he would throw her a knowing glance and tell her that she was either too young to be enlightened or too dumb to understand any explanation. The "sessions" grew more and more participatory. Instead of her being the only naked person in the room, both the nun and the priest also stripped.

It was the first time in her life that she had seen a mature man and woman completely naked. It was shocking at first. She could not imagine that men could look so alarmingly strange without clothes. They assured her that God had meant them to be in this natural state. They explained to her that when Eve ate the apple, Adam's "boy," as they called his penis, became hard and elongated and was meant to be inserted into Eve's girl.

They made a great ceremony out of what they called her own secret initiation into "God's practice," which they assured her would purify her soul and guarantee her a place in paradise. For a twelve-year-old girl, her deflowering was so painful that she fainted and awoke bleeding and raw to a chorus of congratulations from the perpetrators of this travesty.

That, of course, was just the beginning. They tutored her in every aspect of depravity. Some of these acts gave her a vague sense of pleasure, but there was far more pain dispensed as their activities accelerated into unimaginable excess. Still, under penalty of some nameless horror, she remained silent.

She felt trapped and fell into a deep depression, which did not attract the observation of her brother, who was having his own troubles with the authorities, mostly because of his rebellious nature and his refusal to submit to the strict and often senseless rules of the institution. More and more he was vocalizing aggressive tendencies and fantasizing about revenge.

The nun's and priest's discovery of her pregnancy and subsequent abortion at the hands of a brutal black woman were the defining moment of this second chapter of her life. Apparently, the two corrupters had gone through this procedure before.

First, of course, they threatened her again with damnation and eternal hell if she breathed a word of what had happened to her. They went through an elaborate ritual to drive home this point, complete with icons depicting the Blessed Mother, statues of the Crucifixion, candelabra, and an ancient book of Scripture. By then Cynthia believed in these rituals with all her heart and soul.

The abortion was botched, and she had to be rushed to a hospital after hemorrhaging all over her cot in the dormitory. Despite the pain and her very nearly bleeding to the death, she said nothing to betray her corrupters, telling the hospital authorities that she had been impregnated by a man who had been doing odd jobs and had run away as soon as she had made him aware of her condition. By then, innocence had been thoroughly crushed.

The authorities apparently believed her or felt it politic to believe her and sent her back to the institution. They also told her that it was highly unlikely that she could ever conceive children, a classic understatement since they had removed both her ovaries.

Thankfully, the two perpetrators of her misery chose to ignore her, and she settled into a less traumatic routine, although most of the other girls in her group shunned her, and she became an example of how sin punished its practitioners.

Timmy, to his credit, didn't buy the story, and under pressure from him, she admitted what had been happening, sparing no detail.

"He'll pay," he said.

She could sense his resolve. It was a mirror image of her own.

"Her too," she added.

"Her too."

By then Timmy was nearly seventeen and within shooting distance of discharge. Like her, he was exceptionally bright and was able to enter Ohio State on a scholarship reserved for deprived children. He was not going to go without taking his kid sister along, even though she still had two years left before finishing her high school equivalency.

When the ordinary channels declined to allow Cynthia to go with him, Timmy visited with the priest who had abused her. It did not take him long to obtain permission.

A few months after they had left the institution and taken up residence in a tiny apartment in Columbus, she read that the priest had been found stabbed to death in downtown Cleveland, apparently the victim of a mugger. The newspaper story said that he was castrated. She did not require any further explanation.

"It was a good touch," she told him.

"Not too theatrical?"

"I hope he was alive at the time."

"He was."

She searched herself for any sign of remorse or conscience. Happily, she could only take personal pleasure in the event. Her only concern was that Timmy evade apprehension.

"And her?"

"In due time," he said with a smile.

Six months later the nun was burned to death. Her car had mysteriously caught fire. Both terminations were harbingers of Timmy's future profession.

If Cynthia had learned anything from chapter one of her life it was that innocence was, as her mother might have said, a state of grace. And once lost, it was gone forever, as she had learned in the following chapter.

It taught her, too, that there was an inside and an outside to a human being, one seen by others and one seen only by the individual. Although they acted in tandem, the external side shown to others was almost always different from the internal. Both sides, however, were dedicated to their own private agenda. In her case, it was to control her own destiny, control it absolutely—by whatever means necessary.

In a sense, her loss of innocence freed her from any moral

strictures. Conscience and compassion totally disappeared from her psyche, releasing her from errant and endangering emotions. She was liberated from the stress of inhibition, allowing her to analyze her actions and weigh them on the basis of her own self-interest only.

Her outside self became the instrument to further the goals of her inside self, which contained the essence of her expectations. And what were these expectations? Total independence from any form of enslavement, material or emotional.

For years Cynthia's antenna had been tuned to the frequency that would provide the means of her liberation. When Tom Ford called her in for an interview, she knew that he had picked up the signal she had been broadcasting most of her life.

Chapter 12

As always when a deal was in progress, the room was crowded with people. A merger was in the works between one of Max's European companies and a company most of whose directors were innocently unaware that the purpose of the merger was to downsize the company, fire its executives, and gobble up its cash flow.

Most of the details had already been arranged. Those directors in on the deal were to be secretly compensated for their cooperation. The other directors present were soon to be overwhelmed and outvoted. There was an hour of give-and-take, mostly theater, Tom being charmingly adamant and wearing as always the velvet glove over the iron fist.

It was the tradition during these events for Max to call at some crucial moment and deliver a speech to the participants on the speakerphone—sop to the troops, the father addressing his flock. Tom had timed it so that the impending trip on the yacht would be a celebration of yet another coup.

Tom looked at his watch. Max would have been informed when to make the call and would usually make it during the time frame of the meeting. Eschewing the boring details, which he hated, Max's little speeches were designed to be inspirational pep talks, carefully calculated to inspire those who were selling their company—and not into the scam, into truly believing that they were making a fabulous deal.

Tom carried out all the paperwork and nitty-gritty, including signatures. He had Max's power of attorney and designed the contracts so craftily with so many hidden nuances that sellers would not discover their victimization until months later.

Tom would push the button activating the speakerphone placed in the center of the conference table. Max's rich baritone would fill the room with the usual platitudes, the greeting, the pep talk, the future. Tom would have heard it all before, ad nauseam.

When it was over, the people in the room would applaud, an odd spectacle, since half of them—although they didn't know it—would be gone by the end of the year. Max always ran a tight ship, needing the cash flow of the target company to pay for the acquisition.

But when the present conference reached the point of adjournment with no call from Max, Tom glanced toward Cynthia and raised his eyebrows in what he hoped was a gesture of expectation. Had the moment arrived? Cynthia had ordered the job with only a rough six-month time frame in mind. No additional informational follow-up was required. Once the parameters were set, she and Tom were to be completely out of the loop.

It fell to Tom to make the obligatory pep talk, which relied on the words he had heard Max use so often.

"Believe me, gentlemen, this deal will resound to your favor. What we have done here today will ultimately turn out to be the quintessential deal of your lives."

Bet your ass, Tom thought to himself as he uttered those words. A year from now, they would be crying the blues, with most of them downsized out of the company.

***

Later, after the meeting, Tom and Cynthia met in another office next to the conference room. This was Tom's business office, which adjoined Cynthia's. It consisted of a suite, including an adjacent large private area fitted with a pullout studio couch, bar, and bathroom. He felt more comfortable in these quarters than in his Manhattan apartment.

"What do you think it means?" he whispered to Cynthia, as she proffered him a truffle, English imports, his favorite snack, almost an addiction. He took one and popped it into his mouth.

"We're still within the time frame," she said.

"Too long a wait."

"Patience, Tom. We agreed."

"It's still nerve-wracking," Tom said popping another truffle.

He slumped on the couch, kicked off his loafers, and put his stockinged feet on the cocktail table. Cynthia poured vodka over cubes of ice, handed him a glass, and sat down beside him on the couch. They clinked glasses.

"To dear old Max," Cynthia said.

"Hopefully the late departed."

"I'll drink to that."

Their eyes met over the lips of their glasses. Between

126

them, as always, was the unspoken.

"Might mean you won't have to take that cruise," Cynthia said, looking at her watch.

"From your mouth to God's ears. It's like being trapped on a floating prison. There's no escaping him. He becomes ubiquitous."

"Not too many hours before you have to leave," Cynthia said.

"I suppose Angela should be at the Bel Air by now," Tom said.

"I assume so. She was booked for Friday night." Again she looked at her watch. "It's Saturday in France."

Part of her job was to supervise Angela's travel arrangements.

"What do you think it means?" Tom said after a long moment.

"Means?"

"You know what I'm talking about. Max knew the time when he was supposed to call."

"Yes, he did."

"Is it done?"

"We could call the boat?"

Tom sipped his drink and studied her.

"Not yet."

"How long has it been?"

"Five months," she whispered.

He shook his head.

"It's nerve-wracking… the waiting." He sighed.

"Patience," she replied with a smile. "These people know

their job."

"You're still confident it will happen?"

She nodded, offering a sly smile as she sipped her drink.

Her free hand began to slide along his leg, to the inside of his thigh. Lately, she had begun initiating. It concerned him, but he had said nothing to inhibit her, although he was always alert to any changes in her attitudes and actions.

He felt the quickening in his crotch, the spasm of the rising process. He was certain that she had already secured their space, ordered calls to be held. Ms. Bilton and Mr. Ford were conferring. It was not an uncommon occurrence, and they were reasonably certain that their charade, while not foolproof, was effective.

They attributed this to their own masterly deception, his clearly demonstrated and genuine devotion to his family, her severity in dress and manner, eschewing all cosmetic improvement, and offering a persona that suggested sexual indifference to either sex.

Besides, they took no chances. An outside maid service cleaned their offices. Cynthia was hawklike in her surveillance. This did not mean that people were blind idiots. There had to be suspicions, rumors, speculation. That could not be aborted. All they could do was manipulate theatrics to portray themselves as the odd couple, all business, a poor sexual bet.

From the beginning, he had put the administration of this deception in Cynthia's lap. At all costs, their arrangement must be kept from Angela and the children. It was another condition of Cynthia's job, but also another vulnerability for Tom Ford that had to be addressed.

As a lawyer, he knew very well the expanded lexicon of what passed for the new fairness, especially in terms of women. Cynthia, too, was well aware of the shift that had taken place in the marketplace and the courts.

By all legal definitions, she could be defined as a sexually harassed woman, trading, among other things, her body for employment. But Tom Ford was not a man to leave an unsheathed sword of Damocles hanging over his head. His solution had been to make her part of it, raise the stakes for betrayal, make it too prohibitive. Had he done that? Only time would tell.

With her free hand, she raised the glass to her lips and took a deep swallow, then put the glass down and deftly undid his pants and rolled down his underpants. Kneeling on the floor between his legs, she kissed his erection and moved her tongue teasingly down the shaft.

Tom had come to enjoy these little surprises. He thought of them as selfless little devotional episodes. Experience and his earlier instructions had taught her where her ministrations were most welcome. It was always a turn on to watch her transformation. The severe spectacles put aside, the drab outfit stripped away, the hard full body revealed.

To further please him, she had learned to play the slut, a role she either had picked up elsewhere or had deliberately studied and emulated. She had certainly developed an interesting sexual repertoire.

Looking down, he watched her lips and tongue enthusiastically at work. He reached for her breasts, toying with her nipples. Her hand reached down to her clitoris, which she visibly massaged as she palliated him. Everything was done silently, with hand signals and body language.

Sometimes, he was able to watch her clinically, observing her actions without any diminishment of his own pleasure. At first, when this had begun, he had wondered if she was faking her enthusiasm. In her place he would have done the same since it was the satisfaction of the receiver that was at stake here. Nevertheless, he accepted her pleasure in it.

At times it did concern him, as if her concentration on her own pleasure and personal enthrallment hinted at some deeper betrayal, especially when he observed her grinding away on top of him, in slow circular motions, her eyes closed, focusing on the mechanics of the act, as if his erected penis was a disembodied object for her private amusement.

He hoped, of course, that he had kept his irritation well hidden from her. It would not do at all for her to view him as an egoistic monster with no regard whatsoever for anyone but himself, even if it was true.

It was a possibility that he refused to dwell on. Compartmentalization, after all, required enormous discipline and a massive recycling of perceptions. Experience had taught him that to do this effectively, he could never allow his guard to drop or his alertness to diminish.

Every observation was a clue and every nuance a cause for analysis. Suspicion was endemic to the process. Trusting no one, perhaps not even himself, was a given. Emotion was a mischievous enemy. Everything human, in others and in him, was adversarial.

He often speculated about what was in Cynthia's mind. Such musings were obligatory, since what was in her mind, or in the mind of anyone in his orbit, represented potential obstacles. What did she really think of him? Not that it mattered, since he would undoubtedly distrust her explanations. If he was she, he knew, his judgment of him, Tom Ford, would not be favorable.

From the beginning he had told her that he would judge her only by her behavior, her willingness to play the part he had conceived for her. Her execution of that role, so far, was more than satisfactory. She had performed with great efficiency. Her thought processes, as revealed to him, were logical, her analyses always keen, and she was willing to expand her skills.

Since she had committed herself to no life outside of his, she had ample time for study and self-improvement. Her expertise in computers grew, as did her knowledge of business, securities law, currency exchange, arbitrage, commodity speculation, and any and all matters associated with Tom's dealings.

She could slip easily from role to role, all fashioned by him. She was always deferential and obedient, even in the capacity of business adviser, which she had seemed to develop on her own.

But always remember, he told her often, not only in words but in the myriad other ways people communicate: You are important and convenient. A case could also be made that you are necessary. But you are not—repeat not—never, never—indispensable.

"Fuck me, please," she cried suddenly, turning, getting on her hands and knees on the floor before the couch, displaying her eagerness for his special preference. Lately, too, she had become a more aggressive stage manager in these episodes. It was, he decided, something to think about, although this was hardly the moment.

He placed himself against her buttocks, and she took his penis and guided it into her sex, letting it settle until she moved in a quickening circular motion, as he seconded her with his own rhythmic strokes while she expertly caressed his testicles.

She was working herself into a frenzy of gyrations, which always signaled that her pleasure was coming fast, his as well. Cresting together, a process that had taken much practice to perfect, had always been the goal of such an exercise. Coming at the same time, he had learned, vastly increased the depths of his thrill. Apparently it did the same for her, not that it mattered to him.

He was cresting. He felt it coming, the charge crawling up the sensory spine, moving swiftly to ignite the explosive pleasure.

"Ready?" she cried, setting his erection in the grasp of the connecting link, nipping it with her internal muscles.

He squeezed her nipples, the final hot button of their body language.

At the moment of impact, the intrusive buzz of the intercom—the auditory shock, not exactly aborting but repressing the full cycle of completion.

"Damn," he muttered, disappointed.

The buzzing was repetitive, urgent.

"Fire her ass," Tom cried, disengaging, his heartbeat calming. Naked, she moved to the phone.

"Yes," she snapped.

Tom watched her expression, expectant. Always when the phone buzzed unexpectedly, he wondered whether it carried the news he hungered for.

"From the boat," Cynthia said, smiling. "The good captain."

Tom nodded.

"Yes. I'll put him on," Cynthia said, eyebrows raised, unconsciously patting the nude flesh of her flat stomach. She handed Tom the phone. He felt the perspiration induced by his sexual effort cooling, but he was not conscious of his nakedness.

"This is Ford."

"The chief is missing," the agitated voice of Captain Stokes crackled over the line. Tom's face lit up.

"Missing?"

Tom nodded and then looked into the eyes of Cynthia Bilton, penetrating deeply. Done, he mimed. Done.

"He was sleeping on deck… it was hot as blazes…"

"Just gone? The ship searched?"

As he spoke, he did not avert his eyes from Cynthia's, their stares frozen. With great difficulty, he feigned concern. Her reaction was oddly inexplicable. She cupped his genitals and held them, and he did not brush her hand away.

"Stem to stern, Mr. Ford. Stem to stern. Everywhere. I sent a man under as well. Not a rivet was left untouched. I swear… I don't understand. He must have gone over."

"No sign of foul play?"

"None."

"Just disappeared. Just like that."

"It's a fucking puzzle, Mr. Ford. I mean we really looked; we're bug-eyed from looking. We were careful, too, you know, of not disturbing things just in case of… only thing we can think of… he just went over. Just went over… you know, where he slept when it got hot. Went over the rail… that's the only thing I can think of. I… I don't know what to do."

"No one else has been called?"

This was a fundamental question. Actually, a stroke of luck. A less perceptive person might have called Max's office in Switzerland, setting things off in confusing directions, perhaps even a ridiculous attempt at cover-up. The captain had known instinctively where to turn. Good for him. One had to set the agenda swiftly.

Tom was well aware of the inevitable power struggle that would ensue. There was family, Max's wife and daughters particularly, other colleagues, and retainers. He was prepared to defuse that quickly. Indeed, he had paved the way. This was the moment he had waited for.

Now, at last, he could put everything into motion. Only he, Tom, knew where all the proverbial bodies were buried. Tom's circuitous paper route had created the heir apparent—himself.

He would, as earlier calculated, quietly gather the reins, playing the reluctant heir, showing not a sign that he had lusted for the role. The blueprint had carefully been drawn in his mind and on paper. And no one knew, no one—except Cynthia.

"No," Stokes assured him. "You're the first… you being his lawyer and such…"

"Very good, Stokes, very smart. It won't be forgotten."

"Jeez. Gives me the willies. Never thought this could happen."

"You heard nothing?" Tom inquired, his mind groping for another place, another compartment.

Yet he did not move her hand, caressing now. An observer might think her action ludicrous, which it was. Yet it seemed right, in a bizarre way, metaphysically correct on two levels. On one it represented a kind of acknowledgment, a tribute, a gesture of celebration. On the other—an ultimate irony—she had his balls in her hand. He liked that idea, liked the delicious risk of it, a testing of her trust.

She had moved closer to him, her full naked body against his equally exposed flesh. She nibbled at the lobes of his ear.

"Not a fucking sound. Considering his bulk…"

"Not a splash?"

"Negative."

"Not a single untoward sound."

"As I said… negative." There was a long hesitation. "First thing they'll think it was one of us. I know we're in for it."

"You think it's possible that one of… your own?"

"Anything's possible, Mr. Ford. I can't see it myself. Hell, they'll point to me first off. Fucking stew out here. You know what I think… was one of those freak accidents. He got up, lost his footing, and—"

"You heard no scream? No cry for help?"

"You see. That's the way it will go for us. You heard no fucking scream? You heard nothing? How can that be? I'll tell you how." He was getting agitated. "Because we were underway, and the fucking motor was humping, that's why."

"I'm just asking, captain, not accusing." He said the words between lips formed into a wry knowing smile, his eyes turned to Cynthia, who returned his gaze.

She continued holding him, caressing, as if it were his due. His mind was racing with questions.

"When did you realize?" Tom asked, lawyerly now, imposing the interrogation that would soon be repeated by the local authorities.

"Not so easy. It was about six when Jack, my first, the man on watch, did the rounds. The sun was up on the horizon, he said, which figures at that hour. Saw he was gone. Wasn't so unusual. Sometimes he'd go back to his cabin in the middle of the night. He was a night roamer. We all knew that, didn't we? Not a good sleeper."

"So nobody checked his cabin?"

"Not then. I told you. It was not unusual. Seven the steward brought his coffee. Jack said he had gone to the cabin. Only he wasn't there."

"So it was seven," Tom pressed. He had no idea where he was going except to prepare the captain for what was to come. Repetition was calming. He would want it to go smoothly, letting the legalities hang in the air. Without a body there was no way of ascertaining much anyway.

"Yeah, about seven, Mr. Ford." There was a long pause. "What I need is orders. What to do here?"

"You just can't avoid the police, captain."

"I can see that."

"I won't give orders," Tom said. "But I will give advice. Tell them the truth, the absolute truth, according to your own perception, and instruct your men to do the same. I will call Mrs. Hamilton first off. It will surely hit the media. I will have to inform all employees."

The blueprint called for no crude attempts at information management. He needed to be calmly efficient. This was a global media event. And the press had to run its course.

There would be the rumors, the usual speculations, some logical, some off-the-wall. The tabloid press and television would have a field day. There would be fireworks every-where, and he looked forward to the display. After all, it was his display. He had set it all in motion. He looked to-ward Cynthia and nodded.

"Brilliant," he said.

He hung up softly, taking a deep breath. Cynthia, look-ing into his eyes, was still caressing him there. And he was reacting.

"What an elegant idea," he whispered, thinking of the way in which dear old Max was dispatched.

She nodded her agreement, sinking to her knees.

Chapter 13

"Did I wake you?" Tom asked.

Angela had not been sleeping in alpha mode. Rather, she had been floating on a gentle river in a dreamlike but comfortable haze through which she could glimpse the living alabaster haunches of a man. The man moved blithely, unashamed of his nakedness, his face not containing the fixed intense stare of her David but, instead, the moist shining eyes of the man she had sat next to at the Maugham Bar the night before.

In her dream, she had been exploring the nakedness of the man, his flesh alabaster smooth, her concentration tracking downward to that other place, the massive genitals heavy and engorging, rising in a massive erection. The sight of it, the knob emerging, had just begun to set off charges inside her when the persistent buzz sounded, and she jumped to a sitting position, startled, panicked as if she had been caught red-handed, captured in a blazing spotlight by unseen pursuers bent on punishing her for her filthy thoughts.

But the panic quickly eased as she became conscious of her surroundings and alert enough to see by the digital clock that it was just shy of 4:00 a.m. The fantasy, both the good and the bad, quickly disintegrated like a mirror exploding, and a whip of pain jabbed at her chest.

A call in the middle of the night brought only news of

calamity. The children! Was there a more powerful way to be punished for such imaginary guilt-inducing pleasures?

"Nothing scary, I promise," Tom said. Her accelerated breath must have given her away.

"Not the children?"

"No, of course not. Something else has happened." He did not wait for an inquiry. "No, not to me."

She sucked in a deep breath, expanding her lungs, holding the air like a puff of smoke and then expelling it with relief.

"Where are you?"

"At the office. A strange thing has happened. Max has disappeared."

"Disappeared?"

She was not moved by the shock of loss, only the mystery it presented. Max was the one constant of their lives, its enduring inevitability. Max was, had always been, a ubiquitous, all-pervasive spirit hovering over them. Another stab of guilt descended to wound her. The news made her feel, well, joyous, although she tried to smother the sensation with an overlay of concern.

"Are you certain?"

"About his disappearance? Yes."

"Max doesn't disappear," she said dismissively. "He's playing, teasing us. Max doesn't die. Max is forever."

She saw his image in her mind, fat, his unhealthy roseate pallor, a deep-inhaling smoker, an overeating and overdrinking junkie. Max was bent on defying the odds, on living forever.

"It doesn't look good," Tom said in response to her certainty.

She wondered whether that meant he was still alive or dead or… it was exasperating to contemplate… both dead and alive.

Tom explained the situation.

"Are you saying that he just fell overboard?" Angela asked, aghast at the story.

"We don't know."

"Maybe somebody pushed him," Angela said, showing her disrespect. "He did have enemies."

"Many. But it doesn't sound like it. No," Tom reiterated. "Probably some freak accident."

"You think he's really dead?"

She knew her question implied distrust of anything to do with Max. He would be perfectly capable of planning his own disappearance.

"The captain reports he's not on board. Leaves only one possibility."

Angela sensed that Tom had completely downgraded any semblance of hope to a certainty that Max had, indeed, disappeared into oblivion. It crossed her mind to ask him how it affected them, their future, but she decided not to raise the point. Instead she asked, putting it in vaguer terms, "So what happens now?"

"I've got to be the man putting his finger in the dike. I've decided to stay close to the office," he said, underlining the alleged burden it presented.

"So no yacht party," Angela said stupidly, regretting not

inviting Aunt Emma to come along with her to France. Now she was alone. She wanted to convey a sense of disappointment, if only for respectability, but she suddenly realized that this was a difficult task. She was, in fact, relieved that the yacht party would be canceled.

"I guess I'll just roll on home," she sighed.

"Why not stay the few days?" Tom suggested. "You've already made the arrangements. Besides, I'm overwhelmed here."

Remembering the man in the bar, a thrill shot through her. Her heartbeat accelerated.

"Might be a good idea." She paused for effect. "Unless you think I'm needed." She was being deliberately ingenuous.

"Nothing you can do, I'm afraid."

She stretched her body in the bed, actually enjoying her lack of discomfort. Max had enabled them to live like royalty. Shouldn't she be, if not concerned, dutifully mournful? Then why was she feeling exhilarated, free? She decided not to hold the sensation up to analysis.

"Well, it is pleasant here," she said cautiously. "Florence was exhausting."

"And I'll be busy as hell monitoring the situation."

"Well, then… unless you think I can be helpful back there." The redundancy was deliberate on her part, as if she were testing his permission and making him a collaborator in her fantasy.

"I'll keep you posted," he said.

"Poor Max," she sighed. Such a condolence, she supposed was obligatory.

"You never know. Things happen."

"So they do."

She looked about the spacious, luxurious suite all done up in blues and reds. Nor could she deny a familiarly delicious sensation that recalled the "incident" in Florence.

"It could keep me down here at the office for days," Tom said.

"I suppose I could use the rest," Angela mused. "Florence was exhausting."

"We'll stay in close touch. You just rest up."

His sweet air of consideration prodded her conscience, which made her angry with herself for entertaining… she searched for a phrase… forbidden thoughts. A second after the conversation was terminated, she resented this attitude and shooed away the sensation with a startling vehemence.

Flinging aside the satin quilt, as if she were shedding her identity, she let her lightly clad body bathe in the chill of the air-conditioning. Feeling goose bumps break out on her legs, she got out of bed, found the thermostat, and shut it off. Then she drew the blinds that covered one wall and opened the French doors to the tiled patio.

The air was moist, humid, as if the Mediterranean was dissolving, although occasionally a hot gentle breeze made an effort to find her. But a canopy of stars burned brightly in the moonless sky. Stepping out into the patio, she removed her nightgown and stood nude, listening to the lap of the waters against the rocks below.

Standing there, letting her thoughts simmer, she felt

herself disconnecting emotionally from bonds she once thought were unassailable. Images of children, husband, friends, acquaintances, seemed to diminish in memory, then vanish into the moist air.

Replacing these was the dominant recollection of the "incident," the profound moment before the giant icon of desire. It continued to baffle her as she explored its effect, the explosive connection, beyond mere aesthetics, as if the soul of the statue had spoken out to her alone.

What did it mean? Was there something inherent in Michelangelo's choice of this biblical figure that spoke across the centuries? David the giant killer, David the king. She remembered the biblical myth, David's obsession with Bathsheba, another overwhelming sexually magnetic impulse. He, perhaps with Bathsheba's complicity, had devised a way to murder her husband and have her to himself. Had that been the true passion? Such ideas were troubling, and she dismissed them.

Chapter 14

After a while, she saw the false dawn begin, the light spreading an orange glow over the vast stretch of charcoal dark water, turning blue as the real dawn came, then the bright aqua sun-drenched daylight.

She returned to her room and showered, carefully soaping her body, rinsing, then oiling her smooth flesh for softness, overlaying that with suntan oil for protection, with special attention to her rarely exposed breasts. This, after all, was France.

In the early light, she could see the pool area from her window, accessible by funicular, reached by a walk through an exquisitely manicured garden rich with nurtured plants, colorfully flowering. She called room service and requested service at poolside, juice, coffee, croissants.

Then she slipped into the brief black string-bikini bottoms she had bought at Bloomies. Inspecting herself in the mirror, she noted the natural tightness of her flesh, her flat stomach, the tight buttocks, the still shapely and high firm breasts, the nipples mysteriously erect. With a tiny dab of lipstick, she rouged the areolas around them, feeling a pleasant throb of sexual excitement as she did so.

She liked what she saw in the mirror. She felt attractive, seductive, festive, as if she were going to a fancy ball. So far nature had been kind, the etch of aging gentle. There was, after all, a genetic relationship with the well-preserved Aunt Emma.

She covered her breasts with the small matching top. Traditional American modesty was always inhibiting when one was initially confronted with French bathing mores. As always, it took some getting used to, although she knew she would shed the top at the first sign of other bare breasts, if not before.

Throwing a short terry-cloth robe around her shoulders, she took the elevator to ground level, walking down the wide staircase of the veranda to the path through the fragrant garden to where the funicular began its sloping journey from the cliff's peak to the pool.

As she walked, she felt the sensation of being observed, and she turned to look back at the hotel. From where she was, she could see the baroque beauty of the building's façade, perched charmingly on the Cap as if it belonged there.

She knew, of course, that her observation of the structure was a silent ploy to mask her real intention. A man stood watching her from an upper balcony, his body bisected by the balustrade, revealing him bare to the waist.

Despite the distance, she was absolutely certain he was the man who had sat next to her the night before. Her body's reaction told her that, and she savored the giddy pleasure of the excitement.

He waved. Because of the sun's angle, his view of her was clearer. Shading her eyes with her hand, she returned the wave, wondering if she was showing too much enthusiasm for a casual greeting.

Suffused with the remembered thrill of adolescent flirtation, she let the energy of her wave subside. Then she turned and, walking with a conscious, perhaps exaggerated, swing to her hips, hoping his eyes followed her, she moved along the path to the funicular station. Entering the cab, she pressed the appropriate button, and with her glance still fixed on the balcony where the man stood, she let it lower her to the pool area.

Aside from the handsome male attendant and the waiter setting a little table under an umbrella, she appeared to be the only guest at the pool terrace. Not for long, she assured herself with a deliciously expectant certainty. He would come. He could not resist her. God, how she enjoyed this titillating fantasy of her assumed sexual magnetism.

"Une, madame?" the waiter asked.

She only half nodded, correcting herself quickly.

"Perhaps deux," she said, mixing her languages without embarrassment. "Oui, deux," she repeated, offering a broad smile and removing her robe with a flourish, enjoying the brief glance of the waiter's admiration.

The waiter carefully placed the umbrella for maximum shade and then set two places. She settled into her chair and waited, occasionally glancing toward the funicular for signs of movement. The waiter brought out croissants for two in a silver dish and orange juice and coffee in silver flagons.

"And bring a bottle of Dom," she said, remembering last night and how she had shared his. "For mimosas."

The waiter nodded and disappeared as the attendant wrapped two nearby lounges in towels. Deux, she repeated to herself, a tiny giggle rising from her chest.

He will come, she assured herself again, listening with alert concentration for the sound of the funicular's mechanism. She felt the tremor of unfamiliar sensations in her body suggesting the memory of the "incident," and she noted that her nipples continued to be erect.

Suddenly she was assailed with a brief and unwelcome intrusion of memory. In all the years of her marriage, these sensations had been dormant. Sex with Tom wasn't even worthy of the description. Images of their copulation arose briefly in her mind, mere mechanical observances of the marriage ritual, boring and lifeless.

She had, of course, blamed herself. She had felt unattractive, without luster, unmoved by the look and feel of his body's proximity. Her principal anxiety during these moments, thankfully rare, centered on the length of time it would take before the obligatory activity terminated.

At a time like this, why had the subject even crossed her mind? It was an unwanted intrusion. She felt another tiny giggle rise in her chest as she remembered the sensation, the letting go, the exploding fireworks of pleasure that burst in her body. She pressed her thighs together and imagined again the alabaster maleness of the giant sculpture. Was another orgasmic eruption on its way?

The sound of the funicular's grinding mechanism interrupted her concentration, and the sensation receded but not far. Shielding her eyes from the glare, she looked upward at the oncoming bright canary-yellow cab moving upward, progressing to the summit. There, she could see a robed figure waiting. A man. Although he was too far away for recognition, she knew instinctively that it was he.

The cab stopped at the summit. The man got in and the funicular began its round trip toward the pool. She strained her eyes to get a better glimpse of the man. Then, as if she had secretly willed it, she recognized him. In a reflex that sent hot trills through her body, she removed her top.

There he was, dropping from the sky, coming to her. She shivered with delight. David, her David, was coming for her, hungering to embrace her. She reveled in the fantasy and felt her body respond erotically.

He stepped out of the cab, hesitated a moment as he raised a hand to screen away the glare, then moved toward her. She watched him come, graceful, beautiful, his curly blond hair burnished by the sun, his face a wide oval, his chin strong and upturned. Even his brow, rippled by a frown, like David's, seemed to emphasize the perfect slope of his nose, straight and delicate, the bridge thickening slightly then resuming its narrowing flow to the sensuous nostrils.

In his gaze, she sensed a level of scrutiny, again not dissimilar to David's concentration, as if he were seeking to find the vulnerability in his protagonist. Study me, she urged soundlessly. Find my vulnerability. It is yours for the asking.

She was barely able to differentiate between the living man and the statue as she struggled to repress any outward signs of sexual agitation. Be calm, she urged herself, summoning all her inner resources to discipline her mind and body. He must not see the state she was in.

Then suddenly he was there, standing above where she sat, in silhouette, the glow of the sun behind him. He removed his robe and her eyes were unable to avoid a study of his hard muscled body, particularly the bunched weight of his crotch showing the clear outline of his genitals behind their blue spandex covering, the mossed trail of hair that crawled from his navel to the inner sanctum below. She had the urge to follow the trail downward with her tongue.

There he stood, the angle of his body, she imagined, in the same configuration of the stance of the Michelangelo masterpiece, the giant David, her David, brave and arrogant, the well-turned legs firmly planted, the broad shoulders set, the right higher than the left, the arms, muscled and alert, the hard ripple just below the surface of the flesh, and the buttocks, the thrilling roundness of the buttocks.

God, she wanted to reach out and embrace him, bury her face in the promise of his pouch, caress the smooth tight buttocks with her hands, offering a mighty hug. In her imagination, she saw the erotic imagery bursting like fireworks in her brain, as the pictures of fantasy expanded and deepened into three dimensions, and she saw the bulging snake of his phallus enter her body, filling her soul.

Thankfully, her sunglasses were hiding the greediness of her eyes, although she knew that her erect nipples were a bold display of her hidden desires. In fact, she enjoyed the idea of this tangible revelation, wishing she had the courage to show him more, actually searching for a response in the outline of his penis beneath its covering. She felt herself blushing hotly, hoping that he would attribute the sudden extreme of color to the sun's rays.

Aunt Emma, Angela was convinced, had, in their brief encounter in Florence, taught her subliminally how to see the male, instructing her subconsciously how to look, how to observe, how to feel and imagine, and how to convey and receive the essence of the sexual message that had culminated in the "incident." How else was she to interpret the origin of her transformation?

At that moment, she believed she was communicating in the manner of Aunt Emma's design and she felt suffused by what was unmistakably the white heat of raging lust. At that point reciprocity was a cherished hope, vulnerable to a many-sided interpretation. She looked for signs, noting with some optimism that the nipples on his bare chest, like David's, were also erect.

On another level, the present confrontation as it was now occurring had another, more frightening meaning. Was she the same person who had left the safe and familiar just a few short days ago? Or some other manifestation, an outlaw now, on the edge of some abyss, about to jump and take off into another dimension, an environment where the landscape and language were completely unfamiliar and dangerous?

Had she the right to do this, she wondered, to remove herself from the center of her world with all its discipline and responsibility and enter this other wild and forbidden place? Aunt Emma, for all her conscious and subconscious instruction had given her no guidance on the matter of how to cope with the passage, leaving her a lone traveler without passport or instructions.

That was the old Angela agonizing, she decided, ejecting the speculation as if it were mere wrapping on a chocolate bar. Nothing, but nothing, was to spoil the pleasure of the sweet.

The waiter brought the bottle of champagne in a silver bucket and placed it on a stand beside the table.

"Time to return the generosity," she said in words that, in the light of what was actually happening in her mind, seemed common, prosaic.

He glanced at the champagne and nodded his understanding, as the waiter gripped the bottle to lift the cork, which popped as it came out.

"Mimosa?" the waiter asked.

"Whatever the lady's pleasure. I'll join in that."

Their eyes met and he smiled, showing white even teeth. She noted that his eyes, in the bright light of the sun, glowed a kind of dark green, recalling a meadow in late summer. What, she wondered, was the color of her eyes, an autumn brown, suggesting to him?

The waiter poured two thirds of a glass of champagne for each of them and topped it with orange juice.

Still standing, the man reached out and touched her glass with his then drank, as she watched the muscles in his neck and his Adam's apple bob to receive the liquid.

"Please sit down," she said, offering a smile, watching his eyes wash over her breasts, surely observing the erect nipples. He bent his body onto the chair opposite, and they were separated across the little table.

"I see you're an early riser," she said, still holding her glass.

"I am today."

"I'm glad. The company is welcome."

"I agree," he said.

She felt the intensity of his glance and wondered if her own was equally as intense. With some effort, she dropped her gaze, deliberately resisting this sense of recklessness that, she was certain, demanded to consume her. She wanted to reach under the table and caress him. What am I thinking? she admonished herself, groping for some anchor to steady her.

"My husband woke me with a call from New York. Apparently our host has stood us up."

There, she thought, stupidly. Would the evocation of her spouse bank the conflagration rising between them? Did she want to?

She searched his face for some reaction, but his expression gave nothing away. Having never entertained the idea of adultery until now, she felt, at least for the moment, that she had to cleanse herself of any vestige of guilt. Not that she actually felt guilty, only the habit of guilt, the residue of her old life.

It was another thing Aunt Emma had neglected to teach her, how to jettison the inhibiting chains of guilt.

As she battled with herself, torn between the past and present, her old self and her new, she thought of the proximity of his flesh, his knees just inches away from hers under the table. She had to fight away the desire to move forward, to touch him, skin to skin.

"My husband is Max Hamilton's lawyer," she said, again stupidly, unable to let it go. "More than that. His alter ego."

"Is he?" Champion said. She felt the power of his gaze, studying her. Had he this urge to touch her?

"Surely you must have heard of him?" Angela persisted, her eyes lifted to his again. "He's one of those global tycoons, a multibillionaire. He seems to have disappeared."

Champion shrugged, showing little interest in the subject, conscious that she was dancing around the real business between them. When their eyes met, she felt the heat of his glance, although she still had not mustered the courage to engage him fully.

"You haven't heard of him?" she asked, for no apparent reason except to fill the silence.

"Vaguely," he said.

"My husband, Tom,…" she began, as if it were necessary to reinforce her barricades, more for appearance than protection, "…well, in the light of what's happened…"

She paused, suddenly realizing where she was heading, but she could not find the will to stop herself.

"The little cruise is off. He has… my husband…" She said it with special emphasis, hoping in her heart that it would seem like an invitation, "…to stay in New York."

The words were blurted, expelled in a rush and, for the first time since he had joined her, she imagined that she could read his reaction. It was clearly one of approval, which both frightened and pleased her. As if to mask his own feelings, he, too, averted his eyes, and picked up his mimosa for a deep sip.

The alert waiter was immediately at his side filling his glass. As he approached, Angela emptied hers and proffered it for a refill, certain that it was a deliberate fortification for what she had to say.

"He said… well, I might as well stay on here at Cap Ferrat for a few days. We weren't scheduled to go home until sometime next Friday, I think. I'll have to check my tickets."

God! Did her words sound as they were intended, as an invitation? Invitation to what? To lose herself in his arms, to allow herself to be consumed by his body? She deliberately didn't look at his face, fearing that her own sense of his interest was inaccurate.

Her mind groped for rationalization. Damn her past, her upbringing, the constrictions of a boring life. But then, she told herself, it was only fair that she invoke Tom's suggestion. She knew exactly where her logic was taking her. If something did happen here, she could now assure herself, Tom would have to share some of the blame. After all, he was the one encouraging her to stay on. He was throwing her into her David's arms. She shivered with expectation.

"It's certainly a lovely place to be," Champion said, moving his glass in an encircling gesture. He lifted it in a kind of toast. She lifted hers, and they drank.

"I guess I shouldn't complain," she agreed.

"He must feel certain that this… tycoon… will not turn up," the man responded. She hoped his remark indicated that he was worried that the missing Max might suddenly reappear in the full flush of health, and the cruise would proceed. Please no, she begged silently. Let this happen.

"Yes, he does," Angela said, rushing to reassure him. "I believe he thinks that Max Hamilton is gone forever."

"Does it upset you?" the man asked.

"Am I upset?" Angela asked rhetorically, tapping her teeth with a fingernail. "I hate to see anybody die… I mean in that way. Of course, no one is certain, but he is still missing." She paused searching for even more fidelity in her answer. "Besides, he was not part of my immediate family, and he did live life up to the hilt. I'll say that for him." She looked up suddenly. "No," she said. "I'm not terribly upset. He did live on the edge, and he was, after all, my husband's employer. There is that to consider."

She tried remembering the man's name, but fearing that he would think that not remembering reflected a loss of interest, she did not pursue the matter. Then it occurred to her that he had not volunteered a name. Had she told him hers? She had forgotten.

"By the way, I'm Angela Ford," she said reaching out her hand.

"I'm John Champion," he replied then took her extended hand. It was the first touch of his flesh, and it seemed to burn with a tingling electric heat. Also, she noted a pause in the movement, the grasp lingering.

When their hands had disengaged, they finished their champagne, and the ever-alert waiter rushed to repour. She was already feeling the buzz.

"You're welcome to join me for breakfast," Angela said with some embarrassment, since places were already set for two, and there were obviously enough croissants and coffee for both of them.

Champion looked at the two settings.

"I'm not intruding?" he asked, belaboring the obvious.

She contemplated an explanation for the double setting and then retreated from the idea, hoping he would not pursue it. Had he understood that she had ordered it for him in the first place? She felt a sudden attack of panic. Did she seem too obvious, too vulnerable?

"Not at all," she replied, suddenly discovering that their conversation had taken on an odd formality as if it were part of some preordained ritual. Of course, she had no illusions about what was happening. Her body told her that. Again she wanted to reach out and touch him there, feel his reaction, as if she needed an advertisement of his desire to reassure her.

The waiter poured coffee and they nibbled at their croissants. A nervous anxiety stimulated loquaciousness on her part. Without originally intending to, she told him about her children, her life in Oyster Bay. It spilled out of her, a cascade of facts, as if she were running through a checklist. As she spoke, she felt that she was, symbolically, expelling her other life, putting it aside in the telling.

By contrast, he was quiet, and, despite her avalanche of words, not forthcoming about his life. She preferred that. She didn't want him to have a past. Rather, she yearned for him to have been born whole, just as he was, a living replica of the David.

Meanwhile, other guests began to descend from the funicular to the pool, and the chaises longues began to fill.

"I'm running at the mouth," she said suddenly, fearful that she might really be boring him.

"Not at all," he said. Actually, he seemed to have been very attentive to her nonstop monologue, certainly more than the facts of her life deserved. Her inner intelligence was appalled by the sheer banality of her history. She sounded like someone she had no interest in knowing. Where were the adventure and the passion in her life? Aunt Emma had a life. Hers had been a crashing bore.

They finished the champagne and their breakfast, and as the waiter cleared the table, they moved to the two chaises longues set up side by side nearby.

Before he stretched out, he took a tube of suntan lotion from the pocket of his robe and began to smear it over his body. Behind her sunglasses, she watched him with increasing excitement as his hand glided over the reachable flesh. She wished she were his hand.

He sat down on the lounge with his back toward her, then turning his head, he offered a smile and handed her the tube.

"Would you do my back, please?" he asked.

She was certain that the request was a deliberate seduction ploy on his part, and although she hesitated to comply for the sake of propriety, she longed to do it. She sat on the edge of her chaise and squeezed out the cream on his broad back, letting her hand slide over the smooth surface. It felt good, and she wondered what sensations her hands were giving him. Since his back was toward her, there was no way to read his expression, and his body gave no sign that her ministrations were providing him with the hoped-for pleasure.

As for her, she was beside herself with excitement, wishing she could move her hands over every inch of his perfect body. Finally, the lotion was spread and absorbed, and she had little excuse to continue. Before he could turn around, she dropped back to her lounge lying face up, while he turned on his stomach, and leaning on his arm looked up at her.

"I can't remember when I've done this," he said.

"Me neither," she agreed. "I never seem to have the leisure. Besides, the sun is the enemy of the skin."

"So I've heard."

She could feel his eyes washing over her. If she were wearing clothes, she would have to admit that his stare was undressing her. As for her, she surveyed the curve of his tight buttocks and fantasized about caressing their smoothness.

"And you," she said after a long pause, fearful that her lack of curiosity about him might suggest a lack of interest. "Why are you here?"

"Business," he replied. He had turned to face her, supporting his head on his palm. She waited for more of an explanation but none was forthcoming, which, despite her previous feeling, seemed unfair, since she had told him a great deal.

"Where are you from?" she asked.

"I divide my time between Europe and America."

Again she noted his vagueness. A man with secrets, she speculated, letting her thoughts reluctantly construct a history. He was married, of course, with children and, considering the cost of the hotel, quite successful, used to the good life. His wife, she supposed, was going to join him after his business was concluded—something like that.

She decided, too, that he was probably a man who knew women, someone experienced in that department, an expert. Certainly, judging by her own reaction, women would be enormously attracted to him, and, she supposed, she should be flattered by his interest. Or was she exaggerating the intensity of this?

"Have you been here long?" she asked.

"A couple of weeks."

"How long will you be staying?"

"Perhaps a week or two more."

"And then?"

"Depending," he shrugged.

The vagueness and brevity of his answers baffled her, and she began to fear that if she persisted in her questioning, he would disengage. And yet, he lay beside her propped on his arm observing her with continued interest.

She retreated into silence, closing her eyes behind her sunglasses, trying to fathom how she had reached this point, wondering if she would be considered the aggressor in this strange encounter.

It was all very confusing, she decided, not knowing how

to react. She needed Aunt Emma to tell her what to do. Perhaps, she decided, this entire episode was merely the product of a hyperactive imagination, a fantasy gone amuck. She was a wife and mother, wealthy and secure, she assured herself. All right, she had been tempted to have herself a fling. Max Hamilton's death had created the opportunity.

It was the kind of situation that, coupled with her experience in Florence, had suggested possibilities. But it was all self-generated. The subject of these possibilities, or was he the object, was making no effort to take responsibility, making her uncertain whether she was disappointed or relieved.

Was he naturally passive, she wondered? Or was she the coward, advertising her inhibitions, constructing silent barriers? Why didn't he take the matter in hand, seduce her with sweet words and innuendo, batter her with his insistence, relieve her of any responsibility for her actions?

Her mind reeled with a variety of explanations. He might be gay, his interest more platonic than sexual. She shuddered at the idea. What a waste, she told herself, with an inner giggle of irony.

Or maybe this was simply one of those events that had a very simple explanation. He was lonely, very shy, and she had been thrust into his company by chance, which provided merely an opportunity for friendship without effort. He does not like being alone, she concluded. He wants a companion, merely a friend.

She felt a sense of generational regression. Wasn't this the way the women of past generations were supposed to feel and act, passive and inert, objects to be pursued? Perhaps the programming imprint was too indelible to erase.

In the animal kingdom, she had learned from watching television shows, the female deliberately displayed herself, moved her tail invitingly or gave off some scent to invite the male.

Or was he teasing her, satisfying some cruel urge to silently humiliate her with his false promise. Behind her sunglasses, she observed him, his tall muscular frame in casual repose on the lounge as he watched her, inspected her, without embarrassment.

She noted the line of dark hair crawling up his tight belly from that place below. The weight of his pouch had shifted in size and heft, the outline of his organs fuller, more defined.

She was close enough to reach out, caress him into erection, plant her lips lovingly along the smooth shaft. God, he was teasing her, she decided, flustered and confused, exhausted by repression.

"Would you like to go for a drive?" he asked, emerging from the long silence. She contemplated the idea, holding back her decision, hoping he would, at the very least, exercise some persuasion. He didn't, choosing instead to merely wait for her reply. His reticence was maddening.

"Why not," she said, not exhibiting much enthusiasm.

Two can play at this game, she told herself.

Chapter 15

They drove up to Saint-Paul de Vence, where they had lunch at La Colombe d'Or, a wonderful restaurant with an excellent view of the countryside.

As they drove, she tried again to draw him out, but his replies were as vague as before, although she enjoyed their physical proximity. He wore white slacks and a solid dark-green sport shirt that matched his eyes.

They ordered salads and roast duck, he seconding her as he had done at poolside. The waiter recommended a local white wine. He waited for her nod before ordering. The table was festooned with arrangements of colorful vegetables on elegantly patterned tablecloths.

"Have you been here often?" she asked.

"Yes."

"It is beautiful."

"Very."

"And much cooler up here than below."

"Much."

And yet the absence of verbal reaction did not detract from the intensity of his inspection. She knew she was soaking in his gaze, had been soaking in it from the beginning.

When her eyes lifted to meet his, she could imagine passionate communication, but his face seemed devoid of any promise of further action, as if she were simply an object of admiration, a bloodless inanimate object.

After trying any number of ploys to draw him into articulating any revelation about himself, his work, the facts of his life and existence, she finally surrendered to the idea that he was hopelessly nonverbal. But the condition still did not diminish the intensity of her attraction to him.

They finished lunch, walked through the quaint town, around the perimeter, then drove down again into the sunset.

By then, she accepted the silence. There was no point in pushing the verbal envelope. But his look continued to testify to his interest in her, and yet he made no effort to touch her.

If their flesh met it was accidental. Of course, she wanted to reach out, hold his hand, touch him in some way, but, for some reason, her inhibitions held.

"Dinner later?" he asked when they had disembarked at the hotel lobby. She had expected a more intimate invitation and had prepared herself for consent, worried that she was not yet ready. Did he sense that? she wondered. Or did he fear rejection?

"Are you sure?" she asked, testing his commitment to the idea.

"Very," he nodded, smiling. "And you?"

She offered her own smile and nodded consent, almost by rote, as if it were a foregone conclusion. By natural progression, they seemed to have become a couple. As if to bind them further, he took her hand and moved to kiss her on each cheek. The sudden closeness, a polite and familiar ritual, made her feel weak in the knees.

He continued to hold her hand for a long moment as their gaze met. She felt a shiver of excitement and all the physical signs of arousal. They disengaged. Slightly dizzy from the encounter, she managed to get back to her room.

The intensity of her excitement was instantly inhibited by the flashing red light on her telephone informing her of a message. It could only be from Tom, a fact confirmed by the concierge. She was to call immediately.

Did his message spell the end of her fantasy? Was it about to be downgraded from erotic expectation to innocent diversion? She could not contain a rising sob. She shook her head and jammed a fist into her palm, her glance fixated on the telephone, as if it contained the clarion call of her conscience, the death knell of her erotic future. She was assailed by second thoughts.

Perhaps it was a signal of caution, a kind of stop sign, telling her that she must accept the boundaries of her role in life. Despite the evidence of the "incident," Aunt Emma had raised impossible erotic expectations. With trepidation, Angela picked up the phone.

It did not take long to get through to her husband.

"They found Max," Tom told her.

Although she had resigned herself to the inevitable, she was briefly panicked by the idea that this might mean the yacht party was to be reinstated.

"Dead as a doornail. Drowned. Apparently the boat was close enough to shore. With the tides right, his body came ashore above Cannes. It's now in the Cannes town morgue.

I arranged for Max's jet to pick up Mrs. Hamilton and her daughters in England and bring them to Cannes. They should be at the Carlton any minute now. Mrs. Hamilton will have to officially identify the body. They're doing an autopsy."

"How… was it an accident? Or what?"

She had replied to the news by rote, offering the expected response. The fact was that she couldn't care less. Her only issue now was to remain here with Champion.

"Not certain yet," Tom said abruptly. "I've talked with the authorities. There's no obvious sign of foul play. Of course, because it was Max, they would want to be absolutely certain. Max was insured for millions. Can you imagine what the tabloids and TV will make of it?"

"Juicy stuff, I suppose," Angela said with indifference. "Is Mrs. Hamilton broken up over this?" Angela asked.

"In a way, I guess," Tom said. "She was, at least in name, his wife, the mother of his children."

"He was such a bastard to her. And never faithful," Angela persisted, aware of the irony of her own brief dabble in that direction.

"That doesn't change the circumstances," Tom said with some impatience. "Besides, it's irrelevant now."

She dismissed pursuing the idea. What relevance did it have to her? She felt miles away in spirit from Max's death, accidental or otherwise.

"So dear old Max is gone," she said.

"Afraid so."

"It could have been suicide," Angela mused.

"Could be. No note was found."

He seemed uninterested in pursuing the question further.

"What does it mean for us?" she asked, referring to the impact that it would have on their lives, not really caring. It seemed more an obligatory question than one whose answer was crucial to her future.

"More work. You know Max. He had his fingers everywhere. I'm his executor. I've got to see that things go smoothly. The fact is…" He paused and cleared his throat. "…I'll be running things from now on in. Unless… well, there's the girls. They could be a problem."

Her experience with Tom's shorthand told her he was referring to Max's daughters, who had passionately hated their father. Both Angela and Tom had spent a great deal of energy and time hand-holding Mrs. Hamilton, Max's long-suffering, mousy, and abused wife.

Angela had felt a great deal of pity and compassion for the poor woman and had been enlisted by her husband to maintain a warm relationship with her during the rare times when they were thrown together. She had understood the daughters' virulent hostility. Max had ignored and abandoned them, and it had taken all of Tom's persuasive powers to get their father to be overly generous to them, both in their lifetime and in the provisions he had made on his death.

"I'll have to be flying in today to meet with them," Tom said, sparking her alertness. She felt suddenly panicked by the growing sense of lost opportunity. This was not what she wanted. Not now. Her throat constricted and her heart-beat accelerated.

"Today?"

"Believe me, Angela, I'm not looking forward to it. I spoke briefly with Mrs. Hamilton, who seems out of it. She's obviously under the influence of her daughters, who may be advising her. It could get nasty. They need to be placated, I'm afraid. They have some knowledge about what Max has provided. It's a King's ransom, Angela. Still, I'm not their favorite character, and they could make the situation a nightmare by doing something stupid and ruin everything. Considering what I have on my plate back here, it's a real bitch."

The turn of events triggered Angela's anger, which she found difficult to repress. Nevertheless she remained cool, determined to find a way to keep him from coming to France. Her mind rapidly explored countermeasures.

"I have a suggestion, Tom," she said, as a plan formed in her mind.

"A suggestion?" He seemed genuinely surprised. She had rarely, if ever, offered advice in business matters.

"Well," she began hesitantly, her confidence growing as she spoke. "Considering the hostility his daughters have always shown to you, I am here, Tom. I can be there in a couple of hours or less. Perhaps smooth the way. Or they might not be as hostile as you think. Blood is thicker than water, Tom. I'll talk to Mrs. Hamilton and the girls, offer condolences and assess the situation. It might not be as bad as you've imagined."

She waited through a long pause, listening to his breathing.

"It's a thought," Tom replied. "I'm not sure—"

Angela quickly broke into his hesitation.

"I think maybe a woman's touch is needed here. Before you waste your time, I can see them and report back. This is a delicate time, and as you say, if Max has been generous, it might be better not to… well… inflame them by your presence. I mean… well, it could make things worse."

"You might have something there, Angela," Tom said. "The timing might be wrong for me—"

"Absolutely, Tom. I can leave immediately. Be there in say…" she looked at the clock on the night table beside the bed, "a little over an hour."

"I don't see any downside," Tom muttered.

"If things look sticky, you can always fly over in one of Max's jets. What are a few hours to make sure?"

"There are technical matters to discuss," he began.

"This is not the time for any technical matters, Tom. This is… well… an emotional problem."

"You've got a point."

"Say the word, and I'll get ready," Angela said, literally holding her breath. She was acting by instinct now, buying time. Time for what? Without any set plan, she plunged forward.

"Women understand these things, Tom."

She waited through another long pause, hoping her gender appeal might tip the balance.

"I need to know whether they're planning any legal action that will inhibit the orderly arrangement of Max's affairs. If that's on their mind, I'll have to come immediately and forestall them. I need to know the landscape. Do you understand?"

"Of course, I understand. Now I'm even more certain that I should go."

Was she pushing too hard?

"It's so crucial, Angela," he said.

"I won't let you down," she replied hurriedly, feeling on the verge of victory.

"Okay then. But remember. You must call me as soon as you've assessed the situation. I mean immediately after you've seen them."

"Absolutely, Tom. Just as soon as I've seen them."

"I'll be waiting," Tom said.

"Believe me, Tom, I won't let you down."

Still holding the phone after he had hung up, she waited for her heart rate to decelerate. She felt a brief twinge of guilt but quickly repressed it. The only thought in her mind was contacting Champion. She was put through immediately.

"It's me," she said when he answered. "Would you mind dining later? Something's come up."

She hated the idea of missing a moment with him. But at least she had precluded the possibility of an abrupt end to their… she could not think of an appropriate word.

"When?"

There was a long moment of silence between them, as if neither wanted to make the first move to commit.

"Well, I..." she began finally. "I have to go to Cannes, you see. Seems they've recovered the body of Mr. Hamilton. I have to visit his widow and his daughters. They're at the Carlton. Rather grim duty, I'm afraid."

She waited anxiously for his response. Again there was a long silence.

"I could drive you," he said finally. "We can have dinner after you've done your business."

All along, she had been hoping he would make the offer and seized it instantly.

"Really? Are you sure...?"

"I want to," he said. "I... I want to be with you."

The admission sparked a thrilling sense of danger. So far what was between them had gone unsaid—until now. She pondered a reply in kind.

"Yes," she said cautiously. "I'd like that."

She was, in fact, ecstatic.

Chapter 16

After he had hung up, Champion thought about his offer. It hadn't been intended. In fact, nothing concerning the woman had been intended. For the first time in his recent life he felt unmoored, tossing helplessly in the vortex of a whirlpool. Being with her, in her aura, had become the absolute priority of his existence.

A part of him said, Fight this. Emotion is the enemy in your business. But against this overwhelming wave of compulsion, no defense seemed possible.

The night before, when he had discovered the strangely coincidental connection with Max Hamilton, his first instinct was that someone had set him up to be a stalking horse in pursuit of the client who had ordered the hit.

It was, after all, suspiciously accidental, broadly hinting at some directing authority making it happen. How convenient to have an empty table beside him available. Then, as if it were prearranged, enter a beautiful femme fatale who engaged his interest, then mysteriously tantalized him as if it deliberately and scrupulously scripted, just as he had prepared his killing scenarios. He could not quite shake the feeling that he was being sucked into a magnetic field that had entrapment written all over it.

Despite all these sinister speculations, his response to her was happening with relentless forward motion, overriding all sense of caution, a caution that, up to now, was a bed-rock of his motivation. How was it possible, he wondered, for his body and mind to be so mesmerized by this woman? Did she possess some secret psychological or even chemical weapon to vanquish him? It defied logical analysis. To flee was the only sensible operative alternative. What was holding him back?

Certainly he had never contemplated or experienced such unfettered emotion. Once he had thought of his inner world as an ice floe, incapable of melting. Suddenly it had entered a quite unexpected torrid zone, transforming and rearranging his body cells.

This morning when he had walked out on the balcony, he had known absolutely that she would be there in his field of vision. Her wave, acknowledging his presence, had sent shivers running through him. And he knew, with the same certainty that the sun rose and set, that she would be waiting for him at poolside, a place for him already set next to her, his breakfast ordered, waiting.

All his well-laid plans, the carefully concocted set piece of the aftermath had dissolved, erased from his mind, lobotomized. Always, at this point after a mission, his thoughts would be concentrated on disappearance and evasion, putting distance between himself and the event.

In a week or so, he would have been off, zigzagging from destination to destination, then disappearing into one or another of the safe houses he had established for himself in various parts of the world.

After a month or two in one of them, he would bounce to

another, always on the run, adopting and removing identities at will, waiting for the next assignment to emerge. At intervals he would check in with Parker to see if any more assignments were in the offing.

In one swoop, all this effort to recast himself as merely a wandering killing machine, a thinking object without compassion, conscience, feeling, or a moral center, a deliberate disconnect from humanity, was now in jeopardy. The woman, Angela, whether by design, accident, or finding the weapon to penetrate his genetic code, had interdicted these efforts.

Even as he remained helplessly in her orbit, his mind searched for ways to break the spell. As a test of tactics, he had imposed on himself a conversational screen of extreme caution. Still he could not be certain whether his motives were protecting himself or preserving the fiction of his life.

He began to fear that, confronting her, he might find himself unable to construct a history of himself that would be believable. Worse, in his effort to prove his candor, a totally alien idea, he might actually confess how he really conducted his life. The fact that such a temptation occurred to him was frightening evidence that he was beginning to spin out of control.

The change in him was profound, and, despite the obvious danger, he was mesmerized by what was happening. She had cast a spell over him and he could not find either the strength or the will to escape from it. He was well aware that human history had endowed such feelings with words—love, passion, desire. Thus far in his life though, he had never understood what they meant or what experiences they described. He had supposed himself to be out of that loop—until now.

Worse, getting involved with the life of his victim, however peripherally, was anathema in his profession. In the killing business, such conduct was fundamentally against the rules of engagement. After a hit, strategic withdrawal was the only option. And here he was violating the caveat, ignoring consequences, looking for trouble. The one human instinct that he had always accepted was survival, survival at all costs. Now his instincts were clawing at his will. Leave it alone, he urged himself. Run. Flee. Escape.

Later, driving in the Jaguar, with her beside him, he whipped his fears to some neutral area beneath the surface of consciousness. The inner voice of caution grew faint. Whatever the risks and despite his inherent suspicion, distrust and ignorance of any emotional engagement, right here beside her was the only place on earth he wanted to be.

The traffic on the Promenade des Anglais was heavy with tourists, and they proceeded at a snail's pace until they passed the airport, and the road opened.

But caution and suspicion were hard habits to break. His conversation continued to be guarded, almost reticent. He had never learned the language of trust.

It took some effort to concentrate on his driving. All his senses seemed magnetized by her presence. For the first time in his life, he found himself confronting the possibility that his aloneness, once his armor, was melting in the heat of this powerful assault. Without it, he felt naked, vulnerable, exposed.

He knew he was spinning into new and unexplored territory, another consciousness, triggering other fears. Was she experiencing the same powerful sensations? Suddenly this was the central question of his life, spawning a holograph of uncertainties. Had she shown any signs of mutuality? Did her body ache with the need for his physical presence? Or was this some wild narcissistic fantasy of his own concoction? Did she feel the same sense of loss when she was away from him?

He berated his ignorance in these matters, his inability to find the internal levers of control. What if her response to him was tepid, nothing more than a superficial dalliance? That, he vowed, would be unacceptable. Unacceptable? Could he will her into mutuality? And if not, how would he excise her from his consciousness?

"I really appreciate this," she said breaking the silence, as the Jaguar picked up speed and headed toward Cannes.

"My pleasure," he replied, hating the polite formality of the response. What he wanted to say was that he needed to be here, that her presence was the single most important priority of his life.

"Tom, my husband, wanted me to assess the attitude of Hamilton's widow and her daughters." She seemed to check herself. Nor did he want or need any explanation. This was not the aftermath he had planned.

The husband again, Champion was thinking. She had raised the specter of her marriage numerous times in their short acquaintance, as if she had set up her own natural barrier.

His profession had taught him that barriers could not be wished away. They had to be circled or scaled or simply erased. Indeed, he could not deny to himself that it had crossed his mind that he could skillfully find the professional means to eliminate the barrier. He rejected the idea instantly, on the grounds that it could corrupt the exquisite sense of purity he was experiencing.

"Lucky that you were so close by," Champion said.

"Certainly convenient. I saw no need for Tom to travel such a distance if it wasn't necessary."

He felt her eyes observe him and briefly turned to meet her gaze. But just as he turned, her eyes drifted to view the passing terrain.

"He wanted to fly over immediately," she said, still evading his glance, talking to the roadside sights. "I suppose he expected me to fly back with him."

"Would you have?" he asked.

"Probably. He might have insisted."

"And you always obey his wishes?"

"He's my husband."

"I see," Champion said, searching for a neutral comment, hiding his disappointment.

"I don't want to leave here," she said abruptly, with a girlish giggle in her voice. "Not now. It was my idea to forestall him." Was that a declaration of some sort? A tease, perhaps? Again suspicion reared itself, and he looked toward her. She turned, their eyes meeting briefly. This time it was he who forced his eyes away, flicking his glance back to the road while hers continued to observe him.

He made no comment, trying to hold back false hopes within him. He wanted to reach out and touch her. But he held back, fearing rejection.

"I'm supposed to test the waters for him," she murmured. "He handles all of Hamilton's affairs you see. The family could be a problem, especially the daughters. He wants to be sure there will be no legal surprises."

"Sounds like he's trusting you with a great deal of responsibility."

"A rare event."

They pulled up to the Carlton entrance. A uniformed attendant took his car.

"I'll wait at a table on the patio," he said.

"I appreciate this. I'll try not to be too long."

He moved onto the patio and took a table under an umbrella. It was late afternoon, still hot, but the patio had begun to fill with people.

He ordered a Campari and soda and began to settle in and watch the passing crowd. It wasn't long before she had come back, looking grim and pale.

"Bad news. They don't want visitors," she said, looking downcast.

"Odd," Champion said. "Did they announce you?"

Angela nodded.

"There was a gaggle of paparazzi in the lobby waiting for a glimpse of them. I told the concierge that it was urgent and official, that I was with their lawyer. They called upstairs, and I was identified and barred. Apparently they have security, a couple of guards according to the concierge. I don't understand it. I did have a reasonably good relationship with Mrs. Hamilton and her daughters. Now they don't even want to speak to me. If I tell him, Tom will be furious, and you can bet he'll be on his way." Her eyes locked into Champion's. "I have to see them, John, and see them now."

"Well then, we must do something about this," Champion said. His mind was slipping into a planning mode.

"Can we?" Angela asked, her eyes pleading.

"Obstacles are only puzzles to be solved."

"Believe me, John. I'm open to any solution."

Reaching out, she touched his hand, and he eagerly responded. Their eyes met again. He mulled the situation.

"And if you do see them?"

They exchanged glances.

"I do not want him to come here. Not now."

He could see she was conflicted. Then he reached for her hand and brought it up to his lips, kissing her fingers.

"Nor do I," he said.

He rose, left some francs on the table, and, taking her by the arm, led her back into the lobby and confronted the concierge.

"We must see her," Champion explained, assuming an official intimidating air.

"I'm terribly sorry," the concierge said with frigid politeness. "We must follow our guests' instructions. I've given Mrs. Hamilton the lady's name. She has declined to see her."

"This is urgent," Champion said.

"Apparently not to Mrs. Hamilton."

"You've given her the name. Mrs. Thomas Ford."

"I have."

"But I must see her," Angela said. She shot Champion a look of frustration. His own was growing, his mind groping for ways around this problem.

"I have my orders, madame."

Champion removed a five-hundred euro note from his wallet. The concierge glanced at it.

"What is her room number?"

"It will do you no good, monsieur," the concierge whispered, still looking at the note. "There is security. Two men."

"We'll take our chances."

The concierge glanced around him for a moment. Champion palmed the money and put out his hand, passing the note.

"Three hundred forty," he said, looking over Champion's shoulder. "But I must deny giving it to you."

"Of course," Champion said.

The concierge bent his head close to Champion's ear.

"S'il vous plait, monsieur. No trouble."

"Oui, mon ami," Champion said, glancing at Angela.

"I don't understand any of this," Angela said, as he led her by the hand to the bank of elevators, picking their way through the crowd of reporters and photographers.

There were others in the elevator. They remained silent and exited on the third floor. As the concierge had told them, two beefy guards were visible, one posted at the elevator and another at the entrance to the suite. The guard eyed them curiously and with barely a glance at him, Champion guided Angela in the opposite direction toward the rear of the hotel.

"Where are we going?" she asked.

He did not respond, observing the floor layout. He spied a maid's linen closet.

"Wait in here," he whispered, gently leading her into the closet. Inside, he enfolded her in his arms and kissed her deeply. He felt her body melt into his as their lips touched, opened hungrily, joined. An ecstatic thrill jolted him, and he felt her shiver with equal intensity.

The feeling was totally foreign to his experience, as if suddenly the discipline, control, and distrust of a lifetime had seeped out of his psyche. I am not alone anymore, an inner intelligence communicated. I am part of her and she of me.

He knew instantly that he had surrendered to an idea that he had been fighting since the night before. It was as if a virus had entered him and rendered him powerless against its fury. He felt himself letting go, surrendering to a force over which he had no control.

"And you?" she said when they had disengaged.

"Wait, please. Trust me, Angela."

He moved back toward the elevator, walking slowly, nodding to the beefy guard who stood observing him as he came forward smiling. Suddenly, he spun the man around gripping him in a headlock, twisting his arm behind his back. Not a word was spoken. The guard in front of the

Hamilton suite came forward, reaching for his gun.

In a much practiced move, just as the other guard was an arm's length away, Champion pressed the man's carotid artery rendering him instantly unconscious, and pushed his body forward putting the oncoming guard off balance. Kicking the guard in the crotch, Champion let the man fall forward, then with his two hands locked, swung upward under the man's chin, jolted him, and took his gun.

Instructing the man to carry his partner to a utility closet near the Hamilton suite, Champion then ordered him to tie the other with electric cords he had pulled from the vacuum cleaners. Then he stuffed rags into their mouths.

That done, he brandished the gun near the conscious guard's face.

"I could easily kill you both this minute," he said. "I am going into Mrs. Hamilton's suite and will leave them unharmed. If you do anything to interrupt this meeting or make your situation known, I will kill you and them. Do you understand?"

The conscious man nodded. Champion carefully closed the door and walked quickly to where he had put Angela. Again they embraced, clinging to each other, their kiss deep.

"We can go now," he said gently.

"The guards?" she asked.

"They have given us permission. But we can't stay long."

Taking her arm, he led her to the entrance of the Hamilton suite.

"Where are the guards?"

"They've gone for an aperitif," he said, winking at her, certain that she hadn't a clue as to what had transpired.

He was aware, of course, that he was getting in far deeper than he had ever imagined. It did occur to him that he was about to confront the wife and daughters of his victim, the man he had dispatched to oblivion for profit without a second thought. Even now, he felt nothing for the dead man or his family.

"I could wait here," he told her.

"No," she protested. "I need you with me."

"Who will I be?"

She thought for a moment.

"A colleague of Tom's," she told him. Their eyes met. He sensed her hesitation. It was, he knew, a defining moment. She nodded, and the die was cast.

His mind groped for a name. "Bell," he said, thinking of their hotel, Bel Air. "Yes, Bell." He had locked into the idea. He was in his element, planning, exploring ways to transcend obstacles.

"Bell, it is," she said, smiling thinly, straightening, obviously collecting her courage.

She knocked. There was movement within, sounds coming closer, then a voice coming from behind the closed door. Angela looked toward him, and he nodded, fully conscious now that she was deferring to his leadership and her willingness to obey.

The door opened a crack. He could see a woman's face, then the door began to close. He put out his foot to stop it from closing.

"I must see you," Angela said.

"Where are the guards?" the woman asked. She was obviously one of the daughters.

"They were bribed," Angela said.

"Bastards."

They waited through a long hesitation and then the door opened. Angela had known both daughters and had maintained a proper but distant relationship with them. She recognized this one as Victoria, the oldest daughter. She was severely dressed in black, with a hawklike face, eyes deep set and wary. She was hardly welcoming.

"We left word—" she began.

"Let her in Victoria," a woman's voice called from within the suite. She was an older woman, sitting on the couch, pale, somewhat tousled, and obviously agitated. The resemblance between the two women was clear. They entered the suite, and Angela quickly introduced Champion as Mr. Bell, her husband's colleague.

"But mother," the daughter said. "We agreed."

"No harm in this, Victoria."

"I'm terribly sorry, Gertrude," Angela began, embracing the grieving wife. The younger woman took a place beside her mother on the couch. "I was in Cap Ferrat. My husband—"

"Yes," Victoria said. "Your husband did call. He was his usual unctuous self." Another woman came in from the bedroom, the other daughter, Elizabeth. She was heavyset, running to fat, like her father.

"It was awful… about Max," Angela said, addressing all

the women simultaneously. "My husband was supposed to meet me, and we were to join him on the yacht tomorrow as a matter of fact." Champion noted her awkwardness as she plunged into the disjointed explanation.

"With his bimbos," the fat daughter said.

"Elizabeth!" Mrs. Hamilton cried.

"He treated you like shit, Mama. It has to be said. It's over. You can't live your life in denial anymore."

"He was my husband and your father," Gertrude Hamilton said, but it was obvious the fight was out of her. "He has been very generous to all of us."

"Generous?" the fat sister said. "Hush money, I call it. We're being paid off while others take the bulk of the spoils. Well, your husband has a real surprise in store for him."

"As you can see, Angela," Victoria said, "we've always known how we were to be provided for after my father's death. Now that it's happened, don't expect us to simply surrender our rights. We believe we have a case here to pursue full control over our father's assets, his entire business empire. We are not going to sit still for what has been arranged."

Champion watched the proceedings, feeling detached.

"I'm here as a condolence call on behalf of myself and my husband," Angela said with an air of indignity. "Mr. Bell here is a colleague who I asked to accompany me. I have no knowledge of the business arrangements." She glanced at Champion. It seemed a signal for him to speak.

"I can only say," Champion said, again noting the absurdity of the situation, "that your husband and father has been extraordinarily generous."

"I'd like to know how he died," Elizabeth said.

And I can tell you that, Champion thought.

"I'll bet he was murdered," Victoria spat through tight lips. "He deserved to be."

"Victoria," her mother rebuked, rolling her eyes.

"Without a doubt," the heavyset daughter echoed. "Considering his legion of enemies, he screwed everybody he ever touched. However he was dispatched, it was an act of charity."

"Elizabeth!" Gertrude snapped.

So I have provided a service to mankind, Champion thought, amused by the interchange. He felt a heightened sense of the absurd. His act, in this venue, turned out to be a mercy killing. He tamped down an ironic chuckle.

"There is no evidence," Gertrude Hamilton protested.

With difficulty, Champion forced himself to remain detached, although he could not resist acknowledging his own professionalism. Yet he felt, from force of habit, endangered. He should have been miles away from this place. He assailed his weakness and stupidity, although a quick glance at Angela was enough to dispel his doubts, at least for the moment.

"Oh, they were very clever about that, Mother," Victoria said with authority. "They wanted it to look like an accident. I say he was pushed overboard."

"No question," the fat daughter said, looking at Champion, who felt obliged to speak.

"We'll have to wait for more conclusive findings," he said,

very lawyerly, conscious again of the irony of his predicament. Despite this, he felt no connection with the events other than his attachment to Angela.

"Tom is committed to protect your family's interests," Angela said. "He told me so…" She paused. "He… he is ready to be here himself at a moment's notice, but since I was so close…"

"Tell your husband to stay home. We just don't trust him," the fat daughter interrupted. "He was part and parcel of my father's venal business life."

"That's for sure," Victoria said belligerently.

"You can bet they fixed it so that our family will be screwed," Elizabeth said. "We want no part of him."

"I don't know what to say," Angela said, obviously vexed and uncertain. There was no question that Tom should be here, using his persuasive powers on these embittered people. "I had no idea—"

"Well you have now, and you can report that to your husband," Victoria said. "We have retained a very high-powered lawyer in England to fight this. We are against any arrangements allegedly made during my father's lifetime. We are the rightful heirs to everything. We want nothing to do with your husband and his manipulations. We are certain that he fixed things with my father so that he can take over all his enterprises."

"Tom wouldn't do that…" she began but then hesitated, asking herself, Wouldn't he?

"He's always thought of your best interests," Champion said, his eyes roaming to each woman in turn. He hoped he looked sincere. These women were conspiring against his most fervent desire. An accurate report on what was occurring here would surely bring Angela's husband to Cannes posthaste. And he'd find a way to see them, although without the tactics that Champion had employed.

Angela and he exchanged glances. Hamilton's daughters were obviously determined to fight. On another level, he would agree with them. From this encounter, the identity of Parker's client was becoming clear. Who benefited the most from this act? Tom Ford, of course. He doubted whether the daughters had anything to do with it. Although it briefly crossed his mind, he was certain that Angela had no part in it as well. They exchanged glances again. No, he decided. No way.

"Is this your view as well?" Angela asked Gertrude, who sighed and shrugged.

"I stand with my daughters," Gertrude said with a sigh of resignation.

"Mother will not be a rug to be stepped on anymore," the fat one said. "It's time we stood up for our rights."

"You should let my husband explain…" Angela began, suddenly realizing again that it was counter to her desires.

"It will do him no good," the fat one said. "He was my father's flunky."

"You can tell your husband," Victoria said looking at Angela, then turning to Champion, "and his colleague, that whatever legal folderol he has created will be nullified. Our lawyer, a Mr. Lloyd, will soon contact him, simply about that. We have nothing else to talk about. Please leave."

"Surely, you should hear Tom's side," Angela said, turning to Mrs. Hamilton.

"I'm all confused," Gertrude Hamilton said, averting her eyes.

"I'm sorry, Gertrude, really I am," Angela said.

"You can tell your husband we'll meet him in court," Victoria said.

"If he does come here tomorrow, will you see him?"

"I doubt if that would do any good," Elizabeth said.

"Why don't you both just leave," the fat one said.

"You needn't be impolite, Elizabeth," Mrs. Hamilton said, her voice reedy. Obviously, Champion observed, this was a woman whipped to submission by her late husband, and now her daughters were repeating the process.

"My husband will be here in a few hours," Angela said, her voice trembling as she glanced at Champion. "You can tell him these things yourself. As I said, I'm here on a personal basis."

"I appreciate that," Gertrude Hamilton acknowledged.

"All right then, you've done your duty, now leave," the fat one said. "And yes, if your husband arrives, we'll tell him exactly what we told you."

Champion shrugged. He could not think of anything to say, his mind already searching for some explanation not only for his presence but also for the situation with the guards. In for a penny, in for a pound, he thought remembering Parker's little homily. He could foresee nothing but trouble for Angela.

"I guess we've exhausted the subject then," Champion

said, signaling with his eyes that it was time to leave. Every moment was now a diminishment of the time he would spend with Angela. He was also beginning to feel uncomfortable about the guards escaping their bonds.

Angela rose on this signal.

"Once again," she said. "I offer my condolences to all of you."

They moved toward the door.

"And we'll deal with those greedy guards," Elizabeth said as they left. "Damned frogs."

In the corridor, Champion led her swiftly toward the staircase. Angela was too self-absorbed to question his choice. They walked quickly through the lobby to the entrance where Champion called for his car.

They said nothing as they waited for the car. Once inside, he embraced her, and they kissed deeply.

With her leaning against him, her hand caressing his thigh, he drove the car toward Mougins.

"Now what?"

"He's waiting for my call," Angela sighed.

"Then you must call."

She folded into his arms as he drove.

"I know a little place outside Mougins," he said.

"Hurry."

Chapter 17

For Angela any deliberation seemed irrelevant. She acknowledged to herself that she was in the grip of something that could not be stopped, something urgent and relentless. Her mind, she knew, was incapable of rational thought. And she didn't care. She knew she had to call Tom and was desperately trying to work out some explanation that would inhibit his trip to France.

"They have no telephones where we're going," Champion told her.

"Good."

"There," she said pointing to a phone kiosk. He pulled up beside it and they embraced once again. Finally, she got out of the car.

Using her credit card, she called her husband's office.

It surprised her how quickly Cynthia was on the line.

"He's awaiting your call," Cynthia said, and then Tom was on the line.

"What took so long?" he asked.

"Traffic," she said. "It's the height of the season."

"Well then?"

She drew in a deep breath, recognizing that this was a defining moment, perhaps the most defining moment in her life.

"There is no need to worry, Tom," she said, quelling a

slight trembling in her voice. Telling lies had never been her forte, and even now, it pained her to do so.

"No problems on the horizon?"

"None."

"No wavering? No threats of further legal action?"

"I… I didn't see any sign of that."

"Did you talk to both daughters?"

"Oh, yes."

She swallowed hard, then coughed to clear her throat.

"And you saw no indications that they would be less than cooperative?"

"I told you, Tom. There's no need to worry."

She bit down on her lip to keep it from trembling.

"And Gertrude?"

"Gertrude is… grieving."

"Really? Grieving? That's a laugh. She should be celebrating."

"Max was her husband," Angela managed to say.

"Some husband," Tom said.

There was a long pause on the line.

"So you think they'll be cooperative?"

"I believe they will."

"You're certain of this, Angela. No doubts whatsoever."

"That's my assessment, Tom."

She turned to look toward Champion, who was watching her. He smiled and waved. It was exactly the encouragement she needed to proceed.

"I… I believe they have absolute faith in your judgment, Tom."

She closed her eyes tightly as if she were taking in bitter medicine.

"So you think I can skip the trip?"

Her heartbeat accelerated.

"Up to you, Tom. But I see no need to shore up their co-operation. That part of it seems fine. You said you were busy with so many other details.... I—"

"You can't imagine," he interrupted.

She looked toward Champion again.

"I really appreciate this, darling," he said. "You've been a great help. This means a great deal to our future."

She had no interest in what it meant to their future. At this moment, Tom and her old life with him seemed distant and without meaning. Perhaps Hamilton's daughters were right. Perhaps he had manipulated them, all of them. Even her.

"I'm glad," she said, her attention drifting. She was feeling her irrelevance to his life. There was still one piece of unfinished business to transact.

"I think..." she began, looking again at Champion, "... it's quite pleasant here. Aunt Emma and I really knocked ourselves out in Florence. It would be nice to spend a few days resting here."

"By all means, darling. Hell, take the week. When were we set to come home?"

"Friday, I think," she whispered, her knees feeling weak.

"Well, darling. Have a great rest. See you in a few days. You've done yeoman service, darling. Yeoman service. Gotta rush. Have a good one."

"I damned well will," she said to the phone after she had hung up. For the first time in her life, she felt a sense of total liberation. Am I me? She asked herself. Really me?

He was watching her as she came forward.

"Fat's in the fire," she said.

"No problems?"

She shook her head.

"None," she said. "I told him all was quiet on the western front."

"You didn't?"

"There'll be hell to pay."

"I hope so."

They embraced against the car, oblivious to the passing traffic. She felt his hardness against her and caressed him there. Disengaging they got into the car.

"How fast can this baby go?" she asked as he accelerated the car.

"Fast. Like a bird."

"Fly it then."

He turned off the main road to Mougins, onto a dirt road. After a bumpy few miles, he stopped in front of a stone house.

"Wait here," he said.

He was back in a few moments jangling a key in front of her. They went into the house where a roundish little woman greeted them with a happy smile.

"Madame Elaine," Champion said. "The proprietor, cook, and maid all in one. We are her only guests." He winked at Angela. "I pay her a king's ransom for the privilege."

"Enchanté," Angela said, realizing that the woman spoke no English.

They ascended a wooden staircase, and she found herself in a room with low-beamed ceilings, a high double bed, a chair, a sink, and a shelf of assorted crockery.

"It's not the Carlton," he said. "But the lady does provide room service and there is a bathroom in the hall with a big claw-foot tub."

"I love it," Angela said. "Besides, it has all the equipment we'll need."

Nothing in her life had prepared her for this. Even Aunt Emma's hints and explanations, while clues to some sensual nirvana, some pleasure dome on earth, merely scratched the surface of her expectations. She had, indeed, entered into what Aunt Emma had called a dream of passion.

They tore at each other's clothes searching for the touch of bare flesh, finding it.

It was as if some immediate validation of their urgency was needed, without the civilized niceties of what was referred to as foreplay. Her entire life, she was convinced, had been foreplay for this moment, and all experience was reduced to this single animal need.

He led her to the bed where she lay down on the spread, her body open, moist and ready to receive him, drawing him forward by a grip on his penis, inserting him, gripping his hard buttocks, absorbing him tightly inside her, seconding every stroke of his commanding lead as her body convulsed with sensations of pleasure beyond even the wildest flights of fantasy.

She heard a symphony of sounds, strange, inchoate, primitive. Only later, after the shock of this experience had, for the moment, spent itself, did she realize that these were their sounds, the pounding music of their ecstasy.

It was miraculous, she discovered, as the day advanced, the way their bodies magnetized, communicated. There was nothing but openness between them as they indicated their pleasure and encouraged each other in ways that she did not think were possible.

As the colors in the slits of the closed shutters turned from white to orange to impenetrable charcoal, they coupled insatiably.

Orgasmic spasms of pleasure merged. In her embrace, he was her David, her marble man transformed into living flesh, filling her with the power of his manhood. It amazed her that they could make love like this without tiring, wanting more, as if they had transcended mere animal attraction.

Was this the true passion? she wondered, alert for signs. Or the transitory lust that Aunt Emma had suggested, the mere counterfeit "cock fever." Again she felt frightened, vulnerable.

They opened the shutters and watched the stars sparkle in the moonless night, yet never moving from fleshly contact, as if any separation might compromise their attachment. At some point, Angela knew, there would have to be words, a dialogue, an investigation. Surely this mysterious, cosmic event between them needed reflection, explanation, validation.

Only as it became light again did some hint of time and

place find its way into her consciousness, but no details of her past or future filtered into her mind, which, through dint of discipline and concentration, kept her in the now, the present, a place of passion without consequences.

Madame Elaine came up in the morning bringing along a dimpled smile and a tray of breakfast, eggs and ham, croissants, and cups of chicory-laced coffee in big cups. They bathed together in the big tub, enjoying the steamy joy of it until their fingertips wrinkled, returned to their bed, and made love again.

The spears of sun shafting through the open shutters made his eyes seem greener as they met hers. She noted in herself the lucidity and fidelity of her observations of his physical attributes. She saw each dark hair that threaded downward from his navel with such clarity she imagined she could count them. When she lifted his palm to kiss, she saw every line etched in his flesh. No part of him went uninspected and unseen.

"I need to know," she mused, hearing again the echo of Emma's conversation. Was there mutuality here?

"Know what?"

"How you feel." She stumbled for a moment. "I mean is this just... well... a case of temporary insanity?"

He seemed to grow thoughtful, then smiled. She felt herself pressing the point, burrowing deep, determined to find the key to her actions. And his? Had she invented this out of the whole cloth of Aunt Emma's words, from which had come the "incident"? Was this merely the power of suggestion?

"I don't know. This has never happened to me before."

She grew speculative. Doubts gathered. Had she been manipulated into this position by his cleverness? Seduced?

"Never? You seem so worldly, so experienced, so confident."

"Not in these matters, darling." Darling? She savored the word. "Believe me, this is new ground." He paused and inspected her.

"And you?"

"Me?

"May I tell you how I feel?" she asked.

"Tell me if you need to," he said, never letting go of her eyes. Yes, she thought, she needed to.

"I feel…" she began, groping for the defining word. "New." She nodded. "And scared to death."

He leaned toward her and nodded also.

"You're not alone," he said, with double meaning.

"I've thrown caution to the winds," she began, conscious of the cliché, leaving him the blanks to fill in. She admitted her own naiveté, her sheltered past, but she wasn't a complete fool. The risks she had taken were self-evident. She had a life, clearly defined. A place. Wife, mother, home. What risks had he taken?

"Have you?"

"Have I what?"

She could sense that he understood, but needed time to frame an answer.

"Thrown caution to the winds?"

He was slow to respond. Finally he nodded.

"Are you married? Have you children? Are there others who depend on you?" Her aunt had told her that her own true lover had sacrificed a family.

"None of the above," he said with, she noted, some reluctance.

"No one?"

He shook his head. But he volunteered nothing more, which was troubling. Was he lying? She would be devastated.

Perhaps he was in the grip of that fever Emma referred to, the counterfeit. In that case, she thought, this was merely a passing phase, a burst of lust. Nothing more.

"What is your life like?"

"Empty," he replied after a long pause. "Until now."

She wanted to probe more deeply, but she feared disappointment. Despite their intimacy, her mind had not yet defined him. But then, he wasn't giving her much to go on. Retreat, she told herself. Enjoy the oasis, the brief refreshment. She was simply having her first affair, had discovered her erotic center. What more did she want?

No, she decided, determined to fend off an inevitable letdown. This was not the true passion, the real thing.

"Is it a dilemma, you think?"

"What kind of a dilemma?"

She tried to empty her mind of possibilities she could barely understand. This is a form of temporary insanity after all, she assured herself. She forced herself to consider the reality of her position.

"For one thing," she said, "there's the big lie." She giggled. "And explaining you."

He seemed to suck in a deep breath, as if he were relieved that she was shifting her curiosity.

"We'll have to think of some counterstory," he said.

"Have you any ideas?"

"None. Not now."

"And the big lie itself. The discovery of my utter deception of the attitude of the sisters Hamilton and their mother."

"That's the easy part. You were coerced by the mysterious Mr. Bell."

"I was?"

"He threatened you. You had no choice.

"And has he kidnapped me, kept me captive?"

"Yes."

"Sexually abused me?"

"Repeatedly."

She started to giggle, reaching out to touch him, her fingers beginning at his navel, tracing the ribbon of hair downward.

"Why? What was his motive?"

"You can't be sure of that. This Max Hamilton was undoubtedly immersed in intrigue. A great deal of money is at stake. He posed as a colleague of your husband. Held you at gunpoint. Forced your compliance."

"He wanted to muddy the waters?"

"Something like that."

"You make it sound very authentic," she said, coming to the end of the ribbon, caressing. Perhaps he is avoiding any information about himself because he does not want to lie? She held on to this idea. Under these circumstances, reality could only be a spoiler. He would explain himself in his own good time.

Instead, she contemplated his scenario. Aside from her own worry at being able to sustain such a lie, however well rehearsed, she realized that, in his scenario, he had also put himself at extreme risk.

"In your scenario, Mr. Bell is a kidnapper and a rapist. These are heavy-duty crimes."

"First, he has to be caught."

"Why put yourself in such jeopardy?" she asked. "I am just as culpable."

"Mr. Bell forced you."

She shook her head and laughed.

"You're giving Mr. Bell too much credit," she said playfully, continuing to caress him. "Worse. You've made me a sex slave."

It struck her that he was not the least bit fazed by the danger. His fearlessness was reassuring. Did it indicate that he, too, saw no further possibilities in this relationship? She felt a sudden surge of resentment and the matter of the deception grew in importance.

She was certain there was harm in it for Tom. All right, she had acted foolishly from Tom's point of view. Perhaps, instead of Champion's coercion story she might concoct one of her own, which now stirred in her imagination. She met this man at the Bel Air, just a casual acquaintance, a brotherly relationship. Tom would believe her there. In her concoction, she would make him a lawyer. He offered to drive her to Cannes. She accepted.

When she discovered that Mrs. Hamilton wouldn't see her, she told him of her dilemma and turned to him for assistance. He came with her, found a way to get to see them and bear witness to their change of mind. Plausible?

She offered Champion the bare bones of her story.

"More holes than Swiss cheese."

"Okay then, I'll tell him the truth. I met this man, lost all civilized control and had to consummate the relationship at all costs. I could not resist him. I didn't care what I had to do to have him make love to me and me to him. Anything to gain my end. And yours." She giggled. "I love it. Let me kiss it." She did, many times, tip to root and below. She had never done this. Ever.

She paused. Then spoke again. "Except that it is not the whole truth at all, only part of it. Do you think he'll buy it?"

"Probably not."

"And you? How would you describe it from your end?"

"Except for the gender configuration, in the exact same way. I could not resist."

She grew thoughtful for a moment.

"I've risked my husband, my life, my comfort, my money, perhaps my children. What have you risked?"

"More than you can imagine."

She felt a sudden grip of fear.

"I don't understand."

"You will. I promise. I will tell you everything. But not yet."

"When then?"

"Soon."

She shook her head and shrugged.

"You must have a life, darling. I may not have learned much about it. But you have lived a life somewhere. Surely you must have filled your time with some kind of living. Tell me, John Champion. I deserve to know."

"Please, darling. Allow me my little air of mystery. I've promised. Trust me."

She considered various possibilities for his reticence, but she did not pursue it, committed to his word. Instead she concentrated on her own dilemma. Could she go back home to Tom? And if she told him the truth, what then?

"Tom would never have thought I was capable of deception," she told him. "He's in for quite a surprise."

"How did he see you?" Champion asked.

She considered the answer carefully, parts of it occurring to her for the first time, straining to present her answer as the absolute unvarnished truth, as if she were confiding to herself alone. Telling it this way suddenly loomed in importance. It was an offering, she knew. If I show him mine, will he show me his?

"This is off the top of my head," she mused, knowing she was seeing things now from a totally different vantage. "I believe he saw me as a passive appendage, an open book, without guile, a naive innocent, unaggressive, without any opinions except in matters of childrearing, managing a house, and, perhaps, flower arrangements. Oh, yes, the God's truth is that he surely saw me as sexually and intellectually uninteresting, bland, unrebellious, a reasonably attractive pampered wife, to be trotted out for respectability when the situation arises."

The rendition surprised her, stunned her, actually. She had never spoken with such candor about her relationship with her husband. But here it was. Had it been there all along?

"And how do you see him?"

"I don't," she said, blurting it, as if it were on the tip of her tongue. "As of today, he is invisible."

"Then why stay with him?"

Was this the real heart of the dilemma? Had she grasped Champion as a tunnel of escape? Again Aunt Emma's words intruded. Had she invented him?

"The question never came up."

She felt herself coming to grips with the hypocrisy of her past. She had been content with her anonymity. She hadn't felt, therefore it hadn't mattered. She hadn't existed. She and Tom had played their roles as good actors in a bad play.

Actually, now that she was dabbling in truth, she had welcomed his absences. They were an accepted part of her life. Obviously, his other life, the one away from her, was far more interesting and exciting than his life with her. Or was it a life at all? Had he drifted away? Perhaps he was never there. Perhaps it was her fault as well. She hadn't grown with her man. So be it. Hindsight was always profound. She realized now that she had spent most of her life, up to now, in hibernation.

And the children? She had been a concerned mother,

and they had been obedient loving children... and yet, the very first chance they had, they were off as far away as they could get. What did that say?

David/Champion, her marble man, alive and pulsating in this room, had awakened her from her long sleep. She was alive perhaps for the first time, living the defining moment that Aunt Emma had described. Was this it? Really it? The hell with everything beyond this. Against what she was experiencing at this moment, her life with Tom was as fragile as vapor. She felt the heavy layer of denial shed itself like a snake's skin.

"And when the time is over, will you go back?" Champion asked, as if taking full advantage of this description of her self-effacement in her other life. Suddenly, she felt frightened. Terrified. Did he mean stay with her? She feared asking, was she being manipulated yet again? She took refuge in humor.

"Fiddle-dee," she joked, imitating Vivian Leigh as Scarlet O'Hara. "We'll think about all that tomorrow."

She tucked away any discomfort about the future in the back of her mind and gripped him there, feeling the warmth, the blood beating beneath the thin sheath of flesh.

"Hard as marble," she said. His hand reached for her.

"Soft as silk," he whispered.

Then they huddled together connected like tantrists, limbs entwined, drowsing, awakening. Time lost all relevance. The past disappeared.

She felt herself floating, joyous and exhilarated, into unknown space, that once elusive dream. He was floating beside her on this—again Emma's words—magic carpet. She clung to him for safety, certain that his proximity would avert all danger, present and future. She questioned nothing, content to be near him, secure in his embrace.

"I must tell you about Florence," she said in a waking moment, taking him through the story as they lay together, obeying this compulsion to empty herself. She told him about her discussions with Aunt Emma then described the incident.

"Can you believe such a thing can happen?" she asked.

"You just told me it did," he said. "And I believe you."

Energized by their rest and having no sense of time, she discovered, after a lifetime of passivity, that it was she who aggressively orchestrated their lovemaking.

She posed him as the David. His compliance was eager and the image he projected provocative and stimulating. She teased him with her body and her tongue, urging him to keep the pose as she excited his genitals to full erection. Her aggression and total lack of inhibition were a kind of epiphany to her, and she pursued it with boundless energy and imagination. She had discovered rapture.

Despite the idea that they were living in this timeless dream, she knew she could not completely deny the reality of time forever. After her own revelations, she made a silent pact to suspend for the moment all attempts at exploring his personal history. Besides it was far more exciting to discuss the miracle of this attraction between them.

"Why me?" she would ask often. His answer was invariably the same as the question.

"Why me?"

It was, of course, the eternal question without an answer. Counterfeit or real? True or false? Temporary insanity or an indelible imprint? The nature of attraction, of love, was as mysterious as why dreams happen.

Joyful acceptance of the moment was the only response. Wasn't it?

Chapter 18

In the swirling aftermath of Max Hamilton's death, Tom Ford spent every waking moment consolidating power over various domains of Hamilton's empire into his own hands. It was purely an interim measure, he assured the various management teams of the vast empire, but as executor of the businesses he told them that he had an obligation to bankers, stockholders, investors, and family members to hold the empire together.

In his mind and in the manner in which he had set up the procedures of takeover, interim meant permanent. He had the power to hire, fire, negotiate, and work out financing terms in which he had sole say. In a bizarre way, he sensed that Max would have appreciated the underhanded and covetous way Tom had handled the matter.

"It is the style of the screwing that counts for something," Max would have said. He could almost hear Max's voice booming into his mind. "If we're going to be fucked, then, at the least, it should be done elegantly."

"I've done my best, Max," Tom answered in his heart.

It had taken years to work out the arrangements. The plan was foolproof with all paperwork prepared well in advance, waiting for the moment of execution.

Because of the manner in which Max had been dispatched, Tom did not have to contend with the avalanche of disputes and arguments that would certainly have arisen if any evidence of foul play were officially confirmed. Apparently it had been ruled out. Such a situation would have meant challenges from all sides, bankers, insurance companies, investors, and security exchanges in all parts of the globe.

In the absence of a note, a finding of suicide would be difficult as well. Nevertheless, he did expect insurance companies to drag their feet on any payout pending their own investigations.

This was one of the main reasons the consent of the family was essential. Their compliance meant that he did not need to consult with them in his various rebuttals to the insurance companies and others to whom Max Hamilton's death had relevance. Their acceptance of the generous settlement terms meant that they were cut out of the loop, dispatched to wealth and powerless anonymity.

With the family checkmated, he could control most matters in connection with Max's death without interference, and he could mount whatever defense was required to maintain his power.

Considering how shabbily Max had treated his wife and daughters when he had lived, Tom considered the way he had handled things in their interest a bonanza for them. Max had flagrantly and cruelly humiliated and betrayed his wife. He had reduced her to a pitiful tragic figure.

As for his daughters, he had long ago abandoned them, showing little interest in their well-being, although Tom had persuaded him, with much effort, to provide for them, at least during his lifetime, through insurance and other settlements, beyond the grave. To his great relief Angela had reported that they were content and apparently had not planned to take any legal action to contest their inheritance. There was no need to pursue the matter further.

In the press of his hectic schedule, Angela had faded from his concern. At some point in the future, he knew, he might have to rethink their relationship, but he did not wish to dwell on it now.

How quickly matters had transpired. After the long wait of months, it had all gone miraculously well. These hirelings knew their job.

Angela's report had brought good news, and he allowed himself to savor their success with Cynthia for the next few days. The apparent success of the enterprise had heightened the effect on his libido. They had spent hours recounting events and reviewing the masterful way in which they had achieved their results.

As agreed, despite all the debugging devices and electronic sweeps they had commissioned, they spoke in hushed tones in ways that could not possibly be deciphered even by the most knowledgeable eavesdropper.

"The man was an expert tailor," Tom told her. "I never thought he could make such a perfect suit. We mustn't forget our original agreement."

"Just as soon as the invoice arrives."

He had, of course, stayed far removed from the assassination process, leaving the legwork and details to Cynthia. In retrospect, he had no illusions about when the method of elimination had been set in motion in his mind. Taking control of the Hamilton empire had, from the beginning, been his secret agenda. Max's distaste for detail, especially in legal matters, offered a license to construct a paper trail of ascension for Tom, which he had created to be triggered by Max's death. Max had actually agreed, never dreaming that the trigger would be pulled long before any natural demise.

"In the event of Mr. Hamilton's death" was the thematic centerpiece of these arrangements, inserted ad infinitum in the massive paper edifice that Tom had constructed for this life after death. It was, Tom assured himself, his magnum opus.

From such pride of authorship, it didn't take a leap of faith to consider accelerating the process of ascension, and he was willing to allow that the first faint spark of opportunity came from Cynthia's revelation about her brother's confession.

As time went on and his relationship with Cynthia grew more intimate, he could recall the conscious effort to seriously explore the possibility of, as he put it to himself, hastening the inevitable.

What Cynthia had clearly implied, perhaps advertised, even that very first time during their original interviews, was that her brother's tapes had outlined a methodology that had apparently illustrated both the process and the people involved. A "primer for assassination," Cynthia had told him then. The words had burned themselves into his mind.

From time to time as their relationship deepened, he would broach the subject, hoping to convey a casual academic interest in the general idea of assassination in the service of policy, public or private. Her response was always measured, cautious, although he was certain that she knew exactly the point of his reference.

"Do you think these things continue to go on?" he would ask her. Soon it became a kind of mantra, and Cynthia, he was certain, could not escape its implications.

"I have no reason to believe otherwise," she would reply.

"The process does have its merits," he would tell her, his meaning hardly subtle. "Especially in intractable situations."

"That was my brother's thesis," Cynthia had explained, "Before guilt became too overwhelming for him to handle."

"And he revealed all, names, connections."

"Everything."

"Do you think they are still in place?"

"Possibly."

His approach was slow, careful. He needed to reveal intent, but just enough to plant a seed in her mind. Since his entire modus operandi was based on general distrust, he was deliberately oblique, needing to establish deniability well in advance of any action.

"How did they get away with it?" he asked one day. It was about a year ago as they sat sipping vodka in her apartment. It was a question, deliberately out of context, designed to assess whether the seeds had taken root.

"They left no footprints," Cynthia said without hesitation.

"But information had to be conveyed," he said.

"Once the assignment was given—how did my brother put it?—the brain went on autopilot. He had been trained to act alone, an anonymous human missile locked onto its target."

"Trained?" Tom mused. "That implies instruction, exercises, classrooms."

"One on one," she said without hesitation. "He was explicit on that point. One person trained one person. The instructor was never seen again."

"Still," Tom had argued then. "You said he was with the CIA, an institution of government. He was, after all, an employee. He had to be paid. Somewhere there were records."

"On the tape, my brother said he was paid in foreign currency." She had looked up at him and smiled. "Outside the dollar system. In rotating foreign currencies."

"Deposited directly into various foreign bank accounts?"
She nodded.

"By whom?"

"His handler. One person. He was the single conduit."

"Considering the unreliability of human beings," Tom had said, his mind racing, "that seems a bit foolish."

"As he explained it on the tape," Cynthia had continued, "the enforcement system was built in. They were, after all, in the assassination business. They had been trained to do their job and leave no trail. Others, too, had been trained to do the same thing. There was no way out alive."

"In other words, he could be a target as well as a perpetrator."

"That's my understanding," she replied cautiously.

"Thus, to protect the system, they sometimes had to kill their own."

"Something like that."

"How many people did he say he…?"

"Twenty-eight. The number is etched in my memory."

"Snuffed. Just like that. Without further inquiry?"

"According to my brother. They were classified as either accidents or suicides."

"Perfect crimes?"

"They had to be. That was the engine that drove the wagon."

"My God. Now I can understand his compelling need to confess."

"Some were a policy hit, some were colleagues, people who did the killing, like him. Remember while he was confessing, he was also attempting to provide himself with a kind of insurance."

"Or a method of vengeance?"

"That, too. Unfortunately neither worked out."

The revelation was chilling—and fascinating. It was also very far from his realm of experience, although as an abstraction, he could understand its logic as an instrument of power.

It taught him that beneath the surface of apparent perception was a shadowy world, reflecting a totally different reality. Indeed, it was a world he fully understood. Instead of the weapons of assassination, he employed tools of his own trade, legal instruments, words, contracts, their motives deeply hidden in layers and layers of carefully contrived language, designed to confuse and conquer, all in the service of self-aggrandizement. The parallels were obvious.

The big question still remained, but he carefully avoided its utterance. He needed to appear passive, to preserve a semblance of deniability.

He wasn't sure why, since any investigation would reveal that he would be the principal beneficiary of what he had in mind. Perhaps it was a moral imperative. He wondered about that, searching himself for any sign of conscience on the matter. He could find none. The prospect of Max's elimination, the death of the man, had no emotional resonance in him whatsoever.

The idea became the dominant issue in his mind, and it was getting more and more difficult to repress his probing.

"And he actually named names?" Tom might suddenly ask her, his reiteration a probing reminder.

"Yes."

"Do you think the apparatus, the same people are still" — he sucked in a deep breath — "in the light of the time frame, still active?"

"Probably."

"How do you know this?"

"It's an assumption. My brother explained that in his business a secure pipeline is treasured, protected, and preserved."

He considered it a victory for his patience when she finally answered the unasked question that hung in the air between them.

"So you think they're still reachable?"

"Have you something in mind?" she probed, half joking. Since she was privy to his paper trail, she would have no illusions about what he was thinking. He hadn't verbalized an answer, watching her face. What he had learned was that he and Cynthia were two of a kind, soul mates in ruthless pursuit of their goals, willing to make any sacrifice to catch the brass ring.

"I might," he said.

She nodded.

"Are you suggesting I inquire?"

"Might be an interesting idea."

"Yes, it might."

"And the economics of such an enterprise?"

"My brother's reference was to two million a pop. I'm just guessing, but I'd say the costs have probably escalated. Say three million."

"Three mil, then. And the risk?"

"According to my brother's logic. People might speculate as to the source, but the job was so thorough the risk was nil."

What, he speculated, was three million against potential billions? Nil risk, however, was a fiction. In this case, the risk was in the solidity of his relationship with Cynthia. So far her loyalty was exemplary, and he had seen to it that she was amply rewarded. He had made her a very rich woman. She would be richer still from this new adventure. From that moment on, he knew, they would be tied together irrevocably and forever.

"Just spare me the details. And concentrate on the re-wards."

"I will on both counts."

At that point, he was enormously pleased with the result. She had delivered spectacularly, had delivered the perfect crime. It seemed apparent that there was little evidence to conclude that Max had been a murder victim. The circumstances of his death, Tom knew, would always remain a mystery, with the media milking the story for all it was worth.

In the last couple of days, some journalists had speculated that Max had committed suicide to avoid the embarrassment of some yet-to-be-revealed crime. Others thought some government intelligence agents dispatched him for some unknown but sinister reason. But the view from the authorities in Cannes, the only conclusion that mattered, was that Max had probably fallen overboard in a freak accident and drowned. Everything was falling into place.

Chapter 19

Their night of rapture in the little stone house had been an idyll. But the morning brought with it a sense of reality. There were practical considerations. They would have to go back to the Bel Air, get their things, and check out. Hopefully, there was still time.

Unfortunately, they could not go back to the little stone house. Parker's ubiquitous network had used it from time to time and knew its location. In keeping with his own survival methods, Champion had created his own safe house in this region as he had done elsewhere. It was tucked away on the edge of the forest near Mont Ventoux. He had planned to use it only in an emergency. What more compelling emergency than his present situation?

Covering his tracks was a specialty, and he had carefully honed the process. In keeping with this discipline, he'd have to return the Jag to the rental company in Nice and rent another. His stolen set of plates would be taken off the Jag and put on the new car.

His first priority was for him and Angela to disappear without a trace. Her husband, he knew, would be tenacious in his zeal to find her, to get at the truth, not only about her obvious false report but also about the mystery man who was with her.

Five more days. It pained him to dwell on it.

Would she return to New York, concoct whatever story suited the moment, and then throw herself on her husband's mercy, face the music, accept the consequences? Or would she opt to stay with him, reject her old life, just as he would reject his? Yes, he thought, he had made up his mind. His transformation was complete.

Such speculation was exhilarating. He could no longer contemplate life without her. But her staying with him had to be her choice, her choice alone.

To return to the Bel Air was a calculated risk that had to be taken. No messages were being held for Angela, which was an encouraging sign. She had not informed the Hamiltons where she was staying. Nevertheless she was dead certain that her husband would soon be informed of the truth of her confrontation with Mrs. Hamilton and her daughters.

They had a lovely lunch in the hotel dining room from which the view of the sea was irresistible.

"Show no affection," he warned her when she reached over to kiss him.

"Why?"

"People talk," he said. "Why complicate things. There'll be more than enough to explain."

He realized he had injected an element of impending separation, as if he were preparing himself, and her, for another inevitability. Their eyes met suddenly and he could see the sadness that hers reflected.

"If your husband is a resourceful man, he will have soon learned that you have betrayed him, and that there is another man in the picture," he told her.

"C'est la vie," she whispered, shrugging.

"And when he asks, what will be your response?"

"I will say…" She contemplated the idea for a moment. "I will say that I was seduced by an irresistible cad. Coerced and anointed his sex slave. That he cast a spell over me, and I could not help myself."

"And what will be his reaction?"

"I don't really care."

"And your report on the Hamilton situation. He will know it was a lie."

"I don't care about that either."

"What will he do?"

"Try to find me, of course."

He watched her eyes drift and the skin of her forehead wrinkle with an unpleasant thought.

"Let's just pretend he doesn't exist. Let me stay in my dream."

"Only if I'm there with you."

"And you are," she whispered, but she could not resist lifting his hand and kissing his palm. She moved her leg next to his under the table, and with her other hand she caressed the inside of his thigh.

"So much for secrecy," Champion said, his eyes meeting those of the waiter.

They had grilled sole and vegetables and a crisp white wine and lemon tart for dessert. The waiter was attentive and, as always, Champion tipped lavishly.

"We must check out now," he said.

He accompanied her up the elevator and to her room. But

when he started to leave for his own, she pulled him into hers and kissed him with her back against the closed door.

In the flash of an eye, he was making love to her standing. She wrapped her legs around his torso and braced herself against the door. It was quick and unexpected and produced a powerful simultaneous orgasm.

"Am I dreaming this pleasure, love?" she asked, as she disengaged and leaned against him standing.

"If you are, may the dream never end," he whispered in her ear, nibbling her earlobe.

"Is it possible?" She sighed.

"Let's make it possible," he said, too fearful to pursue the idea.

He went back to his own room, packed quickly. He was expert at quick removals. Then he emptied the safe deposit box in his room and thumbed through the various passports, driver's licenses, and other documents he had collected to be sure they were all there. None were genuine, and even the forgeries bore fictitious names under the imprint of various countries where a Caucasian face applied. Some of the pictures showed him with dyed hair, glasses, and facial hair.

He checked the money in various currencies, making certain it too had not been tampered with. Subterfuge was second nature to him. He speculated about what Angela's reaction might be to the way he lived his life, then tried to push any disturbing conclusions far from his thoughts.

One thing was certain. Inside himself, he had undergone a psychic revolution. The focus of his life had become invested in another person. He no longer lived for himself alone, and he was baffled by these new sensations of possessiveness. Without her—he was convinced—life would be unbearable.

He paid his bill in cash. She was punctual, emerging from the elevator just as the men were carrying his suitcases to the car. Watching her come through the lobby filled him with pride. She was his.

He watched her glide across the room wearing a lovely red outfit set off by a string of baroque pearls. Her raven dark hair flowed freely on her shoulders and her skin radiated with an inner glow. Almost immediately her eyes locked into his, validating their connection. Only in her presence did he feel complete.

There had been no point in faking their exit. Observers were everywhere. It was too late to disestablish a relationship, although it could hardly be characterized as coercive.

Their baggage was loaded into the Jaguar, tips were handed out, and he drove toward Nice. She moved toward him, slipped her arm under his, and laid her shoulder against him. Her nearness was indescribable. He wished he could drive this way forever. Destination was unimportant just as long as they arrived together.

"Would you like to know where we're heading?" he asked.

"No. As long as it's with you."

Leaning over, he kissed her on the lips, which she opened for him. He had come to love the taste of her as well. Every part of her was an elixir, a miracle potion.

He drove toward Nice. Like a bright emerald, the Mediterranean sparkled in the morning sun. Ahead was the baroque skyline of the Promenade des Anglais. Before reaching the boulevard, he turned right and headed upward into the hills, then stopped along a deserted stretch of road.

"What are we doing?" she asked.

"A precaution," he said.

He got out of the car, opened the trunk, and removed his dispatch case. From it, he took a pair of license plates and, after removing the existing plates, attached them to the car. It was accomplished in a matter of minutes. Then he came back into the car and she moved against him, as if the brief absence had upset her.

"The hotel has a record of the car and the plates," he said, hoping the explanation was enough to satisfy her. "Why take chances of them finding us, spoiling everything?"

"Yes," she said, kissing his neck.

"Do you trust me?" he asked.

"Of course."

"Your trust is very important to me."

"Haven't I proved that?" she said, squeezing his arm, then bringing his hand up to her lips and kissing his palm.

"My life began with you," she said.

"And mine."

"What I want mostly is that everything between us begins fresh and new."

"Of course."

"I mean a new reality. Us."

"Us," he said, as if to underscore his understanding of

this agreement between them. He hesitated for a moment, then drew her closer and kissed her deeply.

"Will you come with me into this new life?" he asked when they had disengaged.

"For now," she whispered.

Not pressing her further, he felt sure he understood what she meant by that. "For now" was a timeline with finite boundaries. For her it might mean the seven days she had carved from her life, daring not to think of any existence beyond that. For him it meant eternity.

"Are you curious about my life?" he asked.

"Yes. As you promised, you will tell me in good time," she said, after a brief pause.

Would knowing about him change things between them, he wondered? In the long run, if there was a long run, she could not escape knowing the truth about him. Any civilized person, indoctrinated in the morality of Western culture, would be appalled.

He made his living killing people. It had been his way of life for years, a life of subterfuge, dissimulation, disinformation, disguise, lies, false names, pretenses, and, of course, money, a lot of money, for a life of luxury. And for what? Excitement? Thrills? Challenges? All of that. The process itself was absorbing, the methodology, the planning, the stalking, the technique of the kill itself, the style of evasion, the disengagement, and the escape. The money, as he well knew, was secondary.

The greatest drawback to his business, however, was not the violation of the moral code, not the idea of disregarding the sanctity of human life, not the prospect of death, or even the fear of incarceration. It was the constrictions imposed on him, the forced repression.

There was no retirement, no escape, nowhere to hide from the mysterious forces that oversaw the business. Commitment was for a lifetime. For a lone eagle like himself, the commitment had posed no threats. Until now.

In an explosive flash of blind, mysterious, and uncontrollable emotion, his old life was obliterated, but not the habits of a lifetime.

He drove through a network of winding narrow streets to Nice's city center, stopped before a car rental agency. He went in and traded the Jaguar for a four-door Fiat, showing a false passport and license. Then he drove to the same deserted spot in the hills. This time she got out of the car and watched him attach the plates he had taken off the Jag.

"A little evasive action," he explained.

He drove the car in a northerly direction toward Mont Ventoux, watching the rearview mirror instinctively. She leaned against him, dozing as he picked up speed. Suddenly, after a long time, she awoke with a start.

"Did you dream?" he asked.

"I am in a dream," she said.

"Are you hungry?" he asked.

"Not for food."

She reached down and caressed his inner thigh. His reaction was instant, and she opened his pants and held him there.

"May I confess something?"

"Of course."

"Aside from my husband, I have never known another man. I have never held another man like this. I have never known such joy."

Her words seemed formal, as if she were reciting a poem. He felt good, more alive than he had ever felt, transformed. For him, sex had always been a disembodied pleasure, a form of masturbation. He had this sudden urge to cry and tears puddled his eyes and ran down his cheeks. It was inexplicable, but he wasn't embarrassed. She looked up at him and, releasing his erection, she pulled a Kleenex from her purse and patted his cheeks.

"Forgive me," he said, pulling off the highway onto a dirt road that led into a wooded area. "I'm overwhelmed."

Stopping the car, they got out and, hand in hand, they walked a little ways along a trail. Then she stopped and leaned against a tree, and they made love again standing up. Despite the position, she held him inside her for a long time.

"Is it possible to stop time?" she asked.

"Only death stops time," he replied, instantly sorry he had said such a thing, equating death with this. Invoking the word seemed to open a door deep inside him, a door that had been locked a long time, perhaps all his life.

He had the urge to tell her how he had abridged time in others. Something disturbing was happening to him. New emotions were crowding into his psyche, rushing through the open door.

He had never felt such a sense of joy and abandonment.

Another totally foreign emotion was emerging inside him.

Then something happened that defied any explanation. He shouted, as loud as he could, at the top of his lungs. It was more like a whooping sound, like "yowee," and reminded him of a cowboy whoop in a western movie cattle drive.

She looked up at him and laughed. Then she shouted as loud as she could in imitation of his sound, and suddenly they were doing it together.

When they stopped, he faced her and kissed her hair, her forehead, her eyes, her cheeks, then lingered long on her lips. When he had disengaged, he started to speak, but she put her fingers on his lips and stopped him.

"I know," she whispered. "It's indescribable."

He nodded and smiled, and then they made their way back to the car. With her leaning on his shoulder and dozing, he drove in silence through Provence. But his mind was in turmoil.

Who was he really? Was he truly the moral nightmare who had served the devil all these years or someone else locked inside him, emerging now, a decent good moral man?

Having someone who was passionately devoted exclusively to him, his needs, and desires was something he never believed might happen to him. Yet, force of habit made him cautious and wary. It was not easy to shed his animal nature, to find his way out of the jungle. Within himself, he battled the demons of fear and the instinctive need to guard himself against unseen predators.

Was Angela real or some force behind an enemy's will? He hated himself for such suspicion. Was it time to throw away his protective armor and give himself to her, fully, completely, to shed his evil outer layers? These were dangerous thoughts for a man in his line of work. In fact, to remove himself from the killing occupation meant certain death. Preventing such an outcome was considered impossible.

Angela had shown no such inhibitions. From the moment he had volunteered to go with her to Cannes, she seemed to have trusted him completely. Such trust was inexplicable to him. Distrust was endemic to his life.

She had offered no protest, just total compliance and eager approval. Like him, she must have calculated the value of their time together, weighing it against the consequences of their act.

"He will not think I am capable of deception," she had told him last night in the tiny bedroom of the little stone house, her thoughts then still toying with justification. She could not put it aside. "I have never betrayed him in any way."

He recalled that she had paused for a long time, lost in her own thoughts as they lay in the euphoria of afterplay. But the theme of betrayal apparently had continued to nag at her. She is afflicted with conscience, he had thought, fully aware that her past was the principal enemy. And his.

"Is this a betrayal?" he had asked.

"What would you call it?"

He had thought for a long moment, his hand lazily patting her hair.

"An inevitability."

She had laughed girlishly and cocked her head thoughtfully.

"Yes. I like that."

"But do you believe it?"

There had been another long silence as he waited patiently for her response. The gnawing fear of separation had begun to take hold of him. It seemed more menacing than anything he had ever experienced before.

"I… I want to believe it," she had replied hesitantly. "But it frightens me."

"Why?" he asked. He had his own answer, but he needed to hear hers.

"Because it means… that we're out of control. No longer in charge of ourselves." She chuckled suddenly. "As if I've ever been in charge."

Her comment had struck an ominous note.

"Do you think I've seduced you?" he had asked.

"It crossed my mind."

He had started to respond, but she had put her fingers on his lips.

"But I'd rather we consider ourselves full partners in this enterprise. Equals. From the moment I laid eyes on you, I knew that this was necessary."

She had leaned over him and trailed the ribbon of hair with her lips, not stopping.

"My marble man," she told him. "My David."

He had sighed and stroked her hair, his mind probing

beyond the immediacy of his pleasure.

"God, I'm happy," she had cried suddenly. He had felt her shudder, and he reached to her shoulders and pulled her upward, reaching her lips. The kiss had been long, their breath holding. He had felt a dizzying sensation. Is this the end of the future? he had wondered. They made love again, remaining entwined.

"Stay with me," he had whispered.

"I am with you."

He had repressed any further entreaty, suddenly shocked at this discovery of his vulnerability. At that moment, he knew that his life was no longer his own, would never be his own again.

This person, Angela, had become his life-support system. Survival did not seem possible without her nearness, her touch, her aura. Despite everything that had gone before in his life, Angela's proximity was dominating.

He had heard of love. How could knowledge of it be avoided? Always it had seemed something that happened to others. In fact, it was completely out of the orbit of his experience. Not that he was ready to define his present situation by what the word signified. Love!

Somehow the word had gotten mixed up with sexuality, which he had always considered a reflex of the body machinery. The physical form of a woman aroused him in an obvious way. There was pleasure and satisfaction in the fulfillment of it.

With Angela a whole new dimension had been revealed. Sexuality had become inextricably tangled with feelings.

He had no wish to ever separate himself from Angela's body and her aura, as if their connection were necessary, and separation was loss, like death. And he was just as convinced of its finality.

But complete surrender to this idea implied that the finality was mutual, that Angela was in the grip of this same overwhelming need. Perhaps, he reasoned, it was the uncertainty that provided the tension, the fear of loss made the idea so powerful and all encompassing.

Even if there was mutuality, he could not deny another reality: that they had come to this carrying all the baggage of their past lives. With her it was family, a husband, children, and all the memories and history that went with them.

With him it was his profession and all its perceived evil and immorality. Surely, if he revealed to her what he did, she would react with revulsion and disgust and wonder how she could feel anything toward a man who killed other human beings in cold blood for profit.

And yet, if this thing between them were to have any viability at all, he would, one day, have to tell her the truth. Complete candor, he sensed, was the ultimate bonding adhesive, and it required that, between them, there could be no secrets, no lies, no subterfuge.

Any curtain that separated them would have to fall. In his case, the question would revolve around whether her need for him would outweigh her disgust for what he did, what he had done. That part of his life would be over forever. His past would have to be obliterated. Hers, as well.

As he drove, he turned these ideas over and over again in his mind, trying to bridge the gap between inevitability and caution, possibility and reality.

In real time, he speculated they had less than a week to sort things out. Five precious days left.

Chapter 20

"Do we know a Mr. Lloyd, a solicitor, from England?"

It was Tuesday. He and Cynthia had spent the last few days in extensive conference calls calming fears of executives in Max's far-flung empire. From the look on Cynthia's face, he was certain that there was urgency to her question.

"Says he's been retained by Mrs. Hamilton and her daughters in connection with the estate."

No cause for alarm, Tom assured himself. Mrs. Hamilton had sometimes employed lawyers in the United Kingdom for local matters. She did have her home and some real estate parcels in the Cotswolds. Tom took the phone, acknowledging his presence on the line.

"Mr. Ford," Lloyd's voice boomed through the phone, the accent Oxford broad. "Prentiss Lloyd here. How are you today?"

"Fine," Tom answered. It sounded like the beginning of an unwanted solicitation.

"I've been retained by Mrs. Hamilton and her daughters. There seems to be a rather odd problem."

Lloyd's attitude was casual, almost flippant.

"A problem?"

Tom glanced toward Cynthia. His stomach knotted.

"I'm assuming that your wife apprised you of the situation?"

"Yes, she did."

"Then you know that Mrs. Hamilton and her daughters will be disputing the settlement and all concomitant matters."

"Disputing…?" Tom muttered, baffled.

"Oh, yes. Surely she must have informed you of the dust-up at the Carlton. A rather ugly scene, I must say. Your colleague was quite out of line in assaulting the two men. He was quite violent."

Tom was too stunned to respond. Ugly scene? Colleague? Assault?

"Are you there, Ford?" Lloyd asked.

"What the hell are you talking about? My wife called with a totally contrary report. She said the Hamiltons were content with the arrangements."

"Content? Is she mad? We had left instructions to bar all visitors. One of the bodyguards is hospitalized. Your man was extremely violent. We are thinking of bringing charges. However, that's not our main intent. Your wife was told in no uncertain terms that we were taking legal action with a view to taking total control of Max Hamilton's enterprises."

"But this is totally contrary to my information," Tom mumbled, swallowing hard. The phone felt moist to his touch.

"I don't believe this." His voice rose so that Cynthia could hear. "The Hamiltons are contesting?"

"But Angela…" Cynthia said, her complexion alabaster white.

"There must be some mistake here," Tom said, trying to

keep calm, a difficult discipline under the circumstances.

"We might be willing to forget the whole episode at the Carlton, Ford," Lloyd said. "We don't want to be sidetracked, but we will be challenging all arrangements made prior to Mr. Hamilton's death."

"What's happening here?" Tom said, hearing the whine in his voice.

"It will become clearer, counselor," Lloyd said.

"Tell you the truth," Tom said, drawing on his natural inclination to be suspicious of any disembodied voice on the telephone. "I don't understand any of this. My wife paid a condolence call on the Hamiltons, and no colleague of mine accompanied her."

"Did she now? That's curious."

"She is not disposed to lying, Lloyd," Tom added, finding some encouragement in the thought.

"Whatever," Lloyd said, chuckling lightly. "Then she's certainly misinterpreted the situation. There was no ambivalence on the question. Mrs. Ford was informed in no uncertain terms. She was given my name as a matter of fact. And her companion was introduced as your business colleague, Ford, a Mr. Bell."

"I don't know a Mr. Bell," Tom said. Confusion was beginning to escalate to anger.

"Well, then," Lloyd said, the chuckle more pronounced. "My advice to you would be to ask Mrs. Ford for a more accurate picture of what really occurred at the Carlton. Obviously, you have been misinformed."

"I don't know what the hell you're talking about, Lloyd."

"Apparently." There was brief pause. "I've taken the liberty of recounting the events in writing. It is being faxed to you as we speak, along with our demands—food for thought, counselor. The fax will have my telephone number. I eagerly await your reaction." Lloyd cleared his throat. "Brace yourself, old boy. We mean to put your feet to the fire. Cheerio."

Lloyd hung up. Tom was stupefied. He looked at Cynthia, whose face reflected the same reaction. In the background could be heard the sound of the fax coming into the office. Cynthia went to retrieve it. Tom began to pace the office, unable to comprehend what was happening. Angela lying? Impossible. Who was this mysterious Mr. Bell? Nothing made sense. He had entered a nightmare.

"I don't think you'll want to read this, Tom," Cynthia said, coming back into the room. Despite the warning, she handed it over. Anger became rage.

"Bullshit," he shouted, as he read the fax.

The paper rehashed what Lloyd had told him of Angela's visit, explaining in more detail the incident with the bodyguards and offering quotes from Mrs. Hamilton and her two daughters. The visit was described in detail, including a description of the man who accompanied her: "a tall, well-tanned, rather handsome man." Good God, he thought. What were they implying? Also alleged was that the information provided Mrs. Ford was hardly ambiguous. The Hamilton survivors, according to the memo, were going to "use every available international avenue" to fight hard to win their rights of ownership of Hamilton's business interests and nullify all previous agreements entered into between Hamilton and his lawyer, Ford.

Tom read the missive, crumpled it, and flung it to the floor. In his present state, his first thought was that it had all the earmarks of a conspiracy. He glanced toward Cynthia.

"It's a setup," Tom told her emphatically. "Has to be."

"It smells like it," Cynthia agreed.

"I provided for that old bitch and her daughters. They would have been set for life ten times over. I don't understand it."

"They want it all," Cynthia said. "Their pound of flesh and more."

"That's it, of course. A woman scorned." Tom shook his head.

"Accusing Angela of deliberately lying? It's totally out of character. Angela? And the man with her? I can't conceive…"

"And the description of the man?"

"A deliberate implication."

"Like throwing salt on an open wound."

"Not Angela. No way."

"You should have gone yourself, Tom," Cynthia said.

He continued to turn it over in his mind. Another man? Angela? Impossible. He had lived with her for two decades. Perhaps it had not been Angela at all, someone posing as Angela.

"She might have had her own agenda all along, Tom. Maybe even a secret lover."

"Don't be ridiculous," Tom snapped. "It's pure fiction,

that's what it is. They'll never get away with it. Never. It's either a setup or Angela has been coerced. I can smell it."

Angela was beyond reproach, naive about such matters and totally dedicated to his interests. She wouldn't understand deception and surely was incapable of such blatant lies. He recalled their last phone call. Not Angela. Not his sweet, pliant, patient Angela.

He made every effort to calm himself and think things through. Lloyd's contention was absurd, he concluded. His story was too far-fetched, his allegations pure fiction. Yet, he was sorry he had let Angela talk him out of going to Cannes. At that point there was no question in his mind that he was being set up, lied to. They were attempting to use every means to wrest control of the Hamilton enterprises. He had no intention of falling for that line.

As for the allegation that a man was present, this had to be patently false. Angela had not given him a moment's insecurity in that regard. How could she? She had little interest in sex. She would be the least likely candidate for an affair.

To all who knew her, she was the epitome of the good wife, the good mother, the honest woman, a generally pleasant and traditional woman. Indeed, she had stayed comfortably, without the slightest sign of protest, in the compartment Tom had fashioned for her.

"Get Angela on the cell," he ordered Cynthia. "I'm sure she'll clear things up. I'm not going to fall for their line. No way."

Tom watched as she began the process, waiting for her

to make the connection, hopeful that the matter would be quickly resolved. Then Cynthia was talking.

"That's impossible," Cynthia was saying. She mimed to Tom that she was speaking with a room clerk.

"I'm terribly sorry, Madam," an officious voice said. "She left no forwarding address."

"Let me," Tom interjected, grabbing the phone. "This is Mr. Ford. Are you telling us that my wife checked out?"

"Oui, monsieur," the man said unctuously.

"I don't believe it," Tom said, his voice rising.

"Monsieur. I have the records here."

"Something is not right here," Tom insisted.

"She has checked out, monsieur. What can I say?"

Tom was fuming.

"I must get in touch with her. It is a very serious matter. Surely she must have mentioned to someone where she was headed."

Again, he recalled their last conversation. It was he who had persuaded her to remain in the south of France and return home as scheduled. But it was she who suggested that she visit Mrs. Hamilton and assess the situation as a favor to him. Nothing made sense.

"I'm terribly sorry, monsieur. There is no record of a forwarding address. However, the concierge may have a better idea."

"Put me through then."

There was a moment's pause.

"I'm sorry. But the concierge is on an errand. I'll see that he calls you back shortly."

"Damn you, frogs. You do that," Tom muttered, giving the man his number and slamming down the phone.

Chapter 21

With her head on his shoulder as they drove, Angela caressed Champion's leg and contemplated this new sense of herself. She had been searching her mind or, more accurately, her internal landscape for danger signals, signs of an uneasy conscience, anything that might be characterized as guilt.

She had no difficulty cataloguing what only a few days ago would be dubbed transgressions.

She had violated all the so-called value systems that had underpinned her life up to then. She had betrayed her husband sexually. She had deliberately told him a lie.

She had run away, at least temporarily, with a man about whom she knew nothing. Her actions were clearly, for her, unprecedented. In the last few days, she had made love many more times than she had made love in her entire married life. Her body had become a lusting firecracker, wildly orgasmic and passionate.

Perhaps in some secret place deep in her imagination, this man, this John Champion, her David, had become the living embodiment of some other part of herself for which she had been searching, some needed piece of her that had to be connected, like a fuse that governed her internal circuitry.

From the moment she had laid eyes on him, had entered

his orbit, she had felt the necessity of his proximity. Had she invented him? He was, after all, a mature man, with a former life lived without her, an idea that she had consciously repelled. What did this former life mean to her? Would knowing change anything? She was, after all, not part of his yesterdays, nor he of hers.

She had also brought her intelligence to bear on this phenomenon. Was it simply a manifestation of what was commonly called romantic love, where her fantasy had created this love object that had become fixated on the physical presence of this man? Was it merely wish fulfillment activated by Aunt Emma's suggestive statements on the power and wonder of what she called "the experience of true passion?"

Aunt Emma's words again echoed in her mind.

"You cannot say you had fully lived and felt everything unless you have experienced true passion."

Could she now say that she had finally had this experience, savored the power of it exactly as Emma had described it: "Transforming, born again a thousand times over"? Or was it, as she had also described it, merely "cock fever"? admitting that it was a vulgar and dismissive condition like a brief flu.

"Without the true passion, it is nothing," Aunt Emma had said. "And it can enter this dream in the blink of an eye."

So she, Angela, was now in the unenviable position of determining whether or not she was involved with the real thing or merely a prey to a form of temporary sexual insanity. If it was the latter, and she was certain it would be revealed to her in a short time, she would use the phenomenon in her pleadings with Tom. It was a condition, she would tell him, like a temporary viral infection. As a lawyer, he might understand. No way, she concluded. He would throw her into the figurative garbage compactor and press the button.

Did it really matter what he thought or felt, whether he forgave her or not? The reality of her marriage was that, at this stage of her life, it was nothing more than a social symbol. She had been liberated from repressing any negativity about that relationship. Tom's agenda had never had much to do with her. As for her children, she loved them, of course. But they were long past the nurturing stage and could easily pursue their lives without her.

And if this was the real thing, the true passion?

"It must be obeyed," Aunt Emma had said.

"To the exclusion of everything?" she had asked.

"Of course," Aunt Emma had replied, looking at her with deep skepticism. "It can't be evaded or dismissed. It is the central issue of the life force. To deny it is a form of death."

She remembered her own confusion at this explanation. It had been beyond her understanding—until now. She was, indeed, presently in thrall to a man, enslaved by her passion, unshackled from what she had thought was her original self, pursuing a kind of manifest destiny, and willing to put herself completely in his hands, and he in her hands, clay to be molded. Without mutuality, what have you got? Again the echo of Aunt Emma.

Suddenly, with the power of the most explosive epiphany, she discovered that she was, indeed, contemplating a total life change, a complete break with the past, with her history, with any of the landmarks of her previous life: children, husband, everything. She felt suffused with a shivery pleasure over the idea.

Why not? she asked herself. All it needed was the courage of her own consent. Perhaps, too, she needed Aunt Emma's blessing?

Watching him in profile, she felt as if her gaze was consuming him. From time to time, she would kiss his face and stroke him. With his free hand he was caressing the side of her neck where it met in the hollow of her shoulder.

Her analysis of her own motivations did not preclude being watchful of his. Was he in the throes of a similar dilemma? Was this the true passion for him or merely "pussy fever"?

The obscene bluntness of her thoughts shocked her. What was the real truth of this thing between them, a condition that obviously put them both in the kind of jeopardy that required such strong measures of evasion?

But the cool contemplation of these events, the application of an objective intelligence, did not, in any way, interfere with the flow of desire. She had no wish to extricate herself from what was happening to her.

He turned off the main highway at a place called Crillon-le-Brave in the shadow of Mont Ventoux in Provence and proceeded along a winding narrow road that led upward through a thick pine forest. Finally, he pulled up beside a small rustic provincial house.

With the sunlight spearing through the trees, the house looked lovely and inviting.

"Perfect," she whispered after savoring the sight for a few moments.

"I rented it sight unseen for six months," he told her as they moved along a gravel path that led to the front door. The landlord had received cash in advance for the whole time. He removed a key from a place above the doorjamb and opened the door. Inside, it was comfortably furnished with prints of old French scenes on the walls.

There was a parlor complete with fireplace and a tall clock that needed winding, a kitchen that obviously had not been modernized since the '50s with copper pots hanging from the ceiling, and a pantry stocked with canned goods. In the small refrigerator were bottles of vintage champagne, wines, red and white, bottled water, and sodas.

"This will do nicely," Angela said, taking out a bottle of champagne, which she handed to him. Popping the cork, he poured the bubbling liquid into two fluted glasses, handing her one.

"To us," he said as they clinked glasses.

"To us," she repeated. They sipped and kissed.

Carrying their glasses, they moved into the bedroom, which was dominated by a four-poster bed with a high mattress and a two-step riser beside it.

"Fantastic," she said, moving on to the mattress. She bounced up and down. "Sturdy, too." She looked at him and winked saucily. She felt an elation that reminded her of her childhood when her parents had given her a present that she had longed for.

He came toward the bed, the height of the mattress reaching his waist. Bending over her, he kissed her deeply on the lips. Moving crosswise on the bed, she came toward him clasping her legs around him. Again, they made love, hungrily, quickly, spontaneously.

She resisted any further analysis of the phenomenon, accepting it as a gift of joy, chasing any thoughts that might trigger anxiety or any other spoiling emotion. She longed for the power to completely blot out memory, reinvent herself as the reborn Angela.

Chapter 22

"This is the Bel Air, the concierge is calling," the operator said.

Cynthia handed the cell to Tom and picked up another to monitor the call. He glanced toward her and shrugged. He was sweating profusely and he was beginning to feel a vague nausea.

Then the concierge announced himself with an apology for the delay, and Tom explained what he needed to know.

"I have to reach her," he snapped. "It's extremely important."

"We would be happy to oblige, Monsieur Ford, but you see, it is impossible. She left no forwarding address."

Tom could sense the man's hesitation. His mind churned with possibilities. Then he looked at Cynthia and suddenly had an idea. If Lloyd and the Hamilton women were conspiring against him, he'd have to go them one better.

"One of our associates was with her," he said cautiously. "A Mr. Bell. Was he registered at the hotel?"

He waited impatiently through a brief pause.

"We had no Monsieur Bell registered. Perhaps you mean…" His voice trailed off.

"Mean? Who?" Tom pressed.

"No, we had no Monsieur Bell," the concierge said, clearing his throat.

"I have no time for this," Tom said, thinking quickly. "Will five hundred dollars make a difference?"

"Well, I…"

"Trust me, please. As I said, this is a matter of extreme importance. I'll wire you five hundred dollars immediately," Tom pressed, sensing that the man was poised to react. "It's that critical."

"But, sir…" The man's protest was mild. Obviously he was mulling over the offer. "You did say immediately?"

"Yes. To whom should the wire be sent?"

The man gave his name and his bank and his home address. Tom waited, exchanging glances with Cynthia. She nodded. Information, he knew, was about to be provided, the veracity of which might be suspect. It could not be avoided.

"They left here yesterday afternoon," the concierge began, timing his comments appropriately, obviously determined to allow the value to match the purchase price.

"They?"

"A Monsieur Champion," the concierge said. "John was his first name. He gave his address as the George V, Paris."

He nodded to Cynthia, wrote down the information, and gave it to her. He nodded.

"John Champion, you say." Tom was puzzled. "And Mrs. Ford… they left together? Are you sure?"

"Oui, monsieur."

Tom forced himself to resist anger. What he needed now were facts, and he forced an elaborate rapid-fire interrogation, the answers coming back as fast as he asked them.

He asked for a description of the man, the kind of car he was driving. Did the hotel keep a record of telephone calls? Those records were private, the man insisted, which cost Tom another five hundred dollars.

In response, the concierge obliged with an instantaneous report from the hotel's computer. No, the man said, no long-distance calls for the man, no calls at all. No, they kept no records of interhotel calls. There was room service by both parties, not extensive. He looked up calls made by Angela. She had called him. That was all.

"They had separate rooms?" Tom held his breath.

"Oui."

Tom, despite his suspicion and disbelief, felt an odd sense of relief. It was a setup. He was dead certain. He would find the flaw.

"Did they spend time together? I mean in the public areas."

"I believe so."

"Are you sure?"

"It is our job to know," the concierge said revealing the existence of an internal grapevine carrying day-to-day information about all the hotel guests. Pampered service at expensive hotels, Tom knew, meant that the service people, the pamperers, knew a great deal about the guests and their behavior.

"Are you certain it was Mrs. Ford? A tall good-looking woman, blonde, brown eyes?" Beyond that, he could not describe her.

"I saw her passport myself, Monsieur Ford. It was she, your wife."

"And the man?"

"I told you John Champion."

"And they were seen in public together?"

As if to reiterate the point and protect his potential earnings, the man recounted that Mrs. Ford and Mr. Champion had been seen together at the pool, at the cocktail lounge, in the dining room, and that they had left the hotel together for points unknown.

"And they checked out yesterday?" Tom asked.

"Oui."

"Together?"

"Oui."

"Meaning at the same time. Each paid for their own bill?"

"Oui."

"What was she wearing?"

He was deliberately belaboring the point, hoping against hope.

"Let me try to remember… oui, she was dressed in a red suit, set off by a string of baroque pearls." The man sounded proud of his memory.

His heart fell. He knew the red suit, and he had bought her the baroque pearls. Only her behavior was out of sync. He could not conceive of her not informing him that she was leaving the hotel.

"Oh, one thing more."

Tom steeled himself for a new blow.

"She instructed us to return her rental car, which we did."

"Covered all the bases, did she?" He looked at Cynthia and shook his head. "She went with him. Lousy bitch," he muttered.

"What was that?" the concierge asked. Tom ignored his question.

"Were they…" — Tom paused gathering his courage — "…affectionate?"

"Monsieur…"

"I need to know," Tom said.

"It is indelicate — " the man began.

"Fuck that, mister. Were they?"

"Oui, monsieur," the man sighed. "It seemed so."

"When did the man check in?"

"He had stayed… let's see… three weeks. His bill came to…" There was another lengthy pause. "In American dollars, nearly twenty-five thousand. He paid in cash."

"Cash?"

Tom's mind raced with questions.

"Who was he? What did he do?"

"He was not obliged to say. He was a man alone. He went out frequently. Came back late most times. Pleasant chap."

"How old?"

"Fortyish. Fine-looking man."

He was providing more information than Tom had bargained for.

"How can you be sure they left together?"

"Our boys loaded the Jaguar," the concierge said flatly. "Madame was in the front seat beside him when they departed."

"You have a record of the license?"

"It's in the computer, along with the numbers of his passport."

"Can you fax a printout immediately?"

"Well, I…"

"Another five hundred will be provided."

Without hesitation he agreed and Tom gave him his fax number.

"As well as both bills and his registration card."

"Of course."

"Is there something more you can tell me?" Tom cleared his throat, hating the idea of the question. "Was there any sign of coercion? Did you get the impression that she went with him willingly? Could she have been acting out of fear for her life?" The questions spilled out in a jumble. He knew he was conveying hysteria, but he couldn't help himself.

The concierge seemed to remain composed, his haughty attitude reflecting a sense of arrogance coated with a layer of superiority. Tom could picture him, dressed to the nines in tails and checked trousers, looking lordly and imperious. How pitiful he must appear to such a man, Tom thought angrily, a cuckolded husband checking up on the infidelity of his wife. Despite his disbelief, it had become too obvious to deny.

"No," the concierge said, offering the expected answer. "I detected no coercion. I would say Mrs. Ford went quite willingly."

He wanted to lash out at the man. The blood thumped in his head, and he felt a flush rise to his face.

"Are you implying that they were…"—Tom cleared his throat—"…lovers?"

Cynthia had finished with her phone call. She looked toward him and mimed that there was no record of a John Champion at the George V. It struck him suddenly that she, too, was observing his weakness. It galled him.

"I'm not prepared to make that assertion," the man said with a tinge of arrogance.

"Did it seem like they were longtime..." —he paused and cleared his throat again —"...friends?"

"Not at all."

"I don't understand."

"This is strictly my own impression. But I do not believe Madame Ford knew the man before she arrived here. She had to call our desk to get his name."

It was too incongruous, too far from his nearly twenty-year knowledge of Angela. It was inconceivable that Angela could leave the hotel under her own volition with a man she had met a day or two ago. Angela was too— he searched for the right word—disinterested in that sort of thing, too frigid, never flirtatious. Perhaps Cynthia was right after all, and the coincidental meeting at the hotel was staged. And yet he was scheduled to join her for Hamilton's cruise. Cynthia's allegation made no sense. The disjointed logic was maddening.

"And she left the hotel with this man?" Tom asked again, unable to mask his growing hysteria, and it was apparent to him that the interrogation was getting repetitive.

His mind ranged freely with possibilities. Had he misread Angela all those years together? Could she secretly have been involved with other men for years, escaping his detection? No. Impossible.

Tom had always prided himself on his powers of observation. Few details escaped him. He could detect nuance and subtlety and determine true character and hidden motives. He was certain he could predict behavior. This information about Angela shook his confidence considerably, forcing him into other realms of speculation.

Perhaps Angela knew all about him and Cynthia. Here he was playing his own charade, thinking himself extraordinarily clever in his own masquerade, and here she was, totally aware of what he was doing, cleverly maintaining a sense of serene normality. A brilliant performance indeed. Was she now having her sweet revenge? Why not? What was good for the goose… Perhaps the timing of this act was pure coincidence?

Angela? No way.

On the other hand, in the light of the evidence pointing to this new and startling possibility of Angela being involved with a man then—Suddenly his thoughts dead-ended. His private vaunted family compartment, so carefully reserved as a repository for tranquil family life, was in danger of being swept away forever. Tom realized that the concierge was still on the line.

"This Champion, what did he look like?"

"Tall, muscular, blond, although the hair color seemed a trifle too yellow to be natural. I told you, a handsome man, impeccably dressed. British. Carried a UK passport… although I must say he seemed more like an American."

Warning bells sounded in his head signaling yet another avenue of exploration. The concierge's implication was that this man was not what he seemed. An impostor? Posing as whom? For what purpose?

Hamilton's death had obviously put in motion an intrigue designed to undercut Tom's future plans. It might be something Max himself had conceived, the parting shot of an evil, ruthless man. The "if I can't have it, no one will" syndrome.

Max could be as cunning as a snake, willing to pit people against each other for his own enjoyment. Had they chosen simple unworldly Angela as the weapon of his destruction? Stupid bitch! It occurred to him that he was not at all interested in Angela's safety, but only in the damage she was causing, wittingly or unwittingly.

He had no illusions about his true feelings about his wife. She was there for image, not for emotion, a useful prop. Nothing more. He had long since considered his original motive for marriage a desire to appear conformist, a mask for his ambition.

Yet no possibilities could be dismissed. This could be, after all, merely the handiwork of Hamilton's wife and daughters, determined to extract their pound of flesh and grab billions, to even the score for all the years of misery and betrayal that Max had perpetrated against them. Their agenda was to gain control of the Hamilton empire by whatever means possible.

When the stakes were that high, people could summon up huge resources. Yet he had no doubt that he could outwit them. It had been his hope to avoid complications.

"Is there anything else you can tell me?" Tom said to the concierge.

"Only that I hope you find her." He heard a low cough. "And the money, sir."

"It will be wired immediately."

"Thank you, sir."

Hanging up, he looked toward Cynthia, who appeared as baffled as he.

"What do you think?" he asked her.

"I think," Cynthia said with obvious caution, "that your angelic little wife may be something other than she seems."

He started to frame a denial, then hesitated, still fighting the idea.

"So much for duplicity," Cynthia said.

"I just don't understand it," he cried, pacing the room.

"It's obvious that they've found the right inducement."

"Inducement?"

"It's not money that's driving her. She didn't need that."

"What are you trying to say, Cynthia?"

"A man," she whispered. "They've reached her through a man."

"Angela? Don't be ridiculous."

"This man is giving her something she's never had."

"Angela would never react to the blandishments of a man, not in the way you mean. It's totally out of character. She's a boring, frigid bitch."

He continued to pace the room.

"Whatever this man is giving her, it's working."

"Are you saying that dear sweet little Angela, bland little Angela is?—no way—no fucking way."

"He's got to her, Tom," Cynthia was relentless now.

"They're holed up somewhere. She's betrayed you."

For a long time he was silent, moving about the office. He stopped pacing suddenly, then turned away and moved toward the window. For a long time he gazed vacantly at the late summer traffic choking the streets below.

"I should have flown out there myself," he muttered.

"Yes, you should have, Tom."

"She's gotten in the way, Cynthia. Gummed up the works."

"Yes, she has, Tom. Very much so."

Chapter 23

Cynthia watched as Tom's agitation accelerated. An idea had jumped into her mind, an opportunity.

"They've coerced her," Tom hissed, obviously unable to accept any other explanation. "I know it. Angela wouldn't make a move without consulting me. Not Angela. Somehow they've gotten to her. They're manipulating her."

He seemed to be convinced that mysterious forces had her in their clutches and were using her to checkmate Tom's plans.

Such a theory, she knew, fit in nicely with Tom's conspiratorial view of the world. She let it simmer, playing as always the efficient assistant, as he thrashed about trying to make sense of what had occurred. She was not unhappy about this new development.

It's all part of their scheme," he raged. "Bastards! But why? What would they hope to gain? Angela has no knowledge of anything."

"Maybe they've kidnapped her?" Cynthia suggested.

"For what reason?"

"A negotiating chip perhaps."

"Wrong tactic," he shrugged. It occurred to her that he would be perfectly capable of sacrificing Angela if push came to shove. Yes, she told herself. Wrong tactic.

"What about the man?" Cynthia asked. In that question

she felt a note of optimism. Could Angela have had a secret lover all along? Such a situation would certainly shat-
ter Tom's confidence in the viability of his vaunted airtight
family compartment. That would fit in nicely with her own
agenda. Fearing disappointment she moved it out of her
mind.

"Part of their game. No doubt about it. I feel so fucking
helpless," he said, pacing the room like a caged tiger. He
decided to call Aunt Emma. She was home in Santa Fe. As
always, Cynthia monitored the call.

"So nice to hear from you, Tom," Aunt Emma said pleasantly. "Have you begun the cruise as yet?"

"I'm still in New York," he said pleasantly, ever cautious.
In Tom's mind, everyone outside his orbit was suspect. He
explained what had happened to Hamilton.

"My God. How awful. You must be really harassed, Tom.
I've hardly been conscious since I returned from Italy. Jet
lag." She paused. "I assume then that Angela has come
home. We had a glorious time in Florence."

"Actually," Tom paused, shaking his head. "She's staying on in France for a few more days. You haven't heard
from her by chance?"

"No, I haven't. Isn't she at the Bel Air?"

"That's the point, Emma. I think she's switched hotels. I
thought perhaps she had informed you—"

"Do you think anything's wrong?" Emma said, obviously concerned.

"No, nothing like that. I just wanted to check." He
shrugged. "You and she have gotten so close."

"Yes we have, Tom. She's quite a girl. I'm sure the accommodations at the Bel Air were not to her liking." She giggled lightly. "You've spoiled her, dear. It's high season. They might have overbooked. You're not worried are you, Tom?"

"Not at all. I just thought… if you do hear from her, would you call my New York office?"

"Of course I will." There was another long pause. "And if you hear from her, ask her to call her silly Aunt Emma."

"I could have done without this," he told Cynthia, after his conversation with Emma.

With his mind racing from one conclusion to another, she tried deliberately channeling his thoughts to the negative side of the puzzle harping on the distinct possibility, which she believed, that Angela had betrayed him. But why? That was the essential mystery.

During the next hour, Cynthia had obediently called every luxury hotel on the Riviera from Menton to Saint-Tropez.

"She could be dead," Tom speculated.

"What would be the point of them doing that?" Cynthia said, feeding his conspiracy theory and inserting the suggestion. "That would reduce their leverage."

Finally, he called Lloyd back. With Cynthia listening, they recorded the conversation.

"All right," he said. "I'll buy."

"Buy what?"

"You know exactly what I'm talking about."

"I haven't the foggiest, old man."

"Mrs. Ford."

"What about her?"

"Don't play coy with me, Lloyd."

"Coy with a shark, sir? Are you mad?"

"Just state your terms."

"Well, well. So you do see the light," Lloyd said. "We're ready to negotiate if you are."

"What I see is your venality," Tom said. "How did you get her to go along?"

"She and the girls are the legitimate heirs. You weren't going to fob her off with the proceeds of an insurance policy, which barely covers a fraction of what Max was into."

Cynthia was amazed at the cross-purposes of the discussion. They were both talking on different planes. Lloyd hadn't a clue to what Tom was talking about.

"You know what I'm referring to, Lloyd. Where is my wife?"

"Your wife?"

"Acknowledge it. You might as well know in front. It's not negotiable."

"Not negotiable?"

"I don't know what you've done to her. But I'd strongly advise you to cease and desist. It won't work."

"You've lost me, old man."

"I'm talking about Mrs. Ford. It's obvious you've got her to go along."

"I wish you'd make yourself clearer, my good man."

"I give you fair warning."

"Really, Ford—"

"Don't be an ass, Lloyd. Coercing my wife by whatever means or using her as a bargaining chip is absurd. We can't let this matter hang. We've got nearly a hundred companies in twenty countries with management on edge and waiting for direction. An internecine fight between owners will do no one any good. But I will not go ahead until you produce my wife."

"I don't know what to say."

"Think about it," Tom said, breaking the connection.

Cynthia tamped down her elation. Tom's fiercely guarded family compartment was exploding, forcing him to mix it with other aspects of his life, with her. She was, of course, ecstatic. It was the one area of Tom Ford's world she had not yet invaded.

Admittedly, she had long harbored aspirations of one day moving into that territory. From the beginning, he had set the ground rules, and she had obeyed them to the letter, fearing that any untoward act might trigger suspicions that would inhibit her progress toward her ultimate goal.

Inside her mind and thoughts, where she husbanded her secret agenda, she had been on the lookout for opportunity. Finally, from an unplanned and miraculous source, it had come. She would never be satisfied with the crumbs from Tom's table, regardless of the sums offered. Cut from the same cloth as Tom Ford, she wanted it all, everything.

Once it had seemed unattainable. Now it beckoned. Marriage first, then a visit to Mr. Parker, and she would be the surviving widow. Her ultimate plan had always turned on this possibility. Now it had offered itself as a bonanza. The little lady had signed her own death warrant one way or another. If Tom did not consider her betrayal grounds for divorce, then she could always find a proper alternative. Her first option, of course, was to let nature take its course. The little bitch had obviously broken out on her own.

She had no illusions about Tom's inherent lack of trust, except in that vaunted family compartment. Happily, that myth was in the process of disintegration. Nor had she expected this sudden good fortune. Her own secret interpretation had, up to now, been heavily tinged with wish fulfillment.

To herself, she gloated over this new wrinkle. Tom had mythologized this exemplary wife and mother as if she were a saint. Cynthia had listened to this galling exposition ad infinitum, especially in times of afterplay when they had physically exhausted themselves with sexual acrobatics.

Cynthia's own view was that the woman's principal virtue was accepting her husband's absences without question and satisfying herself with the meager representation of his sexuality as the proper conduct for a devoted hard-working husband. Judging from Tom's insatiable libido and their powerful and frequent sexual episodes, she could not imagine anything being left for Angela to—if not enjoy—validate.

Sensing this weakness in her archrival, Cynthia bore down on Tom by illustrating her sexual prowess, initiating little titillating surprises that kept the sexual edge between them well honed. To achieve her goal, the total possession of Tom Ford, she had vowed to employ every weapon in her arsenal.

The real adversary, Cynthia knew, had been in Tom's mind, embodied in the romantic myth of so-called family values. To Cynthia, the real Angela was a fool, naïve and shallow, lacking any insight into the bedrock nature of Tom Ford, a bland and boring female without any perception or complexity, totally isolated from the reality of her husband's life. This latest version of her shallowness merely illustrated the woman's naïveté and fragility. Obviously, she had been seduced by some fortune-hunting gigolo with lots of patience and a big wand, someone who had the skills and motive to turn her on. It must have been difficult work.

Angela, Cynthia reasoned, had simply been at the right place at the right time, having caught Tom's eye at the moment of his greatest vulnerability, a season of youthful insecurity and uncertainty; then having borne his children to fill in the blanks of his family-fortress fantasy. She doubted if Angela had the slightest clue to Tom's inner life or, for that matter, any imaginative inner life of her own.

To Cynthia, Tom was a true predator, with a gargantuan appetite for power, without a shred of conscience or morality, a cunning, cruel, conspiring, self-obsessed, greed-besotted voluptuary. It took one to know one.

He had no toleration for being thwarted and, conversely, could never be sated even after achieving his own even more ambitious goals. In her view, he had not learned the value of "enough." She was certain she had. Enough, for her was having all that Tom had acquired up to and beyond the death of the bloated Mr. Hamilton.

Under Tom's polished exterior, so carefully contrived

through an uncanny ability to convey confidence and credibility that he was perceived by others as self-effacing and devoted solely to Max Hamilton's interests, a middle man who was able to interpret the roaring acquisitional ego of Max Hamilton to others and twist them to his own advantage.

He had given up all clients except Max and had finally stripped him of everything, even his life. Tom had consumed him and assumed him. Cynthia had observed this entire happening and had become an essential part of it, the decisive instrument of Max's death.

From the moment of her own epiphany during the interviewing process, she knew that fate had brought her to this man, to Tom Ford, who was to become her life's feast, as if some devilish fate had served him up for her to cannibalize. Actually, the true epiphany had come earlier when she had heard her brother's taped confession. Without realizing it, he had given her the game plan for her own sortie into upward mobility. She had grasped the opportunity.

Since the condition of her employment was to give up everything, to strip herself of all extraneous desires and channel her body and soul into the service of Tom Ford, she had devoted every moment of her life to doing just that. Such intimacy gave her the ability to ply her real agenda, studying him, analyzing him, dissecting him, probing for the soft underbelly of his vulnerability.

She knew him now, as a watchmaker knows his clock, every beat and nuance, discovering in the process that she was a mirror image of his most savage and single-minded attributes.

The revelation of her brother's professional life gave voice to her own inchoate theories that she, like him, had somehow been born with genes that, like microchips made from human cells, had been programmed by exposure to their ugly early history to perform acts without any inhibition of conscience or compassion.

She characterized the end result, triggered by the microchip, as a special talent, born in the genes, and embellished by experience, like that displayed by a musician, artist, or writer. Her brother's death, she had decided, was the result of a fault in the chip that weakened the genetic pattern, especially in the area of conscience.

To her, the ultimate test of this theory was the competent manner in which she went about the process that led to the elimination of Max Hamilton. It never failed to amuse her how Tom had utilized her knowledge and given her the means and opportunity to go forward. She appreciated the irony that her brother's tape-recorded diary, his legacy, this symbol of his fault line, had led her to the one man who could deliver on the contract to eliminate Max Hamilton, Parker, the killer-broker.

The recording had provided an assassin's primer complete with road map. She had followed it zealously, following his instruction to the letter. Her brother's tape had provided Parker's name and number. She hadn't been totally certain that the number was still operable, and it had been somewhat of a surprise to find that it was still functioning, lending credence to the theory that if it wasn't broke, don't fix it.

The high-tech revolution had created superhighways of interdiction, but left the back roads free of hindrance or surveillance. After some attempts from a series of Manhattan pay phones, she finally found her mark.

After a cryptic explanation revealing her sibling relationship, Mr. Parker directed her to call at various intervals, instructing her finally to meet him at a pub in, of all places, the Chelsea section of London. She obeyed without question, armed with carte blanche from Tom Ford and the power and means to negotiate the contract.

Mr. Parker of the disembodied voice on the pay phone was a balding little man with Coke-bottle glasses, thick moist lips, a sallow complexion, and a musty-looking trench coat. He sat at a corner table of a lager-smelling pub that had seen better days, presided over by a consumptive-looking barman with a roseate complexion and rotted teeth.

Mr. Parker was sipping on a pint of dark stout with a dying head of foam. The pub was peopled with a working-class crowd huddled around the bar and a few seedy couples occupying the surrounding tables.

Most of the customers had the pallor and bloat of those unduly conversant with the results of the brewing process. The atmosphere struck her as completely incongruous to the business at hand.

Parker invited her to join him in a drink, and she ordered a sherry more out of form than necessity. He made this choice known to the barman then waddled heavily to the bar to collect both drinks. Observing the man, she was surprised that he looked so much less sinister than she had imagined, considering that he was quite possibly the instrument of untold deaths, including her brother's.

From time to time a pay phone in a booth nearby would ring. No one answered and the ring continued until the caller lost patience. Parker would briefly look toward the phone, then shrug and return to their conversation. Obviously, this was the pay end of the communication system. It was laughable in its crude simplicity. The other customers, undoubtedly used to the intrusion, paid no attention.

She was not surprised that his very first words were devoted to her sibling relationship.

"He was a good man, one of the best," he said, not unkindly. Since he undoubtedly knew her brother's history, she presumed he would have access to her own history as well, including her present employer.

It amazed her that he appeared so shockingly ordinary and nondescript, as if he went to great pains not to distinguish himself from any of the other customers in the pub. Under other circumstances, she might consider him a whimsical figure, more than slightly ridiculous.

"I'm not surprised he gave you my number," he said, shaking his head in a good imitation of someone who might have cared. "Nor do I care. Enough time has elapsed. If you were going to use it to betray us, you would have by now."

"I would never go to the authorities," she had replied.

"The authorities," Parker chuckled. "That would hardly have mattered. My dear lady, the authorities created us. For them it would be an embarrassment of monumental proportions to the institutions themselves and, I can assure you, they would quickly brush it aside as a mad fantasy."

He shook his head and lifted his glass for a deep sip, then continued.

"Your brother started out, as we all did, as a civil servant, a piglet at the public swill." He seemed determined to pursue the matter. "Who would dare admit that we had ever existed as an instrument of public policy? My dear lady, we can only be characterized as objects of denial, anonymous functionaries, no more lethal than a file clerk.

"Is it possible that anyone could admit that civilized nations would employ such rude tactics, deliberate cold-blooded and illegal means to eliminate enemies of national goals? Unheard of. It is one thing to repent and reveal to a beloved relative, but under no circumstances would such a confession have credence in the hallowed halls of the so-called authorities.

"Dear lady," he said with a light chuckle, "we are still involved with the authorities. Freelancers now. We barter services for access. Marvelous experience thrashing about in the hubris of their data banks, we know everything they know. More important, we know what they do not know."

"I assumed that," Cynthia responded.

"Good show," he said.

Parker upended his drink and swallowed the dregs, and then, slapping the glass on the much-abused table, he continued.

"Well then, to business. I must assume you have rationalized in your mind the reasons for the assignment. You see our work defies all the assumptions that underpin our society: morality, legality, ethics, the sanctity of human life. Even the motives for the deed are suspect. Some of our customers offer noble goals, satisfying themselves by indulging in the fantasy of the greater good. Eliminate the corrupt, the greedy, the spoilers, and you eliminate the evil. Some acknowledge that the deed is for personal gain, for swift problem solving, or simply to remove a bottleneck to progress. It's all the same to us."

"I hadn't bargained on such instructive philosophy, Mr. Parker," Cynthia said, wondering what he really wanted to convey. At that moment it came to her. He was hawking his raison d'être, informing her that he was totally aware of her motives, and, for reasons of his own, he wanted her to be aware of his.

"It proves there is a human side to every business. Even ours."

"Now that we've disposed of that," Cynthia said. "Can we get on with the business at hand?"

"With pleasure," Parker said. Again he signaled to the barman, lifting his glass. Then he waddled to the bar and carried a full pint back to the table, sipping as he walked. Sitting down again, he spoke below a foam moustache, appearing even more incongruous than before.

"I expect I need not reiterate the terms," he said. "That part, meaning payment in advance, is, as stated in our brief phone conversations, not negotiable."

"I wouldn't be here if I hadn't accepted those terms," she acknowledged. She had estimated that it might cost as much as five million. She had been wrong. The price was six with another three million if the death was declared ac-cidental. "Of course, I'm expecting you to instruct us in the intricacies of the money trail. And, of course, the matter of risk."

"Integrity is the very soul of our business. It is based upon absolute trust. I can assure you that there is no risk to you in the fulfillment of this contract. Moreover the other inherent risks are, you might say, practically nonexistent. Rarely has a professional been caught and tried. One was once and was dispatched in his cell. Are you reassured?"

"I appreciate your trying to put me at my ease," she said with a tinge of sarcasm. His obliqueness was beginning to wear on her.

"Our business depends upon personal satisfaction and word of mouth."

Again he chuckled, obviously pleased with his humor.

Just like that, she heard her own voice say internally. It seemed so banal. Even the subsequent negotiations ap-peared to be little more than if the transaction was across a retail counter. And the incentive plan proffered by Cynthia seemed like an offer on television. "And here's a chance to double your money."

"A verdict of accidental death would simplify matters tremendously," she told him. "And as we agreed, it will considerably improve the fee."

"We love incentives," Parker said.

"In that case, the incentive payment will be based on the rendered service. In other words, after the fact."

"How can it be otherwise?"

"We are also people of integrity," Cynthia said, unable to resist.

"Now for the other side of the coin, dear lady. The lucky winner of the lottery."

"You've heard of Max Hamilton?" Cynthia asked cautiously.

"Well, well. Then again I did not expect a street urchin. The Max Hamilton. Wonderful! A genuine mogul, sharp in business, pockets full of filthy lucre. We adore challenges."

"He moves around. Jets and boats. Country to country like a bee gathering pollen," Cynthia said, noting that she was picking up Parker's speech rhythms. "I'm prepared to fill you in on his whereabouts."

"Wonderful, dear lady. Often we have to fend for ourselves in finding our—how shall I say—quarry. However, no matter, we are quite resourceful. We are trackers par excellence. High tech, low tech, all around tech. Seek and ye shall find. We have the resources, the people. Nothing escapes our notice. We have, as they say, the maximum access allowed, inside, outside, and around the so-called law. We can be quite omnipotent."

It was hardly the atmosphere for such boasting. The man reeked with the appearance of inefficiency.

"Unfortunately, in this case, the act—considering the prominence of the man—will create a media event. These people are magnets for that sort of thing. Tricky business. The authorities become so much more tenacious."

"Hence the incentive," Cynthia said.

She realized suddenly that they were not talking in whispers. An interested party with reasonably good ears could make out what they were saying from the distance of one table. At that table sat a boozy couple that seemed totally indifferent to everything, including each other. Parker seemed to sense her discomfort, and as if in arrogant defiance, raised his voice.

"A verdict of accidental death implies an official ending. In cases of this kind, one involving a celebrity, there is often no final curtain. Sometimes they are allowed to drag on for years as an unsolved crime."

"The verdict must be official to qualify," Cynthia said.

"In that case," Parker said. "We've got to give you our best man. A lone wolf, as they say, our most competent killing mechanism."

"I assumed that from the beginning."

"Good," Parker said, putting out his hand. She took it, feeling the clammy moistness pass to her flesh. As a ploy to release her hand, she reached for her glass, then raised it, forcing him to follow suit.

"To a successful conclusion," she said, drinking the contents of her glass in one swallow. He raised his pint, touched her glass, and drank. She stood up.

"Chances are we will never meet again," she said.

"Never say never. We thrive on repeat business."

His words still resonated in her mind. He was right.

Chapter 24

Time had lost all meaning. She had the sensation of having lived a lifetime in three days.

Each evening, they had driven to the nearest town, just a few kilometers from the house. There, they would walk for a while holding hands, then take a table at one of the sidewalk cafés, where they sipped Pernod and watched the warm glow of sunset orange silhouette the low mountains.

As Friday, the day scheduled for her departure, drew nearer, she was conscious of a growing hysteria building inside her. Postponement was no longer an option. So far she had deflected any further talk of staying on. She could not deflect it for much longer.

He bent across the table to kiss her. She noted an older man sitting alone at a nearby table. He looked up from his newspaper and smiled appreciatively.

"Where are we going?" She sighed, the pressure of time too strong to keep bottled up.

"Your choice," he said, watching her face, their eyes meeting, holding, penetrating as deeply as their imaginations could take them. Was that fair, handing the decision to her?

"And you?"

"I know where I want to go," he said.

"Where?"

"With you."

"Feelings change," she said, regretting it instantly. It was an idea that provoked anxiety. She watched frown lines crinkle his forehead.

"Not this."

"How can you be sure?"

She watched him mull the question, which lay at the heart of everything that had happened, was happening. As he contemplated, his gaze never left her face. Was he assailed by the same cold wind of fear? Everything was transitory. Nothing lasts. She felt suddenly frightened and longed for the reassurance of Aunt Emma. Only Aunt Emma could possibly understand what was happening. So far she had resisted calling her.

"I'm sure," he said flatly.

They lifted their glasses and drank and sat silently together as the sun slowly disappeared and the lighted streets began to fill with people.

He called for the check, and while he went through the process of paying, she went inside to find the bathroom. She had deliberately not charged her cell but the sight of the pay phone behind the curtain suggested that Aunt Emma was within easy reach. She managed to bridge the language gap and was miraculously put through.

"Angela!" Aunt Emma's voice seemed panicked.

For a second she was tempted to deny it, to explain that she was now the new Angela, that the old Angela was gone. But Aunt Emma did not give her leeway.

"Where are you? Tom is worried sick. He's been calling all week. He's desperately trying to find you."

"I don't want him to find me," she blurted.

"What is happening?"

"I met this man… I… I think I've found it. You know. What we spoke about."

"A man?"

"Yes," she hesitated. "As you said, it happened in the blink of an eye. Like a miracle."

It occurred to her suddenly that she might ask for her to expatiate on the "man," who he was, what he did. Instead, as if to foreclose on that inquiry, she filled in what blanks she knew.

"I met him at the Bel Air. He reminds me of—well, in appearance—the David. He lives well, but I can tell you, Emma, he's… we're in a state of constant joy. It's just as you described it. I think I've found it—totally."

"Have you really?"

"I'm sure of it. Thanks to you, Aunt Emma."

"To me?"

"What we talked about in Florence."

"You must be positive, Angela. You must feel it in your bones."

"I do, Aunt Emma. It's as if I've found a new me. You showed me the road map, Aunt Emma. I know where I am now. Do you remember? Did you really think it couldn't happen to me?"

She waited through a long pause.

"Not after what happened at the Accademia."

"Call it a catalyst." Angela giggled, the panic gone. "It primed me."

"Are you ready for the sacrifice, Angela? It is very difficult to jettison your old life. Tom will be crushed. Are you ready for that?"

"I haven't completely decided. It's not easy as you know." She waited through a long pause. "One thing I did decide, Aunt Emma. Tom is irrelevant."

"Well then, follow your heart. If you don't, you might regret it. It might sound like a corny cliché. But then, clichés are often the truth."

"You made me see things in a new light, Aunt Emma."

"Did I really?"

"Really, Aunt Emma. I now know what you meant," she answered, haltingly, feeling her throat grow dry. "As you said, you'll know it when it comes."

"Yes." Aunt Emma sighed. "I did say that."

"You called it—"

"—the true passion?"

"Yes."

There was a long pause. Angela could hear her aunt's soft breathing, suddenly punctuated by a deep sigh.

"How I envy you, Angela!"

"It's wonderful, Aunt Emma. Just as you said, the defining moment of my life. I may have to see it through."

"Yes, you will."

"To the exclusion of all else…"

There was still another long pause, which she interpreted as a message of uncertainty. It frightened her.

"As long as you're prepared for leaving everything behind."

"I need reassurance, Aunt Emma," she felt her voice tremble.

Again she heard the silence at the other end.

"It's your decision to make, darling. You have to weigh it carefully. Are you certain?"

"You said I'd know."

"Do you?"

"I believe I do. The old life has no meaning. Perhaps it never had."

"Only you can be the judge of that. That's the trick of it."

"I think I've found—how did you put it?—my erotic heart. I… I've entered the dream."

"God, all that highfalutin language. Never mind. It is the truth of it and everything I told you was tested in my life."

"Then it is worth the candle?"

"If you're dead certain."

"Let's say, I'm leaning in that direction."

"So you're not sure."

"I don't know if I can find the courage."

"If it's the real thing, believe me, darling, you'll find it."

Angela felt suddenly alone. She realized that she hadn't been totally forthright.

"There's more to it, Aunt Emma."

"More to it?"

"I think I've hurt Tom in a business way. I've lied about…" She suddenly realized it might be a long and complicated story. "Let's leave it at that."

"It may sound cruel, but once you break the eggs, you've got to live with the consequences. As I told you, it often gets messy. Someone always gets hurt. Luckily your children are grown."

"Someday I could explain it to them. Perhaps in a way, you explained it to me."

"If they love you, they'll understand."

"It's everything you said it was, Aunt Emma."

"However you choose, I wish you gobs of love and luck."

"I know that, Aunt Emma."

Tears moistened her eyes and spilled over her cheeks. She wiped them away with the back of her hand.

"You won't mention that you spoke to me," Angela said.

"Of course not."

"I don't know where this is going, Aunt Emma," Angela said.

"When you do, darling, will you please call your Aunt Emma? It's important for me to know and for us to stay in touch. If you need me, call me. Promise?"

"I promise."

"Just be sure," Aunt Emma said. "Be sure."

Angela felt herself nodding.

After visiting the bathroom, she came out again. He was still seated in the chair gazing skyward at what was now a star-studded canopy. Seeing her, he got up to meet her, and they embraced.

"I missed you," he said.

"And I missed you."

She did not tell him that she had called. They got into the car and headed back to the little house. "Be sure."

Her aunt's words echoed in her mind.

Chapter 25

From the moment he awoke, his naked body draped around her like a spoon, Champion felt the rising tension of expectation. Tomorrow was Friday, the designated day of return on the night flight from Nice. She had promised him that she would decide before then.

"Give me that space, darling," she had pleaded.

It was agony, not knowing, waiting. Worse, he could no longer project a life without her. He weighed a long menu of strategies. Boiled down, any persuasion smacked of subterfuge and manipulation. On that basis, he knew, no future was possible. It was not like his business, in which fate could be deliberately forced.

He searched his mind for some tiny vestige of solace. At least her memory would not include his occupation. Repressing that history had been a terrible trial for him. Above all, he feared her knowing. At the same time, he felt a terrible void, as if his dishonesty had somehow sullied the purity of his commitment.

Perhaps if she knew everything, she might understand the transformation that he had undergone. But there was no way to prove that to her. Was there?

The sun speared through the tree outside the bedroom window, splashing light like random splotches of yellow paint.

He held her, drinking in the odor of her hair, a delicious nutty smell. He lay still, his breathing deliberately shallow. Stay, he begged her in his heart.

Until this moment of his awakening, he had battled time, agonizing over its relentlessness and searching for some way to halt its movement. For him, this experience with Angela was the quintessential moment, the epiphany of joy discovered. He had captured light in a bottle. Darkness had disappeared.

His life could be measured, like the world's, in the before and after. Before Angela and after Angela, the now of his existence. It was impossible to recall what came before her, the existentialism of a life bereft of feeling, a numbness, as if no blood had flowed in his veins. This other person inside him had metamorphosed from flesh to shadow, and he had discovered long ago that he had severed himself even from that shadow.

Now he was flesh again, reconstituted. Although they had promised themselves to avoid history, it was impossible to totally separate themselves from memory, deep memory, before they had acquired the baggage of adulthood.

It was her idea to explore those events and impressions that took place before the end of innocence. And it never failed to amaze him how rich and absorbing such exchanges could be. He found, too, that plumbing these depths of themselves increased the bond between them.

He had to go back further than she, because he could barely remember innocence and what it meant. It was true that once he had been aware of feeling. After all, he had not been born emotionally dead. He hadn't thought of such things in more than thirty years. He felt renewed, reborn, alive again. Lover's talk could probe deeply with the sharp explorative strokes of a scalpel.

"I remember flowers," he told her. "Bursts of color, delicate petals, wonderful perfumy smells. My mother must have loved flowers. But she was out of my life so fast. By three she was gone, death by disease."

Loss had come early to him, he had noted, as if for the first time. In fact, everything he told her about his memories seemed to emerge for the first time. "And that," he told her, "must count as the end of innocence."

"That's all you remember, the flowers?"

"I suppose if I try, I can remember more."

"Then try."

"The feel of her. I think I can remember that."

He moved his hand to her bare breast, squeezing lightly.

"Yes," he told her. "Something like that. Soft." He smoothed her hair. "Silky."

"And her voice. Do you remember her voice?"

"Only as a song. I can't make out the words."

He surprised himself. He had never dipped so deeply into memory, into himself. Never.

"And your father?" she had asked.

"My father?"

He thought about this for a long time. His father was not an innocent memory, although not to be identified with pain or indifference or neglect. Love, the paternal kind, and death, the murdering kind, was his father's legacy.

He had not seen his mother die and, therefore, he could never associate her with death. She had simply gone away in a large box and, like the other memories of her, they would always be associated with the perfumy smell of flowers.

But memories of his father did not require a massive search through time. They were always ready to be recalled, and images as vivid as the events had occurred within moments of recall.

Predators, they prowled streets. City streets. He remembered cold and dank nights as they, father and son, stalked their prey. They planted themselves in freezing shadows, in doorways, the father scanning the streets, lit by neon bar signs watching for the lone unsteady gait.

The luck of the roll, he remembered his father calling these predatory outings, mostly on cold nights, often snowy nights, when the streets were deserted. Icy nights were best, his father believed. He would prod the child to act, to cross the path of the mark to deflect attention, while the father usually with a brick swiftly whacked the back of the target's head.

Usually the boy would ask the person for money. A simple question, no more. "Got a nickel, mister?" or "lady" as the case might be. They were no respecter of gender. It was all over in seconds. His father would go through the victim's pockets or lift the pocketbook, and they were gone. Never more than one a night and never in the same place twice.

In some seedy backwater hotel, his father would lecture him on the process: discipline and speed. The hit had to be hard, a single blow. The father showed him where, at the very back of the head. They never stayed long enough to assess the damage, although sometimes his father would read out stories in the papers about a man found dead, his skull crushed.

"Poor bastard," his father would comment, shaking his head. "What's the difference how we get there, laddie? Quicker the better."

He remembered war stories. Vietnam. His father had been one of the earliest to go. Death don't discriminate, his father told him. He could remember a whole series of little one-liners like that. Flesh and blood all we are. Dust to dust, meaning nothing to nothing. Oblivion to oblivion. The trick is get out without getting hurt.

And yet it was a life not without affection. His father loved him and had professed to love his mother. If tears were evidence, then the verdict was inescapable. Talking about Champion's mother always stirred his father to visible grief.

Of his father's love he had no doubt, none at all. Your dear old Dad loves you, laddie, his father assured him often. He was never unloving or neglectful. Considering their occupation and lifestyle, it was a confusing legacy. Early on, his father had excised conscience and guilt from his repertoire of emotions. No wonder he could take up a life of killing for profit without regret. This memory was Champion's justification.

Later, he had calculated that that life with his father had lasted for two, maybe three years. His four to seven, he had estimated. They had lived like nomads, one hotel after another. Sporadically, he remembered his father, women, and booze, but only brief passing images. Medicinal and mental, his father assured him. Your mother was the light of my life, laddie.

Then suddenly it was over. In his memory was the wet feel of his father's cheek as his own boyish lips lay against it, the musky smell of an old overcoat, the roughness of his father's hands grasping his. Words, too, came back, the voice, graveled by sadness. Something about a boy needing a stable home, an education, friends his own age, the voice said.

It hadn't made much sense at the time, this "reupping."

"I'm a soldier, laddie. A real good killer." He had winked, groping for levity.

He'd be back, his father promised. Cousin Annie and Jacob and their kids would be his home till then. Only his father never did come back, and the so-called home was more an exercise in endurance and toleration than caring. He never blamed his father for planting him in such arid soil, and the first chance he got he left.

"Skip my father," he told her. "He doesn't conform to your view of innocence."

Someday, when he was certain that history had become irrelevant, he would tell her about the life of this other person. It was more of a hope than a promise.

They rose, showered together, dressed. Then they ground coffee beans, made coffee and brought steaming mugs to the patio that looked out to a pine forest. They watched each other over the rims of the mugs, drawing comfort from eye contact. It seemed unbearable to be physically apart, and periodically they had to touch each other for reassurance, as if the dreamlike consistency of this powerful new relationship needed the validation of the flesh to prove its reality.

Later, after the morning coffee, it was their practice to drive into the town and meander through the market to buy food for the remainder of the day. Today, of course, was different. She offered no hint of her plans, just as she had evaded the subject from the beginning. Thus, aside from the anxiety of time, it was a morning like any other in the past few days.

Then, suddenly, it became different.

"I adored my father," she said, as if she had been mulling it over since he had rejected any reference to his own. "He was the love of my life."

She stopped speaking suddenly, leaned over and kissed him, this time on his eyes. "Until now." Her kisses had shut his eyes, and suddenly when he opened them, her face seemed to have frozen in a strange faraway expression, as if she had just remembered something she had long forgotten.

"What is it?"

"Of course," she said, after a long pause. "That must be it."

"What?"

"Why it happened. The David."

"Your experience in Florence?"

She smiled, her face glowing with revelation.

"Everything has a reason, I suppose."

"Even us."

"It probably still qualifies as innocence," she said, laughing as if she refused to carry the burden of the day's decision. "I'll let you be the judge. But it's a secret that must be told. I don't know whom else I would tell it to. I never have confessed it."

It worried him to hear her tell secrets. It might force him to reciprocate before he was ready or, more to the point, before she was ready to accept them.

His secrets were darker, blacker. She would surely think them monstrous. He brightened suddenly. They wouldn't, of course, be his secrets, but secrets belonging to that other person, the one he had discarded like a snakeskin.

He had often observed what he had assumed were lovers talking together in low tones, intent on conversations that had always appeared to be urgent and important, and he had remembered wondering what was so interesting that it would induce such self-absorption. As this other person, he had experienced the torture of envy. So this is what lovers' talk is about, he thought happily, watching her face.

"This is my secret of secrets," she had prefaced. "And you must promise not to laugh or think I have violated our pact."

"I promise," he said.

"It explains everything."

"I'm listening."

"I was, perhaps, five. We were living in upstate New

York. My father was a high school teacher."

"Too much history," he said, realizing suddenly that he was being playful, another alien experience.

"I was hiding under the bed in my parents' room. For some reason then I loved to hide under beds. It was also so mysterious under a bed, dark. My mother loved dust ruffles. It was morning. I think it was spring. Yes, spring. Mother had sprigs of yellow forsythia in vases everywhere, fresh cut from our garden. They had no idea that I was under their bed."

He smiled as he watched her, reaching out, stroking her arm.

"No. I did not hear strange noises, sexual purring. I did hear the bed creak, and I peeked out under the dust ruffles to see my father's bare feet swing over the bed and plant themselves on the floor almost touching my nose. I saw the feet move then lifted the dust ruffle further. What I saw was the image that connects with what happened in Florence." She lifted a finger and wagged it in front of him. "You promised not to laugh."

"So far it's not very funny," he said.

"I don't mean laugh because of funny. I mean laugh because of—well, you be the judge. Anyway, I peeked out further and saw him standing in a shaft of sunlight, gloriously naked. His body was smoothly muscular. And I saw all of it. Everything. It was my first look at that part of him, my only look. At first it was a shock. These strange objects hanging there from a bed of jet black curls. I stared upward, mesmerized, looking at these objects. Also the way he stood.

The way he held his arms. The way his legs were planted."

"Did the sight frighten you?"

"At first, then it thrilled me. I… I can never be sure about this. But the thrill made me tingle all over. I think I had an orgasm."

"At five?"

"Then in Florence. I saw Michelangelo's David standing there, this giant, naked. There I was, watching it from a similar angle, seeing this perfect marble man, perfect in every way. His phallus, his testicles, large and wonderful. I felt a sudden shuddering ecstasy. Waves of thrilling pleasure washed over me. I had thought at first that it was Aunt Emma's sexy talk that had been the only factor in my arousal. Now I know it was more than that. My childhood memories, my years of repression, and of course, the exquisite erotic beauty of the David. Is that possible? Of course, it is. I'm sure of it. I experienced it. And then I saw you, and I have been suffused with ecstasy ever since."

"But I'm not marble, I'm flesh."

She leaned over and pecked him on the lips. "Now you can laugh. You've just heard my secret of secrets. So there. I have shared an intimacy with you as profoundly private as anything I could imagine."

"Are you suggesting that I'm a stand-in for your father via Michelangelo?" The question masked his accelerating anxiety.

"Sounds perverted," she said with mock coyness.

"Well, am I?"

"It's too mysterious to understand," she said, giggling

girlishly. "Nevertheless…" She paused. "Not every ques-tion has an answer." She shrugged. "There is a connection. Has to be. I think… or…"

"Or what?"

"Maybe I imagine when I am with you…" she hesitated, "…that I am in David's embrace."

He laughed.

"I can't imagine—" He began. But she quickly put her fingers on his lips.

"I can," she whispered. "You think I'm mad?"

He nodded.

"I accept the condition. Gladly."

She giggled, then stood up and insinuated herself on his lap, nuzzling her nose into his neck, and they entered a long silence together.

Watching her, he put aside the banter. Was this her way of preparing her departure, interpreting her attraction to him as a fantasy induced by a work of art, which somehow connected to a childhood experience? Was it too painful for her to approach directly, forcing her to rely on this to ex-plain herself, to justify the transiency of their affair?

Searching her face, he looked for any signs of a decision, either positive or negative. He found none. Only a lover's face, adoring and affectionate. Then why did she feel com-pelled to tell this story about her experience with her father and the David connection, on this, of all days?

He tried to put all this in perspective beyond the realities of her decision. At some point she would have to make it known. Perhaps, he speculated, she would opt to go back, sort out her past life, and return to him. He would not, could not, restrain her beyond her wishes. For the first time in days, he forced himself to consider practical considerations.

By now, he knew, they would have discovered the lie. Angela's husband would be scouring the Riviera for her, certainly enraged and justifiably confused. He needed an explanation. From what he had learned during their visit to Mrs. Hamilton, a great deal was at stake, and the grieving widow prodded by her two daughters was about to make a stand.

From his own earlier research into Max Hamilton's life and affairs, he could surmise a battle royal in the offing, with Angela's husband at the very center of the storm. Although he rarely considered who paid the freight for his various assignments, he felt certain that Ford was at the heart of it, the principal motivator, the one who ordered and paid for the hit.

Based on the bedrock principle of "who benefits most," he was willing to assume that Angela's husband was also the principal beneficiary. The question he asked himself now was how badly Angela's lies hurt the man's plans. Ford's response was a fearsome prospect. It was quite conceivable that a ruthless man like Ford would stop at nothing to gain his objective, including eliminating his own wife.

Tom Ford was undoubtedly a man who indulged in conspiracies and men with that bent usually believed that others were also conspiring against him. He might even believe that Angela was a part of such a conspiracy. The mere contemplation of such a possibility made Champion's blood run cold.

During the past few days, he had pushed such speculation to the back of his thoughts, although he was finding it difficult to keep from surfacing. In a practical sense, however, he was consciously forcing himself to deny the very existence of his pre-Angela self. It was impossible to obliterate memory, and although he had constructed avenues of physical escape from law enforcement authorities, he had not established any pathways to escape from those on whose side he had enlisted. It was common knowledge that no one had ever thrown off the shackles of the organization. He wasn't even certain it was an organization in the traditional sense.

All he knew was that it was ubiquitous, could reach anywhere, find and eliminate anyone. Indeed, he might have been assigned to eliminate former "members." He could never be certain. Parker, ridiculous little Parker, was his only connection, his only conduit. He had never questioned, never inquired beyond what was necessary to accomplish his mission. And he accepted the conditions of employment, which meant that he would forever be a nonperson.

He had struck his bargain with the devil for possibly two reasons. First, it was something he felt he was bred to—dark, sinister, challenging, exciting, on the edge; perhaps there was even an element of nostalgia in it. It was also a way to professionalize nonfeeling, no emotion, a living deadness. With life meaning nothing, what was there to lose? There was also skill in it and, he supposed, satisfaction.

The second reason, he speculated, was economic insulation, meaning enough money to completely foreclose on any issue of personal need and allow him the opportunity, if he so chose, to live a lifestyle of choice at whatever level of indulgence or personal whim. A life of ease and luxury was a periodic choice for him, not a necessity. Considering his early life, he had considered his elaborate lifestyle a form of vengeance. He knew, too, that access from an array of secret accounts could be cut off in a second without recourse. By prior agreement, withdrawals were limited to no more than two million a year, a tidy sum especially since, through clever manipulation, it was not subject to taxation by any government anywhere. Certainly enough to maintain an extravagant lifestyle if he so chose, and he often did.

Of course, it was neither a life nor an occupation for everyone. Participants, like him, had to be loners, without qualm or conscience, orphaned by life, haters who found in this work the key to a kind of selfish personal salvation. Parker characterized such people as maggots of civilization, who fed on the diseased carcass of mankind.

"We are the devil's spawn, old boy," he had said cheerfully. "Enter hither and you acquire a noncancellable lifetime membership. No way out, I'm afraid. We have an exit plan that is foolproof. It goes..." He demonstrated with a chop of his hand across his neck. "Poof."

There had to be a way out, had to be. By the very nature of his transformation, he had resigned from the organization, cancelled his membership. Poof, he whispered. But then life had also taught him that nothing was foolproof.

There had to be ways to live beneath the scrim, to exist outside the line of fire. Had he the cunning and skill to outwit them? No matter if she stayed with him or went back to her other life, he could never go back to his. Never.

Although she showed little outward signs of contemplating consequences for herself, she had to be considering what she had to face if she returned. It would not be a simple process at this stage for her to reinsert herself into her old life. She was the first to break the silence, but only after they had engaged in a long lingering kiss.

"Tomorrow is Friday," he said finally. It could no longer be avoided.

"I know."

He saw the flicker of pain in her eyes. She looked at the tall clock, frowning at the time.

"Our enemy," he said.

She nodded agreement.

Chapter 26

They sat at the usual table at their favorite of the two cafés in the village. The regulars, now familiar with them, looked up and nodded. The waiter, a roly-poly middle-aged man wearing a much-abused tuxedo, brought their regular order of café au lait for two and a wicker basket of rolls and brioche.

Tastes, smells, sounds, the feel of everything, even items as commonplace as the rolls, or the heft of the extra large cups that held their café au lait, encapsulated for her an enriched sense of living. With this man beside her, life was more, feelings deeper, colors more brilliant, sights more defined and enchanting.

She had been especially attentive to any signs of diminishment of the heat of this fire between them. None came. If anything, the intensity of their entwined lives increased. Be sure, Aunt Emma had said.

Even their lovemaking, which she thought at first would be a barometer of romantic longevity and would define the reality between them was, although still as intense as ever, symbolic of something deeper than mere pleasure. There was, she decided, more here than lust or transient desire. By then, she had eliminated the idea of "cock fever."

She was well aware of the risks she had undertaken, and what she would face if she did return. As she had told Aunt

Emma, this event had to be played out, come what may. Had it been played out yet? Far from it.

From the very beginning, she had secretly believed that the experience would provide a hint of its ending. So far it hadn't. The options were still open. She could go back to the States, face the music, find a way to justify her actions, and, if possible, return to the normality of an unfeeling life. Thereafter, she would hold this experience in memory, a kind of brief encounter, revisited in imagination, providing images to warm the cold future.

Or she could go back, wind up her past with some grace and return to Champion, a practical idea that had been rattling around in her mind for days. Would he be there for her when she returned? Or would her absence somehow break the spell?

Tom, of course, would be furious. She would undoubtedly be punished in some way. Perhaps there would be legal repercussions, embarrassing arguments, and hassles. What was that against the experience of a lifetime?

Then there was the ultimate option. Turn her back on yesterday. Against what she was now living, everything else that had gone before in her other life was pallid, lifeless, stupefying. She could barely recognize that person who lived in the skin of the old Angela. Her past, she concluded, was a life of lies. And so the moment of truth had arrived. To be or not to be. She knew it preyed on his mind as well, although like her, he kept the anxiety deep inside himself. Again she searched herself for any sign of remorse or guilt for the action she had taken. She could find none.

The waiter brought a split of champagne and poured the bubbling golden liquid into their fluted glasses. The day's topper, they called it, another part of their daily ritual. To them, champagne was their private nectar, a ritual, both a symbol of their meeting and a glorious refreshment.

Neither of them proposed a toast, obviously fearful that it would sound a note of farewell. They clinked glasses and drank. It was difficult getting the liquid down. It took all her discipline to hold back her tears. She could not show him that.

"Help me," she whispered.

"I can't," he replied.

She stood up suddenly. There was only one person in the world to whom the question could be put.

"Be right back, darling," she said.

Finding the pay phone that she had used when they had first arrived, she used her credit card and mastered the connection as before. A strange voice answered.

"Have I got the right number? Is this Emma Harper's residence?"

"Yes, it is."

"Whom am I talking to?"

"Maggie Thompson, a neighbor. I've been here since—"

"Yes, Maggie," she said pleasantly. "Aunt Emma told me about you. This is her niece, Angela Ford. May I speak to her please?"

There was a short pause, a slight sighing sound, a cough.

"You haven't heard?" Maggie Thompson said. There was no escaping the ominous note in her voice. Angela felt her heartbeat begin to smash against her ribcage.

"Heard?"

"I feel so awful telling you this. She's... well, she's passed on."

"Aunt Emma? Passed on? What are you talking about?"

"It was a shock to all of us, a terrible blow. She... she fell down the stairs, one of those freak accidents. Broke her neck. Died instantly, I'm afraid. At least she didn't suffer. Angela...?"

Angela felt a fainting sensation. The receiver slipped from her grip as her strength ebbed, and she dropped to her knees. The waiter was the first to notice, summoning Champion.

"My God! Angela!"

He knelt beside her and, noting the hanging receiver, quickly replaced it in its sling. She hadn't fainted. He helped her up.

"What is it, darling?" he asked, holding her. She was shaking.

"Is madame okay?" the waiter asked. Some of the customers had turned to observe them.

"I hope so," Champion said. He helped her up and got her to their table. She felt drained, limp. The waiter brought water. She sipped, recovering slightly. The sudden knowledge of her aunt's death had stunned her, like a physical blow to the solar plexus.

"Aunt Emma!" she cried. "I don't believe it. She's dead."

"Aunt Emma?" He seemed puzzled at first. "Oh, yes, the Emma of Florence.

"I… I spoke with her from here… just a few days ago."
She looked toward the phone, as if the horror of the truth
needed further validation to be believed.

"You called from here?" he asked, frown lines appearing
on his forehead.

She felt his glance bore into her, his eyes suddenly feral,
glancing from side to side, surveying the people around
him. His look puzzled her.

"How did she die?" he asked.

"How?"

She was trying to remember. Then the image of her aunt,
lying sprawled and broken came to mind. She shook her
head, hoping the image might disappear.

"You must tell me, Angela," he pressed.

"Maggie said she had fallen down the stairs. An accident."

"Who is Maggie?"

"Maggie Thompson. A neighbor."

Beyond her grief, she noted his interest in details. He
wasn't just inquiring. He was interrogating. She could not
understand this sudden businesslike interest.

"Where does she live?"

"Santa Fe."

"Did you use a credit card to call her?"

What had that to do with Aunt Emma, she wondered?

"Credit card?"

"You must trust me, Angela. Please. Tell me. Did you use
a credit card to call her?"

"Yes, my American Express but—"

"The first time as well?"

She nodded, mystified.

"Did she know where you were staying?"

"How could she? I don't know myself. And if she did know, she would never tell. Not Aunt Emma. Never."

Suddenly ashen, Champion sucked in a deep breath.

"We have to go," he said.

Getting up, he reached out and helped her rise. Putting some euros on the table for the check, he held her arm and gently moved her toward the car. Helping her inside, he walked quickly to the driver's side and got in.

"Go where…?" she began, still unable to fully comprehend what was happening. Aunt Emma dead? "I can't believe it," she said aloud, leaning her head against his shoulder.

"Stay calm, love," he said, gunning the motor. Before he hit the accelerator, she noted his inspection of the side mirror.

"What is it?" she asked.

He moved the car slowly down the street, his eyes still concentrating on the side mirror. When the car reached the corner, he swung it sharply to the right and floored the accelerator. The car jumped forward with tire-burning speed, heading toward the house.

"I think we have a problem, darling," he said as the car reached the top of its speed. "I'll explain. I promise. In the meantime, we have to gather our things and get out of the house as fast as possible."

Questions crowded into her mind, but she said nothing.

Whatever was happening, she trusted his actions. The car moved dangerously around winding curves. She turned to look out of the back window, saw nothing. Another sharp turn brought them to the gravel road that led to the house. When he reached it, he pulled up abruptly.

"Five minutes at the most," he told her. Holding hands, they ran into the house. She threw piles of clothes and toiletries into a single suitcase. He did the same, stopping occasionally to listen and look out the window. She had just started to pack her other suitcase, when he stopped her.

"There isn't time," he said, handing her a dispatch case that contained his laptop computer, while he picked up their two suitcases and they moved swiftly out of the house.

Motioning her to get into the car, he put the two suitcases in the trunk, jumped into the driver's seat, and drove the car swiftly back to the asphalt road, heading in the opposite direction of the village.

"Is someone following us?" she asked. Looking back, she saw nothing but empty road.

"Maybe," he replied.

"But no one is behind us."

"Please, darling. Trust me."

They kept to the side roads that wound through country villages. At one village, they stopped for gas, sandwiches, and a road map. The gas was self-service, and after setting the pump, she watched him inspect the car, check under the chassis as well as under the hood. When the pump stopped, he replaced the nozzle and paid the cashier while she waited in the car.

"Will you tell me what is happening?"

"Later."

"Where are we going?"

"I'm not sure."

It would not be a snap decision, she thought. It had whirled around in her mind for days, despite her desperate attempts to repress the idea of it. Postponement was no longer an option. Fish or cut bait, she urged herself. She had already distanced herself from the traditional, the conventional, the inculcated values she had observed all her life.

With Aunt Emma gone, there was no one to turn to—no one except him.

"Good," she said. "That's where I want to go."

Their eyes locked, and he bent over and kissed her.

Was Aunt Emma prodding her from the grave?

"You are my life," he sighed.

She embraced him and briefly kissed.

"I have something bad to tell you," he said, after they had disengaged.

"What?"

"Aunt Emma's death was not an accident."

She felt suddenly ice cold, and her teeth began to chatter. She moved closer into the crook of his arm.

They drove for an hour in silence. From time to time, he turned his face toward her, bent over, and kissed her. Despite this attention, her mind was on the terrible fate of Aunt Emma. Why? Aunt Emma, who lived life to the fullest. Aunt Emma? What had she done to deserve such a fate? He continued to glance into the side mirror.

There was little traffic along this new road, and he seemed to relax, looking less and less into the side mirror. His earlier actions strongly implied an ominous sense of danger, so far inexplicable. Despite her immersion in these perplexing events, her grief over Aunt Emma's death overrode any anxieties about her own personal safety.

Not an accident? A question arose in her mind that had lapped on the edges of consciousness since she had told Champion about her aunt's death. It had set off inquiries that seemed strange and out of context, like his questions about the manner of Aunt Emma's death and Angela's use of a credit card. What did it mean?

Up to that morning, she had managed to postpone thinking about the consequences of her actions. Now the full impact of her decisions came rushing through her defenses.

She had deliberately stepped across the safety line of caution, was in the process of trashing her old life, her old safe self, surrendering to the juggernaut of overwhelming passion. What did the piper now have in store for her in payment? Was Aunt Emma's life part of that exchange?

"Oh, my God!" she cried suddenly.

"What is it?"

"It seems so... so awful. I'm almost ashamed to think it."

"Think what?"

"That Aunt Emma's death had something to do with me... with what we've done."

She had expected him to dismiss such a thought as an aberration, an irrational assumption, a guilt reflex. Instead he was silent for a long time.

"Tell me I'm being ridiculous," she said. "How could it possibly be related?"

"Unfortunately you aren't being ridiculous."

He turned to face her briefly, then moved his head downward to touch her lips with his, as if to confirm this mutuality.

"I wish…" he sighed, but he did not complete the statement. Suddenly his train of thought was interrupted. He sprang to acute alertness, his eyes narrowing, as he looked ahead, up the road.

Just beyond a turning, a truck was heading downward from a dirt lane cut into the high ground above them. It moved relentlessly, its motor grinding as the driver edged it through the woods just above them toward the two-lane road on which they were driving.

Hitting the road about a hundred yards ahead of them, it turned toward them and moved swiftly along the inner lane. As it came closer, the driver edged the truck close to the line that separated the lanes, forcing their car to move precariously close to the edge of the ravine to avoid a collision.

As the vehicles drew parallel, the truck edged further over the line, coming directly at them.

"Hold on," Champion yelled.

She reached out and grasped the dashboard with both hands. Suddenly, Champion swung the wheel toward the oncoming truck, forcing the other driver to move swiftly to avoid a head-on collision. There was a slamming sound, the screech of metal against metal and a stunning display of sparks. But miraculously, their car was in the clear.

Champion stomped on the accelerator, and the car began a precarious journey along the winding road. Looking back, she saw the truck make a skillful U-turn and begin pursuit.

The suddenness of the near-death experience was just beginning to register in her mind. This was no accidental collision. This was a deliberate attack. By whom? Why? The questions tumbled in her mind. Was all this connected to Aunt Emma? To Mrs. Hamilton? And then the unspeakable occurred. Perhaps Tom?

She looked toward Champion. His expression seemed frozen. He was deep in concentration, his lips taut, his eyes dancing from the windshield to the rearview mirror. Turning, she noted that the truck was gaining, despite the Fiat's speed.

The road ahead wound beside the ravine, which suddenly seemed endless. There was no way to gain a clear view ahead. They rounded curve after curve at high speed, their bodies bouncing in tandem. The truck's pursuit was relentless, gaining at every turn until it was directly behind them.

She could see the driver clearly, thin face, pale complexion, his lips contorted in a cold smile as if he were enjoying the process. Rounding a curve, the truck veered to the inside lane, the strategy obvious, to force their car into the ravine.

The driver of the truck was apparently depending on its greater heft to do the job. But it occurred to her, even in the terror-filled moments of the attack, that the heft made the truck less maneuverable than the car.

Again and again, the truck smashed against the side of the Fiat as Champion fought the wheel to keep the car on the road.

Beside her, Champion was surprisingly calm, although his inner tension was evident by the perspiration that had sprouted on his face.

"Brace your knees against the dashboard," he called to her, glancing at her briefly, nodding gently as a comforting gesture. The truck continued to slam against the side of the Fiat with accelerating momentum, making it increasingly difficult for the car to hold the road. They were within inches of the edge of the ravine.

"Hold on," Champion shouted, as the truck swung toward them recklessly.

She closed her eyes and felt the pressure on her knees against the dashboard as the Fiat decelerated abruptly. The reverse force threw her across the front seat as he turned sharply and sped upward into a narrow break in the woods.

Behind them, they heard a loud crashing sound, then the reflection of a fireball, which briefly lit up the sky behind them. Their car ground to a halt within a hair's breadth of a tree that blocked their way.

For a long moment, they held their position. Champion slumped over the wheel, fighting to catch his breath. The momentum had wedged her into an awkward position with her legs twisted under the dashboard. It required a great deal of effort to extricate herself. Miraculously, she was unhurt.

She turned toward him just as he lifted his head. Noting an open cut over his eyebrow, she fished in her purse for a tissue.

"Well we've established one thing," he said.

"What is that?" she asked, as she put the tissue over the wound, dabbing it. It wasn't deep, and the blood was beginning to coagulate. Their gaze locked.

"There is a contract out on your life."

It sounded like a line in some bad movie. Contract? The concept was miles from her understanding.

"A contract on my life?"

She did not understand the nomenclature. Was he referring to a business thing? She studied his face. He seemed pained, conflicted.

"There are those who would like you... well, gone."

"Gone?"

"God, I wish I could avoid this," he whispered. "Dead, darling. They want you dead."

"They?"

She was confused. Who were they? Such possibilities never intruded on her life. But then, nothing she was currently experiencing had ever intruded on her life. Yet the evidence of their near-escape was compelling.

"None of this makes sense," she said. Despite the security of his nearness, she was becoming conscious of a numbing fear.

"Not in your world, darling."

It was impossible for her to correlate.

"Why me? Because of what I've done? Does it warrant...

my death? What can anyone gain from killing me?"

"I can't say."

"But you would have been killed as well," she said, sensing in herself a growing protest. The idea of his death seemed a greater blow than the prospect of her own.

"What's one more death to them? Your Aunt Emma, for example."

"Aunt Emma. Why Aunt Emma?"

Tears streamed down her cheeks. He spoke gently, barely above a whisper.

"They had assumed she knew where you were." His eyes searched her face as if he knew he was inflicting pain. She felt her stomach knot.

"Are you saying… dear lovely Aunt Emma. Because I… I didn't tell her where I was?"

He shook his head.

"It wouldn't have mattered. They would have killed her anyway."

How could he possibly assume all this? Again she searched his face for some measure of comprehension.

"How could you know this?" she asked.

He sucked in a deep breath.

"I know how they think. I know their power and their reach. I know them well," he said, clearing his throat. She felt him inspecting her face. She was silent for a long moment, searching for some rational understanding of his remarks.

"Are you saying that you know the people who did this to Aunt Emma?"

He nodded.

"Not in the way you might think. These people are… functionaries. To them it's a job, people for hire, experts with no emotional investment whatsoever. They are paid assassins."

"I still don't understand," she said, trying to tamp down her sobs. "Poor dear Aunt Emma."

"I'm so sorry to have to say this, darling. She had become merely a detour. They were covering their tracks."

She could find no logic in his remarks.

"How can you know these monsters?"

"I know them well. I am in the same business." He paused. "Was. No more."

She felt a thump in her chest, as if her heart was giving up its last beat. A wave of nausea gripped her. She gagged, then her lips began to tremble, and she had difficulty focusing on his face.

"You had to know sooner or later. Either we confront our histories or we live a lie. I can't live a lie any more, and I can't deny my past. I make no excuses, and I'm not proud of it. I've killed many people, most under government auspices. The CIA considered what I did heroic, noble. I was a soldier in a great war. And like any soldier, I killed for my country. In the last few years I have killed for profit without guilt or remorse. I'm sorry I have to tell you."

"I can't listen to this."

"You have to, my darling. And I have to tell you. I can't escape that anymore. I love you with my life. I never thought it would ever happen to me. Nothing means more to me than you. And yet, how do you see me now? I must seem like a monster to you. I see myself as a monster. For me, life has always been… well… meaningless. Until now. Until you."

She tried to find some anchor for her thoughts. She felt disoriented, totally confused.

"Forgive me, my darling. I am not what I seemed to be. I couldn't help myself. But then, I'm no longer who I was. Can you possibly understand? Is it possible to be transformed by—call it love or whatever. I am not the old me. The old me is dead. I could never kill again. Never."

She wanted to comprehend what he was saying. It was so far from anything that she had ever known in her life. Her David, a killer? Could she risk everything for a cold-blooded assassin? Again her poor Aunt Emma's words came back to assault her:

We are talking here of entering a dream of passion that transcends everything, that sweeps away reason, morality, judgment, conditions, appraisals, that defies analysis. Character? He could have been anything. The worst sinner, a moral nightmare or the most lily-white saint, of any race, religion, a beggar or a billionaire, stout or slender, tall or short, of any age beyond puberty.

"There is more," he said sucking in a deep breath. He hesitated, his eyes locking into hers. "I killed Max Hamilton," he said.

The irony of this last revelation exploded in her mind. Her body grew cold and trembled. A tiny scream gushed out of her throat. Had she entered a nightmare? Where had her David gone?

"I was the instrument," he pressed on. "But not the originator. I'm not looking for absolution, darling. I am beyond redemption. If there is a hell for sinners, I am a prime candidate."

He closed his eyes and shook his head.

"Believe me this is the worst moment of my life. I am part of the chain reaction that leads us to where we are…" He paused, wiping away a sudden onslaught of tears with the back of his hand. She looked at him, confused, disoriented.

"Who would do this?" she asked, recovering her balance, growing thoughtful. "Who is so evil…?" She tried to steady herself sensing that there was more horror to come.

"I can't be certain, Angela. But as hateful and horrendous as you may find me at this moment, the man you lived with all these years, the father of your children, would be the principal suspect."

"Tom?"

She was stunned. The revelation had an instantly sobering effect on her.

"Are you saying that he had Max murdered?" she managed to ask. It was all coming so fast, she had little time to absorb the implications of this confession.

He nodded.

"It seems obvious."

She felt her nostrils twitch. Her world seemed to capsize into a whirlpool.

"Aunt Emma? Now me? Are you saying my own husband wants to kill me as well? I don't believe a word of it. Not Tom. Kill the mother of his children? And Aunt Emma?

That makes my whole life a mockery. Tom, a murderer? Ordering Max Hamilton killed? What are you saying? I can't conceive of such a leap of faith. I'm sure he's angry with me, furious in fact. But to have me killed? No. You can't live with someone for more than two decades and suspect him of such a horrendous act. No. I can't believe it. I'm sorry. It's not grounds enough."

She shook her head wildly, as if trying to dislodge the possibility. Where am I? she wondered. And yet, they had both escaped from someone bent on destroying them.

"So it would seem."

"How could he live with such a thing?" she blurted, her mind clear now as if a kind of survival mode had set it. "He's the father of our children. I can't believe he is so evil. To order Max killed? It's crazy. And me? His wife? True, my little lie may have had some impact, but this? How can I hurt him enough to…?"

"I know it's not the world you believed you lived in," he said watching her face.

A sudden rage engulfed her, boiling her insides. The heat of her anger became unbearable. This couldn't be, she railed at herself, desperate to jettison the information from her mind. He tried to embrace her, but she fought against it, pounding her fists into his chest shouting. "Killer. Killer. How could you?" He sat there taking the blows until her energy ran out. Then she waited for some form of reason to return. Logic kicked in. Then questions.

What was happening here? Was it possible he was making all this up for his own sinister reasons? Was he manipulating her? She studied his face. Could she believe this man? This killer.

It will not matter what he is or what he has done, Aunt Emma had told her, crashing again into her consciousness. The worst sinner, the most lily-white saint.

She felt the sudden deadweight of her own false history, the arid desert of lies and denial that she had inhabited. As she dwelled on it, sucked it into her mind, her anger intensified. The sky was falling, closing in on her. She felt on the verge of suffocation.

As if to save herself, she opened the door of the car, jumped out, and began to run up the dirt road.

Her mind roared with conflicting suppositions. Was this the penalty for selfish pleasures? How could she be so naive, so lacking in perception and insight? Maybe I deserve to die, she shouted inside herself, feeling a rising hysteria bear down on her.

She felt her breath come in gasps as she continued to climb. Where was reality? Where was fantasy? As she ran, she felt her mind settling, triggering memory. Aunt Emma had made it clear that the true passion was a blind guide, that nothing mattered except the experience itself, whatever the danger and risk involved.

Hadn't they agreed to ignore the past, forget history, destroy the old baggage? Surely hers, as presently revealed, showed an equally perverse perspective. But to die at the hands of her husband was beyond all reason. It was impossible to believe, impossible to project. Yet if true, it would be the ultimate insult of her entire life.

She began to slow. Behind her she heard movement, and when she turned he was there.

"Can you forgive me?" he said.

"Forgive?" she whispered after a long silence. Her heart was pounding, her breath came in gasps. She paused, looked into his eyes feeling the intensity of his gaze.

"I am no longer the man of my past," he said.

"Can that be possible?"

"Answer that question for yourself, darling."

She allowed her mind to grapple with the question. Was his past, what he did before he met her, really relevant? And hers? Had they really been reborn, truly?

"Why am I here then?" she whispered. She hadn't intended the question to be asked aloud. "And you?"

Like a bell tolling in her head, she heard the vibration of her aunt's voice, entering her mind with an earth-shattering clang: Did love transform everything? Their eyes locked for a long moment.

"As you said," he whispered. "Not every question has an answer."

They embraced suddenly and kissed deeply. When they disengaged, he took her by the hand and led her toward the car. She felt safer now, more rational. Suddenly she stopped and faced him.

"Will they keep trying?" she asked.

"Yes."

"I need to know why."

"We will find out."

Had she entered a dream or a nightmare?

Chapter 27

Cynthia hadn't expected to confront Parker ever again. But here she was five months later, sitting across from him at the same table in the seedy lager-smelling pub, surrounded by what appeared to be the very same cast of odd characters. A dark headless pint of stout stood between them. An untouched pony of sherry was at her elbow on the table.

Tom was scheduled to arrive the next day. A meeting had been hastily arranged with Lloyd at the Savoy. There was no time to lose, Tom had reasoned. Angela's visit with the mysterious stranger, whatever the motive, had further poisoned the well. The Hamilton women were hell-bent to thwart him. The meeting with Lloyd was designed to cut his losses and, hopefully, work out a deal that would avoid any long, drawn-out legal maneuvers.

It would be a showdown for Tom, who was prepared to make an offer to the Hamiltons that they couldn't refuse and to persuade them that the operational supervision of the vast business empire of the late Max Hamilton would be impossible without him. He had deliberately set up a system that only he and Cynthia could interpret. Cynthia was certain that Tom's persuasive powers would prevail.

As always when an important meeting was to take place, Cynthia played the role of advance man, setting things up, handling all "atmospheric" details. She had made certain that the suite that had been arranged for the meeting at the Savoy was letter perfect, well stocked with all the trappings for an important event.

Unfortunately, her own plan, unbeknownst to Tom, had not met with the kind of success she had expected. Now she berated herself for her overconfidence. The Hamilton "elimination" had inflated her expectations.

The autopsy results on Max, both by the French authorities and independent pathologists hired by the Hamilton women, had shown no evidence of foul play. This made an official finding of accidental death mandatory, although it did not silence the suspicion of the tabloid press.

The revelation about Angela's obvious betrayal, for whatever reasons, moved her to act swiftly.

"Delighted to oblige under the usual terms," Parker had told her when she contacted him through their usual method. She pictured him at his table at the Chelsea Pub, looking threadbare and pathetic in the gloomy atmosphere. The sour smell of lager seemed to permeate the phone line.

"It must be swift and sure," Cynthia had told him. "I'm betting the farm on this one."

She was, indeed. It would break her, but, considering the upside, it would be worth the effort.

In her own cryptic and oblique way, she gave Parker the name of the target and the salient details of Angela's odd journey, including Aunt Emma's address in the States and other information that might be helpful.

"Considering the time frame," Parker told her, "I can offer no guarantees."

"That's why I've put in a kicker," she told him.

"A kicker?"

"Double the incentive."

"My, my," Parker said chuckling. "A matter of life and death is it?"

"An apt characterization," she shot back, annoyed by his twisted humor. Yet, despite the monetary compensation offered, she suspected that the challenge meant more to this cramped little man than the money. Having gotten away with this dirty little business for years, he seemed to revel in pushing the envelope.

"Find her and do her," she told him. "The clock is ticking."

It was the best possible psychological moment for such an event to occur.

Nor did she have any doubt that Tom would marry her after Angela was dispatched. According to her game plan, he would have no choice. The risks of not obliging her would be too formidable for him to resist.

The speed with which Parker had pinpointed Angela's general whereabouts was astonishing. Cynthia was elated.

"Never difficult with a credit card," Parker told her over the phone in his usual elliptical fashion.

"Then we can expect swift results."

"We know the general whereabouts. We are pursuing the specifics with diligence,"

But her hopefulness was shaken when she learned from Parker of Aunt Emma's "accident." Tom had puzzled over it then dismissed it from his mind as mere coincidence. Nor did he mourn her passing, since he had begun to suspect that Aunt Emma was deliberately keeping information about Angela from him.

"She might have known exactly where our little lady was," Parker told her when she called on learning of Aunt Emma's accident. "But the old girl didn't tell. Poor thing. Not that it would have mattered." By then the meeting with Lloyd was being negotiated.

"And the man?"

"Yes, we did manage to pry that from her. She did say there was a man."

"Who was he?"

"She was not forthcoming on that point. Our colleague suspects she didn't know."

"So where are we now?" she asked, when she called again the next morning.

"Close."

"How close?" she had asked.

"Very," Parker said. "The credit card is a remarkable tool."

"How soon?"

"If I was a betting man, I'd use hours as my marker," he said.

"From your mouth to God's ears," she said.

"I would leave Him out of it, my dear," Parker said. "I rather think he would disapprove."

She felt buoyed by his optimism.

"I am off to London tomorrow."

"Well then, perhaps we will have a celebratory potion," Parker said.

But when next she called Parker, moments before leaving for London, his report was ominous.

"A temporary balls up, but we're on to them," he told her, his voice reflecting a subtle note of defensiveness she had not detected before.

"We have a time problem, Parker," she rebuked. For the first time since these new arrangements had been made, she felt the cutting edge of frustration.

"I must see you," she said.

"I am your obedient servant."

"I'll be there as fast as I can."

After the Savoy suite had been arranged, she took a cab to Parker's "office" in Chelsea.

"There is something strange going on," Parker told her when they were finally face to face again, offering less preliminaries than on the occasion of their first meeting. He took a deep sip of his lager and wiped the moisture from his lips with the back of his hand. "Very strange."

For the briefest moment, she caught in his expression a tiny flicker of uncertainty.

"Strange?" Cynthia asked, making a monumental effort to repress a flash of panic.

"We had them in our sights," Parker said, without the necessary vagueness of their telephonic communications. He sighed, shrugged, and took another deep sip. It was as if he needed the liquid as fuel.

"The failure to bring the matter to fulfillment is baffling. A car over a cliff is an excellent dispatching method. A perfect little setup. High topography. Lonely road." His jowls shook as he moved his head from side to side. "Perhaps our man's vehicle was faulty. Or…" Again, he paused and lifted his glass, taking a deep draught, almost to the bottom. "…he was up against someone who was aware of his method."

He drew in a deep breath. "Blind luck for our quarry, I'd say. Lost a good man, poor darling."

At that moment he paused again and removed his glasses revealing mousy little eyes, without color, black as granite. They seemed to throw off shooting beams of malevolence. He blew on the lenses and wiped them off with a filthy handkerchief he had withdrawn from the side pocket of his trench coat. She was relieved when he perched them back on his nose, disguising the chilling glint in his eyes.

"Believe me, we do not take such things lightly. An operative is an enormous investment, difficult, if not impossible to replace. It took some doing, but we did not allow ourselves to miss a beat. It didn't take long to find her again."

"And him?"

"Off in a puff of smoke."

"You lost him, but you found her?"

"Then lost her again." Parker sighed, as if he were talking about a missing pet.

Cynthia felt the thump of her heart. It was getting more ominous with each revelation of his narrative.

"She passed through de Gaulle Airport with tickets to New York on Air France."

Cynthia was stunned. Was she coming home after all, the repentant sinner? Her heart sank.

"Was she alone?"

"So it appeared."

She felt the hot glare of his Coke-bottle lenses focused on her, perhaps seeing inside her.

"But, you see, she was not on the plane at the New York end," Parker said, shaking his head, pausing to contemplate his own thoughts. He lifted his glass again, swallowing the liquid down to the dregs. But he didn't signal the barman for a refill.

"Amazing," Cynthia said relieved. "One would think dear little Angela was an escape artist."

"Actually, she made no attempt to hide her own identity."

"And the man?"

We have a name and a description. A tall, handsome blonde man. Albert Phillips was the name on his UK passport."

"Who the hell is he?"

"It's a false document. Albert Phillips died three years ago in Brighton."

She waited through a long pause, noting a curious little smile twist his lips, as if he were playing the cat to her mouse, doling out tiny revelations while holding back the ultimate secret. "There is enough evidence to lead us to believe that we are dealing with someone who is more than simply a bed companion."

"What does that mean?" Cynthia asked, trying to ward off a wave of fear.

"I'm afraid we are up against professionals."

"What makes you think that?"

"Little clues abound aside from the false passports. For example, the plates on the car he was driving are registered to a Japanese businessman whose car is in a storage garage in Paris. Never reported as stolen. The house that was rented: Paid for in cash in advance, six months ahead. No name given. That suggests planning. Then there is the matter of our colleague's demise. In retrospect one might say that he deliberately led our man to this high lonely road for exactly the results obtained. Then there is the airport caper, a ticket not used. Good advice from someone who truly knows the inner workings of the game."

"You make it sound as if you're dealing with Superman," Cynthia sneered. "If he is such a hot shot, why did he allow her to make a credit-card call?"

"My guess is that she was not informed of this prior to its use. Indeed, the lady used it a second time. This suggests that she was an innocent in these matters. My interpretation is that he simply did not know that she was making these calls or did not learn about it until it was too late." His twisted little smile broadened. "But the fact that she hasn't made any more calls using this method leads me to believe that she has now been warned of its danger."

"So now she has been instructed on what not to do."

"More than that. Much more. It can't escape her attention that someone is trying to eliminate her, him as well. She now must surely know that dear Aunt Emma has been dispatched to her greater reward. Worse, from her own experience, she might have deduced that Aunt Emma was deliberately scuttled. And the airport business suggests she is now being instructed in the elements of evasion." Parker shrugged. "By an expert who knows that the people stalking them have ubiquitous access."

"But who?"

"Someone who obviously knows how these things are done."

She inspected his face imagining that she saw in it genuine concern. Worry, in fact. It did not take a leap of faith to understand what might be on his mind.

"One of yours?" she asked.

"It pains me to think about it." The smile disappeared. "Yet it is so out of character." He seemed lost in thought.

"Why?"

He spoke as if talking to someone in space.

"Our people are loners. They travel alone. They work alone. They live alone. They trust no one. They perform their mission then disappear. But never, never, under any circumstances would they carry baggage, especially not a lover. For them, such an involvement is a ticket to the grave."

Her mind started to race with possibilities. Without thinking, she lifted the glass of sherry and upended it in one gulp.

"He probably has total control of her," Cynthia said. "She's not that bright. There's no question that she's been enlisted in the cause of our enemies." An errant thought intruded. "Is it possible that one of your agents might have been seduced by... higher compensation?"

"Anything is possible. But money does not buy immortality, not in our shop. Betrayal and resignation are capital crimes in our world. The sentence is an immediate death penalty."

Parker raised his hand to get the attention of the barman, who, seeing the signal, nodded and poured another pint. "If he's one of ours, he is suicidal." He offered his sly little chuckle, then rose and waddled to the bar to pick up his glass. Her discomfort with this new wrinkle made her detest the man more than she had before.

She tried to picture what his life was like. Wealth alone did not make a lifestyle. He was undoubtedly rich, but she suspected that his existence was pinched and wretched, although she admitted to herself she might be wrong.

Life had taught her that most people were seldom as they appeared. Tom, who projected the image of the good husband and family man, was a premier example of dissimulation. And what of dear sweet Angela, the devoted wife? From the most recent evidence, not at all as portrayed. And she, the dedicated self-sacrificing, flunky whore. Turn us all inside out and what have you? All of us, pressing our secret motives and perceived desires, plotting to gain our objectives.

From what Parker had so far conveyed, it looked as if she was being deliberately thwarted. She did not take kindly to this possibility.

"The problem you see…" Parker said, when he had returned to the table. He paused a moment to suck the foam from the top of his glass. "…is that it's harder to stalk someone who knows he or she is being stalked. Oh, in the end, we get them. We always have. But we are dealing here with an expert evader who could keep us going for days, perhaps months."

Cynthia felt the full weight of her depression, although her mind did spin with ideas, none of which were particularly encouraging.

"We don't have that luxury."

"I'm very well aware of that." Again, the twisted smile rose to his lips, and she felt that his little cat-and-mouse game was about to reach a climax. "Nevertheless, my dear, all this prologue means we must proceed with extreme caution. This time we will be prepared to reinforce our options." He belched then took another sip on his lager. The man was both devious and oblique.

"I don't understand."

"Your little lady is in the UK. She has reserved a room at the Savoy under her own name."

Cynthia was stunned by the news.

"And the man?"

"We're not certain."

"But why the Savoy?"

"What does it matter? She will soon be a matter of past tense."

Perhaps, after all, Tom's original speculation was correct and Angela had been coerced. She was, therefore, a bargaining chip, and Lloyd and the Hamiltons had something sinister in mind to extract more from Tom than he was prepared to give. On the other hand, Angela could be a willing partner in their grand game.

"It has a logic," she said, checking herself from going further. Motives were not Parker's bailiwick.

"There is an aberration here," Parker said mulling it further. "We must assume she is advertising her presence, an anomaly for someone who knows she is being targeted and is apparently accompanied by an expert in the evasion arts. They've already taken out one operative. I can't let this happen again.

"Yes, I understand, very bad for your overall business. My only interest, however, is the woman."

"We mustn't lose time then," Cynthia said, her hopes rising.

"No, we mustn't," Parker said, raising his glass and taking a deep sip. "Unfortunately, we have been forced to employ more people than normal."

"Which will cost more, I suppose."

"I'm afraid so. We are dealing here with a formidable foe. She is under his protection. He knows what he's doing, and we need the insurance."

At that point, she had little choice and agreed to the added compensation.

"Unfortunately, I must expose our very best man to the prime event. If he is thwarted, others will immediately step into the breach. I cannot emphasize how important this operation is to our future."

"And to mine.

"You were quite pleased with our previous work for your people. Believe me, we will get similar results."

"Well, then, let's get on it," Cynthia pressed, somewhat relieved. "My only interest is the woman," Cynthia repeated. "The man is your problem."

"Of course, dear lady," Parker said. "The man is indeed our problem."

Chapter 28

They had slept for a few hours in the car in the parking lot of the port terminal building on the French side. Leaving the car in the lot, they boarded the boat to cross the channel.

Champion knew that any hope of a future for him and Angela depended on finding a way to deflect the contract on her life and his own, an inevitability now that he had chosen to leave the killing arena. He suspected that it was Angela's husband who had put the plan for her demise into motion. To checkmate such a move required, above all, information. He could not react in a vacuum.

Earlier, it took a single phone call to a receptionist in Tom Ford's office to determine that Ford would be heading to the United Kingdom for a meeting at the Savoy. From this, he assumed that Ford might be negotiating with the Hamilton women and their lawyer. A plan was beginning to hatch in his mind.

While they waited for the train at the Folkstone station, he made a pay-phone call to the Savoy and reserved a room in Angela's name.

"Is she with the Ford party?" the reservation clerk asked.

"Why do you ask?"

"Miss Bilton checked in earlier."

"Who?"

"Cynthia Bilton, Mr. Ford's associate. He is scheduled to

arrive tomorrow."

He tucked the name away in his mind.

"No. She is not with that party."

After making these arrangements, he called Parker. It had been his pattern to call him at least once a month to determine his next target. He hoped that Parker would see this call as routine, but his real motive was to glean some information about the status of the Angela Ford assignment and how the death of one of Parker's operatives had impacted on the situation.

"Most fortuitous. Most fortuitous," Parker said when he heard Champion's voice.

"How so?"

"Are you in easy reach of London?"

"Yes."

"Brilliant. We have work for you," Parker told him. Champion had hoped for such a reaction. By now, considering the success of his evasive tactics, Parker might suspect that he was the man accompanying Angela. Worse, the elimination of one of his operatives would be evidence enough that he was defecting, and defection in Parker's eyes was a mortal sin that carried the death penalty. Champion knew he was playing a dangerous game, deliberately putting Angela and himself in harm's way by reinforcing Parker's probable suspicions.

Parker, after all, could not ignore the circumstantial evidence. Hamilton had been eliminated in southern France, and it was no secret that Angela had been in Cap Ferrat. Also, his call at this very moment was too obviously coincidental not to be factored into Parker's speculation.

Parker, Champion knew, never acted in haste. He was not about to lose a trusted operative on mere suspicion. Here was his opportunity for absolute proof.

"Angela Ford," Parker said. "Does that name mean anything to you?"

Champion sensed Parker's gamesmanship.

"Nothing."

"We expect the usual dance. Only this time it's a duo. She is with a man, too clever by half. They must dance together. Both. Do you read me?"

"Clearly."

"Both," Parker repeated. "And swiftly. This is a tricky business. There is no time for your usual careful planning."

He could hear Parker's labored breathing.

"Instructions?"

"Later."

Parker abruptly broke the connection.

"Why are you smiling?" she asked when he had returned from the telephone booth. He knew his tactics confused her, but she did not question them.

"I have been assigned to eliminate you," he told her.

She did not return the smile. Instead, she pursed her lips, and her eyes studied his face. Her attempt at control was betrayed by a little nerve tic in her cheeks and widening of her nostrils as if she needed to suck in more air.

"Well then, here I am."

He forgave her the sarcasm. Perhaps she needed it as a defense mechanism. Nevertheless her response panicked him, indicating that he had not yet earned her unqualified trust.

"He wants me to do your mysterious companion as well," he said.

"Meaning?"

"Yours truly," he shrugged.

"Kill yourself?"

He nodded and smiled suddenly.

"In what order is this to be done?" she asked.

"My option," he said with a wry chuckle.

His light touch seemed to relax her.

"That means that he might not know whom this companion might be," she said.

Champion grew thoughtful.

"Of course he suspects. This means that a backup team has been assigned as well."

"A backup team?"

"Two people. When it comes to enforcement, he takes no chances." He paused, shrugged and smiled. "When their suspicions are confirmed, they will act."

"My God!"

"You must trust me on this," he whispered, letting the words hang in the air for a long moment. They had earlier discussed the issue of running, disappearing together, creating new identities. They would find us, he told her. From them, there is no place on earth to hide.

The London train arrived at the Folkstone station, and they entered the first class compartment. Seating themselves, they were the only passengers in the compartment.

She leaned against him, caressing. He kissed her hair and they sat in silence.

"I still can't believe it's Tom who is…" she said out of the blue, indicating her thoughts. Her words trailed off but he could not escape their meaning.

"Who is Cynthia Bilton?" he asked.

She frowned and cocked her head.

"Cynthia? Tom's assistant?"

He told her what the room clerk had told him.

"Would she know?"

"More than likely," Angela said. "She is his eyes and ears in business."

"Only in business?"

"It never occurred to me…" She frowned and her voice trailed off. "She is a plain, efficient woman, a loyal retainer…" She shook her head. "No, not Cynthia. I couldn't conceive it."

"You could be wrong."

"Why not. I am discovering that most of my life I have been wrong." She looked at him. "Until now."

"It could explain why there is a contract out on your life, Angela."

"So you think they are in this together?"

"It would seem so."

"And I'm the obstacle to their…"

"It does seem logical."

She was silent for a long time, obviously looking inward. This situation was obviously light miles from her previous life's experiences.

"It's so impossible to believe. Tom, my husband of two decades… and that woman?" She squinted as if she were in pain. "Am I the most foolish human being on earth? Where was my insight?"

"Evil people are the most cunning among the human species. When you cast aside moral inhibitions, everything is possible. There is no such thing as honor, decency, and compassion. They can wear a million disguises to hide their real intent."

She averted her gaze, suddenly troubled.

"You would know that," she murmured.

He nodded.

"I was afraid of that," he sighed.

"Afraid?"

"That you would judge me by my past."

"That's the way I'm judging myself," she said. "I hate my old self."

"So do I, my old self. Who was I?"

She seemed to turn the matter over in her mind.

"I'm not the least bit interested in your old self," she said reaching for his hand and bringing it up to her lips.

"Neither am I."

"I'll take what I see."

"So will I."

The train continued to speed through the English countryside.

"What happens when their suspicions about you are confirmed?" she asked.

"It is a bridge I have to cross."

"Not alone," she said.

"Not anymore."

She was again silent for a long time, caressing him.

"Well then," she said. "Since we are both in danger, we must make every moment count."

She lifted her face to his and their lips joined deeply, while her hand unzipped him. Then she got up, and drew the curtains of the compartment.

"Here?" he asked.

"Anywhere, darling. Everywhere."

She raised her skirt and lifted herself on his lap and straddled him and rotated her body in a circular motion. Her tongue darted against his, her body's movements accelerating with the heat of her passion. Their mutual orgasms came quickly, and she stayed in this position until his tumescence receded, and they disengaged. She nestled in the crook of his arm as the train sped toward London.

"Are you afraid?" he whispered.

"No."

She closed her eyes, but he could tell she was not sleeping. Suddenly she said, "All the boundaries you have lived within fall. Nothing is as it was. Consequences mean nothing. You are set free, floating on a magic carpet."

"What?"

"Something Aunt Emma said."

He nodded, knowing what she meant.

Chapter 29

"The Savoy," Parker told him on the telephone. He was calling from a kiosk in Victoria station. "She has reserved a room under her own name."

"And the man?" Champion asked.

"One must presume he is with her," Parker said. He was silent for a moment. "I am expecting a very creative scenario."

Champion knew the shorthand. A murder suicide or a double suicide would do nicely in Parker's book. The testing process had begun.

"And quickly," Parker added, hanging up.

"Fat's in the fire," he told her in the taxi, as they drove toward the Savoy. A few blocks from the hotel along the Strand, he tapped the glass and instructed the driver to stop. He embraced her and whispered:

"Register, go up to the room, and await my call."

He watched her back, receded, and waited to give her time to register. Entering the lobby, he scoped the area and spotted the two backups immediately, one in a chair allegedly reading a newspaper, the other standing at a bulletin board noting the day's events. Instinct, he chuckled to himself. Takes one to know one. He knew that they could not fail to spot him. He was sure that Parker had shown them his photographs.

He had never seen them before but he knew them by instinct. They were both big men, telescoping the method they would use. Something physical. No firearms. Perhaps knives.

Certain now that he was spotted, he went to the bank of house phones and called Tom Ford's suite, letting the phone ring until the operator came on to announce that there was no answer, a stroke of luck. He had expected the Bilton woman to be inside. Then he called Angela's room and gave her the number of her husband's suite, two floors above hers.

He ascended the elevator to Angela's floor then walked up the two floors. Angela was waiting. Without a word, Champion manipulated the easily picked lock and let them both into the suite.

"First things first," he told her.

"I hope I can handle it," she confessed. Together they had roughly calculated the risks. Closure for both of them, completely and irrevocably, was their only hope of a future together.

Champion inspected the suite with a practiced eye. It was obviously the largest and best appointed in the Savoy, with a view of the Thames, two adjoining bedrooms, and a dining room. The table was configured for a conference with places set for a number of people, laid out with lawyerly yellow pads and writing instruments and silver carafes. It was obvious that serious business was to be conducted here.

Champion moved around the suite, his keen eye searching for the best vantage. He knew that luck, skill, and experience were not enough to neutralize the unforeseen. At this point he was relying on assumptions.

He knew that Parker's conspiratorial mind was layered with suspicion. There was no way to fully calculate the imponderables.

What would baffle Parker the most were Champion's motives. Once money was discounted, Parker would be roaming a wasteland, the place where his world began and ended.

The man, Champion knew, could not possibly imagine the power of love. No way. For Parker, conscience, remorse, and greed were the traditional motivators of defection. Not that it mattered. Champion would soon deliberately confirm Parker's suspicions.

Then he heard the door opening. From their present vantage, they could see her but she could not see them. He noted that the woman was plain, nondescript, severely dressed in gray, hardly someone to be cast in the role he had accused her of.

"Her," Angela whispered, standing beside him, watching the woman through the crack in the half-opened door to a bedroom. He felt her sway against him.

"Stay," he commanded.

The woman fastened the chain lock and deadbolt and moved into the suite.

"I've been waiting for you," Champion said.

The woman was too stunned to move. Her complexion had turned ashen.

"Who are you?" she could barely expel the words.

"Parker's man," he said.

Her eyes nervously shifted from side to side.

"I think you have the wrong information." Her voice was tight with arrogance as she found her poise again. He inspected her face, the feral eyes, the determined jaw, the air of cold calculation.

"Do I?"

"This is absurd." She sucked in a deep breath then expelled it in exasperation. "What's happening here?"

"I'm on the job," he said, watching her.

"You're being ridiculous. I thought you people were professionals. I'm paying for this little caper, and I don't appreciate what's going on here."

He watched her in silence, observing her confusion as she made a valiant effort to hold on to her smugness.

"You're looking for Angela Ford. Not me. There must be some mistake. Ah, yes."

She grew thoughtful for a long moment then nodded, as if she had received an epiphany.

"I see what's happened," she said. "There are two Fords you see, the husband and the wife. This is the husband's suite. Thomas Ford." She looked at her wristwatch. "He's flying in from New York. You're looking for the wife. She probably registered as Mrs. Thomas Ford. I get it now." She offered a nervous laugh. "It could be cleared up in moment. Comedy of errors. You'll see."

She tried to put a brave face on the logic as she walked toward the telephone. "I'll call Parker. He'll confirm what

I'm saying."

As she moved toward the phone, he sprang at her before she could reach it and held her by the arm.

"Of course," she said. "Pay phones only. Of course, I understand. We can go to the street, find a kiosk…"

He continued to hold her arm.

"Get your hands off me," she said, trying to shake him off. "Believe me, you'll pay for this."

"Sorry," he said. "I have my instructions."

She continued trying to pry herself loose from his grip.

"But you're in the wrong place," she pleaded. He noted little beads of perspiration break out on her forehead. The arm he held felt suddenly damp.

"Why can't you understand?" she asked, the arrogance slowly giving way to abject fear. "I am your employer for crying out loud. I made these arrangements. Believe me, you're in the wrong place. Just check with the hotel. Can't you see? You've made a mistake."

"I don't think so," he said flatly watching her.

"He said you were his best man, the one who did Hamilton. Believe me, there is a mix-up here."

"No mix-up, Cynthia." Angela materialized in the room. He pushed Cynthia into a chair.

Cynthia was stunned, shocked into a sudden silence. She started to rise from the chair, but Champion pushed her back.

Angela stood before her, hands on her hips, watching her, her eyes giving off sparks of anger. "Dumb little Angela. So you both wanted me dispatched to oblivion, did you?"

"I… I don't know what to say."

"It must have seemed like a good idea," Angela said. "What a monster you are."

He watched Cynthia fight for control.

"Pot calls the kettle," Cynthia said, sneering, cutting a glance at Champion.

"You needn't have gone to such lengths," Angela sighed.

"Win some. Lose some." Cynthia said, her arrogance returning full force. "What does it matter now? I… we had you down as a blind silly little fool. And here you are. How long have you known?"

"You're right, Cynthia. I was a blind silly little fool."

Champion remained silently watchful.

"I'm really sorry, Angela. You could have gone to your grave none the wiser."

"How unfortunate for all of us," Angela said.

"We could have gone merrily along until you gummed up the works. He had the entire Hamilton operation in the palm of his hand. He still has, as a matter of fact, although thanks to you he might have to give away more than he bargained for."

She studied Champion as if she had noticed him for the first time. "Who would have thought it? Tom had her down as a frigid little bitch. Proves nobody really knows anybody."

"Well, we now know where he found sexual solace," Angela said, inspecting the woman with deliberate exaggeration. "Not very impressive." Angela struck him as remarkably composed.

"Where have you been, Angela? On another planet?"

The woman paused for a moment, her gaze roving from Angela to Champion and back. "I see. Not another planet at all. I suppose you've been having affairs like this all along. But this one is... made in hell. Imagine consorting with a killer, the guy who did Hamilton. There's irony for you. And you, stud, assigned to kill your little pussy here. There's a laugh."

"Yes," Angela said. "We had hysterics over that ourselves."

Cynthia eyed Champion up and down. "I'll say this, though. You've got good taste, Angela. Pick him up at the Bel Air, did you? Smell of blood turn you on? Never really bought the idea that you were on their side, although Tom believes it thoroughly." Suddenly she offered a malignant smile and turned to Champion. "Asshole. Why not pop the little bitch, collect your fee, and vamoose. Maybe I can square it with Parker, double your end. Get you a pardon for stepping out of line. What do you say?"

Champion shook his head slowly, his answer clearly articulated. Now she turned again to Angela.

"He's an idiot. Probably got all his brains in his dick. Well, now. What a clever little bitch you are. Tom's got all the ego and brilliance to deal with business, but none with women. He thought he had you properly labeled and shelved, taking you off the shelf on occasion for appearance's sake. Oh, I supposed he loved the children, but even that is somewhat doubtful."

She appeared to be unable to stop her compulsion to talk.

"He's an absolute monster, you know. We both are. But how could you?" She threw her head back and laughed. "Angela, ye hardly knew him," she said in mock brogue. "So where do we go from here. If I were you, both of you, I'd make a deal." She tapped her forehead.

"What sort of a deal?" Champion asked.

"Smart man, your stud," Cynthia said. "No downside. Five million. All I've got. It was going to Parker anyway for your…" She giggled hysterically and looked toward Angela. "For your demise. It was my party. Tom wouldn't have the balls for that. Call it his unspoken wish. It needed no orders from him, although he might make a big show of grief. He had no qualms with me arranging Hamilton's ending, thanks to your stud here. Yes, he's been more than generous, but then I've provided services par excellence. You see, we're made for each other, two peas in a pod. So… stop all this nonsense and lighten up. We can contact my bank now, get it done. I'll call our near-sighted little man and stop the deal. Then you two go off to Tahiti or wherever, and I'll promise never to darken your door again. Leave the way clear for Tom and me. Everybody gets what they want."

Again she focused on Angela.

"We're a natural fit, me and Tom. You say you didn't know that? Maybe not. Or maybe you did and just put it out of your little brain. Where did you think he was spending all that time away from home and hearth. And why not? I give good bed and great head and am a whiz at business myself. He can't do without me. You do your thing with this stud here, and I do mine."

Champion and Angela exchanged glances. Champion looked at his watch.

"Enough?"

"More than enough," Angela replied.

"No second thoughts?"

"None."

"As agreed then."

Angela nodded.

"What's going on here?" Cynthia asked, coming to the full realization of her predicament.

"Do her, please," Angela said. "For Aunt Emma."

"No," Cynthia pleaded. "No. Please. I'll do anything you want of me. Please. I was wrong. Please."

He moved swiftly, reaching into his pocket and pulling out two rolls of tape. Swiftly and expertly, he taped her to the chair then taped her legs together and her hands behind her.

"What will it matter? You're dead meat," she said to Champion. He taped her mouth and eyes then stuffed cotton in her ears.

When she was finally immobilized, Champion and Angela embraced.

"Your husband will find her."

Having foresworn any more killing, he felt somewhat cleansed by the thought, although he knew that Parker would not be so sanguine when Cynthia would lodge her complaint. A disgruntled client was as much of a threat as a defector.

They embraced, and kissed deeply.

"If we ran now, at least we would have some time with each other... before they found us."

He could not argue with her logic.

"Would you rather have a life or a moment?" he asked gently.

"I would settle for the moment," she said. "But I'd rather we took the risk for a lifetime."

He kissed her again then moved her away.

"You must go now, my darling," Champion said. "As we agreed. Have you everything?"

"Yes," she said, like a child presenting herself for inspection. She held up the new passport, the airline tickets, destination Florence, and the large envelope thick with cash.

"I don't know if I can do it, darling." Tears had sprung out of her eyes and were running down her cheeks. He shook his head and looked at his watch.

"Please hurry."

"I love you beyond life," he whispered.

"No," she said. "Nothing is beyond life. And my life demands your presence."

She kissed him deeply. With effort, he made her disengage.

"At the foot of the marble man," she said.

"I'll be there. I promise."

"When?" she inquired once again. Repeatedly asked, it was the question that had no answer.

"Soon."

"I'll wait forever," she said, turning, then hurrying out the door.

Chapter 30

As he knew they would, both men were following him. By now, they had surely checked Angela's room where they had expected to find her body. Again, he passed through the lobby. When he was sure they were following him, he started down the stairs.

Despite the danger, he felt the sweet effects of relief. Angela was safe. Moreover, he had kept the ultimate promise he had made to her. His killing self was over forever.

Cynthia would be silent for now. He was amused by the little drama they had acted out in Tom's suite and, in an odd way, pleased with the knowledge that Tom had not arranged for Angela's murder. He supposed it was a vindication of sorts for Angela's early life choices. Tom was, after all, the father of their children.

He reached the lower level of the hotel where it gave access to a rear entrance that led down to the promenade that fronted the Thames.

Knowing the mind of an assassin assured him that he was affording them opportunity, throwing it in their faces. Walking down the stone staircase that brought him to the level of the promenade, he crossed the street and began a walk along the balustrade. A few feet below was the inky blackness of the river.

The promenade was deserted at that hour. Darkness always chased the casual strollers, and, except for nearby houseboat restaurants, it was not a thoroughfare at night. Behind him, he could hear the approaching footsteps of the men. He patted his pocket, felt the bulge of surgical tape, bandages, antiseptic.

There had been no point in equipping himself with a bulletproof vest. He needed to expose soft tissue, take the gamble that the blade would not hit a vital organ—a mad gamble.

He felt certain it would be a blade, a swift plunging stroke. They wouldn't choose a garrote. That took too much time, even measured in seconds.

The possibilities were self-evident. They would take him from behind, one man. Plunge the knife into his heart, pull it out, then the other to assist in a speedy toss of the body into the Thames.

His body tensed. The footsteps were getting closer. His auditory senses were concentrated. Near a lamppost, he passed through a puddle of light.

Now, he told himself. Come and get me.

In the darkness between the two lampposts, a perfect spot for their purposes, he willed them to make their move. As if in sympathy, he heard the quick clatter of running steps. Waiting through milliseconds, he turned suddenly, just as the point man had lunged. He looked directly into his assailant's startled face.

As he had planned it in his mind, he stepped sideways toward the stone balustrade, keeping his body in range of his attacker. He knew the man would be an expert, plunging the blade into his chest, aiming for his right side, the target heart.

Champion was a student of the human body's killing parts, his stock in trade. He knew exactly the geography of its most vulnerable parts. His movement had deliberately deflected the clean stroke into what hunters call the oven. He felt the blade slide into his flesh. In and quickly out. The sensation was a sharp sting. Aside from the heart itself, he was alert for any arterial tear. He could smell the blood, feel its moisture. His mind raced with the specifics of the countermeasures he must quickly take to avoid a quick death, or a lingering demise by infection.

Again the assailant struck, lower this time, in the area of the abdomen, perhaps the liver. The sensation of pain seemed muted by the adrenaline rush, enough to free the energy to hoist himself to the top of the balustrade.

His plan was to allow the second man his role, waiting for the lift, the push then the plunge into the dark waters of the Thames. He would then linger in the water out of view, wait an appropriate time, then float downriver and eventually rise to the shore, apply first aid, and get himself to an emergency room. His mind functioned only in the context of that focus.

He must appear to his assassins to be dead meat, stabbed to death, and, as insurance, drowned, disposed of, liberated from the consequences of his defection.

But in the split second before he slipped over the balustrade, he felt one more jab of the blade somewhere in his back. He hadn't expected it and felt suddenly faint as a sharp pain shot through him. As he fell, this last seemed the most telling blow of all and his mind mentally x-rayed which part of him it had caught.

He might have fainted briefly, but he was quickly revived by the shock of the river's icy waters. He felt an onslaught of consciousness, prodding his mind to alertness, concentrating on a single goal.

Survival!

Focusing his energies, he struggled to bring himself beyond the pain, concentrating on summoning the will to stay afloat and move along with the tide and reach that point where he could crawl ashore. He could visualize the real objective of the exercise, the clear image of Angela, her face, her voice, her arms outstretched, beckoning. He felt an accelerating physical weakness. Her image began to grow dim, the sound of her voice became faint. He was losing her.

Then suddenly, he sensed that he was outside of himself, watching someone who resembled him, slipping into the wet blackness. The likeness merged with himself, triggering a tiny awakening of consciousness. He was below the surface of the river, choking, fighting to breathe, energy seeping away. He could barely find the strength to will his limbs to move.

By force of will, he popped to the surface, gulping hungrily at the air, faintly reviving awareness. He was floating now, like flotsam, unable to resist the tide that was carrying him helplessly away from the lights of shore.

His body felt numb. The pain receded and his mind

grew clearer. He knew that he had come to the end of his resourcefulness. Defeat was imminent. Yet even in the process of surrender, as the sound of his own death rattle echoed through the night, he could still sense of the power of Angela.

Angela!

For the first time in memory, he felt the extraordinary invasion of guilt. It consumed him, filling him with a fear far worse than the oncoming thunder of his impending demise.

What had he done to her? He had set her adrift, to float, like him, on the rushing tide to her own doom. Hadn't he ripped her away from her sense of place, something he had never had? If fate had not brought them together, she might have remained content. Wasn't it possible to live with contentment, even in a cocoon of falsehoods?

Yes, he treasured their few short moments together. It was the only real trophy of a life lived, mostly without real sensation, of frozen emotions, a life of death. She, their love, the glory and power of it were the only things of value that he was taking to his watery grave.

Don't wait for me, Angela. Forget I existed, he cried out to her in his heart. I have no right to die without you. At that moment he made another discovery of himself. He was afraid to go alone into oblivion.

He looked upward, saw a sliver of moon poking like a flashing light between passing clouds. Suddenly he felt enveloped, gripped by a force outside of himself, and he was aware of a rising sensation, carrying him upward toward the flashing light. Was he hallucinating? Was this the way death happened? Was this rising sensation carrying him to what he perceived now as the terror of oblivion?

Voices! Floating in the abyss. Fading in and out of his mind. And behind them the steady hum of a motor. Were they the voices of ghosts?

"Not much chance," a gruff voice said. "Nearly drowned and bleeding."

"Third I've fished out on these runs. Mugged, stabbed, and heaved into the drink. Old story," another voice said.

"Looks of him, he'll be maggot feed soon."

"Have you radioed?"

"Aye."

"Ask for an ambulance or hearse?"

Before disappearing into the void, he heard the sounds of laughter.

Chapter 31

It was early December, and the Christmas season was already in full swing in Florence. The city's piazzas were trimmed with necklaces of colored lights, and the stores were filled with shoppers. Hordes of tourists were already filling the ancient city for the Christmas festivities.

Insulated from the joyous spirit by the bleakness in her heart, Angela could sustain her hope only by visits to the Accademia where her David, the beloved marble man, eternally triumphant and forever poised to smite the giant, bore the only tangible reminder of her love.

After nearly four months, her obsessive vigil was beginning to wear down her morale, certainly her hopes. Still she could not abandon her vigil. Without him, the future was the enemy.

There was no point at attempting to search for him. Besides, he had assumed another identity. It would be impossible to find him. Besides, she had warned him of the risks. Hadn't they considered all the options? Parker, in an about-face of motivation, might take it into his head to inflict revenge on her for interfering in his business arrangements.

John Champion had, with the exception of his own unresolved fate, been right in all his predictions. Each day she had bought the International Herald Tribune for any news that might possibly be relevant to her. She had been in Florence for a week when she found it.

Under the headline HAMILTON'S LAWYER AND AS-SISTANT KILLED IN FIERY CRASH, the report told of Tom's car losing control on the M2 and crashing through a barrier. There was a reference to the death of Max Hamilton by drowning and a brief speculation on the irony of his lawyer's accidental death less than a few weeks after Hamilton's.

It took all her self-discipline not to contact her children. She cried for days after, not mourning for Tom, who had lost all relevance in her life, but for her children not having the comfort of their mother at this traumatic time for them. They would survive, she assured herself and someday, when and if the dust of her life ever settled, she would contact them again and tell her story, hoping they would understand. As for Cynthia, she wiped all thoughts of her from her mind.

Despite Champion's belief in the necessity of his staged death and his assurances to her, grave doubts were eating away at the core of her denial. Wounds were to be expected, he had explained. His assailants must truly believe that he had died. It took a leap of faith on her part to come to the same conclusion.

In retrospect, Angela could understand how his very presence, the delivery of his assurances woven within the excitement of their lovemaking, between passionate embraces, could influence her consent. She had become convinced that their love provided all the armor necessary for their protection. She should have argued against it, she thought, opting for the shorter duration. After all, didn't intensity multiply time?

Her daily visits to the Accademia resulted only in more and more disappointment. Not knowing what had happened to him was agony enough without the terrible ache of his absence. She felt helpless and alone.

She had taken a room at one of the many small pensiones that dotted the city, hardly a match in grandeur with the hotel room she had shared with Aunt Emma overlooking the Arno. Yet, it was more than adequate. Environment had no meaning for her without him. She could have lived in a hovel. All her thoughts, hopes, dreams, expectations were concentrated on his return. Her heart, mind, and body longed, ached for him.

His presence invaded her dreams where he seemed more alive than in her waking thoughts. In these dreams, she ran the gamut of emotions. Some were overwhelmingly sexual and, at times, she awoke gasping for breath, as if in post-orgasmic hysteria, her nipples aching, her genitals awash with moisture.

Her days were spent sitting on the Accademia benches near the entrance watching everyone who entered. Dominating the gallery, as if he were offering her the embrace of his protection was her marble man, the David, in whose imaginary embrace she had found fulfillment. He, too, seemed watchful, observant, searching the crowds, waiting for John Champion. To imagine this alliance was comforting, hopeful.

She knew she was the object of some curiosity by the staff

of the Accademia. They nodded politely and smiled at her, surely speculating on her motives for being there.

"We can set our clocks by you, senora," the woman who took the tickets at the entrance told her. Beyond just curiosity, she supposed she was also the object of considerable discussion spiced with gossip and ridicule.

For the first few weeks she held herself together by shutting out any thoughts about any future course of action. Not that she could conceive of any. Ahead, without him, was an infinite desert, bleak and forbidding. Without perpetual hope, she would be unable to sustain herself. Oblivion, however she got here, seemed the only viable alternative.

Occasionally, she would catch an errant glimpse of some disturbing impression of herself in the mirror. In the image, she would see despair, loss, defeat. More and more this triad was invading her consciousness.

Without him, she felt a sense of creeping death take hold of her. Was her life over? Even the echoing words of Aunt Emma, who apparently did find a life after the loss of her lover, her one true love, was not enough to revive her optimism. After all, Aunt Emma had remained Aunt Emma. And she, Angela, had taken another identity, had jettisoned her past, had willfully divorced herself from everything that had come before.

She felt no contrition, and her sense of guilt concerning her children began to fade with time. The bond remained, of course, but it had become part of her yesterdays, her old self.

She realized, too, that while passion might have been

dormant or, in her case, undiscovered, it was not dead. Having found it, she realized that within it was the essence of living. Some might call her action selfish. But then wasn't the self, her own self, the universe in which she resided. She had, indeed, entered her own dream, and she vowed to stay there until oblivion descended.

As time wore on she no longer thought much about Tom. He had become a stick figure in her mind. By then, she had forgiven herself for her blindness. What she had not known, after all, had not really existed. She had jettisoned that other life.

As the weeks of empty waiting continued and turned into months, she struggled with herself to keep her hope buttressed. She tried desperately to excise any sense of time, persuading herself that merely hours were passing, not days, weeks, months.

In an attempt to renew hope, she moved to other pensiones, sometimes two in one week. Her newly bought wardrobe was sparse and movement was simple. She tried eating in different trattorias, as if any new environment would erase the sense of time passing.

Getting through the nights proved the most difficult. Her mind spun with scenarios. Was it all really a dream? A mad fantasy? Who was John Champion? Had she invented him to give shape to Aunt Emma's suggestive powers?

She avoided people. At times a man would approach her, attempt to flirt. Her evasion was polite, although it took some effort to hide her disgust. Evenings, from dusk when the Accademia closed, to past midnight, she would aimlessly walk the streets hoping to exhaust herself.

As summer gave way to autumn and the air grew chilled with the onset of winter, her thoughts grew darker. She found herself walking across the many bridges over the Arno, stopping occasionally to contemplate the slate waters rushing to the sea. When she concentrated, she imagined she could see John in his damp grave, and it took all her willpower to tear herself away and move on.

Despite his warning, she contemplated a phone-call search of London hospitals, which reflected the last vestige of her hopes, since the implication of such an investigation was that he was still alive. But here she was hampered by ignorance. What name had he chosen from his grab bag of aliases?

She could feel herself sinking deeper and deeper into despair and hopelessness. By rote, she went to the Accademia day after day. The staff would stare brazenly now. She was certain that she had become more than just an object of curiosity, the butt of their jokes. When she heard errant laughter, she became convinced that she, her absurd constancy, her daily entrance were the comedic triggers.

Once one of the guards asked her in broken English why she came every day. Not answering, she stared him down, until he turned away in embarrassment. Eventually, even the dead eyes of her marble man seemed to mock her.

Was this her fate? she wondered. To be an object of eccentricity? Soon she could barely muster the will to break the pattern of her days. She ate without appetite, slept fitfully, tortured by dreams that were beginning to take on nightmarish qualities. In them, she would see frightening distortions, images of Champion, half man, half stone. One dream showed his broken body, his flesh in pieces, scattered on the ripples of a river, floating like raw sewage.

Around her was the season of joy as people prepared for Christmas, a birth. She could only imagine herself on the fringes of death. She felt rootless, her spirit disabled.

For the moment, though, she saw no alternative for her present role. She was doomed to wait. For how long? She doubted that she would ever find the courage to move on, find another life. There was no future.

Why had he left her alone?

Chapter 32

He lay in a white room, conscious of attachments to his body, the pulsing of machines, whispery voices hovering in the air above him, odd astringent odors.

Images of Angela continued to glide through his mind. They moved with unrelenting speed, and he was incapable of slowing them down. His only real fear was they would stop altogether.

If there was any certainty in his thoughts, it was that he had not yet died, not yet. One of the whispery voices had created a picture in his mind: a man hanging by a silver cord over an abyss.

"He's hanging by a thread," the voice had whispered.

Earlier he had felt sensations of being moved, wheels needing oiling. Then hovering between darkness and light, vague pain. More voices.

"We've removed the kidney. There's liver damage," someone said. "And the infection has spread."

"He's very weak and burning with fever."

"I'd say he's slipping."

"Have you notified his next of kin?"

"Can't be found."

He saw himself smiling.

Still Angela's image persisted, hurtling past him.

Stop, he heard himself plead, a scream in his brain, echoing. He could see his hand reach out to touch her.

Stop!

Then… it might have been later. He had no sense of time. It was she that was reaching out, and he was on the run, running as fast as he could, through dark streets, tunnels, paths through the wilderness. Running.

"Save him," her voice screamed as he ran. He tried to slow down but his legs would not allow that. "What will become of me?" It was a wail, like the wind.

Chapter 33

Still she waited. More weeks passed. She no longer paid much attention to her appearance or her clothes, wore no makeup, rarely looked at herself in the mirror. She neglected rudimentary personal hygiene. She didn't care. It was beginning to dawn on her that he was never coming, that she was doomed to an endless wait, a prospect that she knew she would be unable to endure.

There were times when she imagined she saw him, and her heartbeat would accelerate with expectation. But further observation would indicate that she was mistaken, and she would sink back into despair.

Lately, she had begun to actually confront these men of her imagination, appearing before them, searching their eyes for recognition, only to be met by confused blank stares as if she were a crazy woman.

Had she lost his image in her mind? It was just one more fear to add to all the others. To have him disappear in memory would be the ultimate loss.

As Christmas approached, the city was becoming saturated with the sound of bells, church bells, banging and clanging, tolling their Christmas tunes. She no longer paid attention to dates or time or even seasons. But there was no avoiding the tracking of days until Christmas in this Catholic city. Soon it would be Christmas.

More and more she paused when crossing the Arno on foot. Her latest pensione was on the side of Florence less trafficked by tourists. Every morning she would walk across the bridge and traverse the winding streets to the Accademia.

These days when she stopped to contemplate the river, she could no longer discern his image reflected in the waters but her own. An alternative had entered her mind, and with each passing day it grew from mere possibility to inevitability. Without him, she had no life. At least in oblivion there would be no more anxiety, no more loneliness, no more waiting, no more pain.

The idea grew in her mind until it became an obsession. What was the point of living? Throwing herself into the Arno offered a tantalizing solution, an end to the excruciating pain of separation. After all, she had had her moment.

One day, she resolved to carry out this last alternative. She would simply disappear, expire in the river, leaving no trace. The idea grew in her mind, and she became obsessed with plans for the final event.

It was impossible to sustain her vigil. She had become an object of ridicule. Finally, she could take it no longer. She gathered up all her possessions, her remaining cash, considerably diminished, her false passport, her clothes, any material trace of her life, and checked out of the pensione.

Disposing of her possessions piecemeal in trashcans along the street, she prepared herself for her obliteration. She had never been fingerprinted. No identification was possible. They would discover an anonymous bloated female corpse, perhaps half eaten by fish and unidentifiable. The act, she knew, was a violation of Aunt Emma's caveat, that memory might be enough to sustain one's sense of discovering the one true passion.

She had carefully chosen as the site for the event the least trafficked of the many bridges across the Arno. To avoid any possibility of rescue by some high-minded citizen, she planned to wait until dark to do the deed. She had deliberately picked a moonless night when she could slip unseen into the dark waters.

She had timed her actions to give her one last moment with her beloved David, on whom she had lavished so much hope and optimism.

Arriving at the Accademia near closing time, she saw the giant figure through a mist of tears. The staff regulars, she noted, eyed her with peculiar interest, as if curiosity had won over ridicule.

The bright winter sunset made the statue seem incandescent with a crystalline-white patina. The light radiated throughout the room, suffusing her with an odd sense of joy, something she had not felt for more than six months.

Rather than have this sudden changed mood dissipated by false hopes, she restrained herself from searching the faces in the crowd. Yet she could not shake a sense of anticipation. Here I am, she announced to herself. Save me, love.

But for all her posturing and silly hopefulness, nothing happened. Once again, her expectation was fantasy. Exhausted by frustration and disappointment, she sat on one of the stone benches near the entrance waiting for the gallery to close and send her to her fate.

Had she taken the wrong fork in the road? Many wrong forks? If she had never gone to Florence, never tried to nourish a relationship with Aunt Emma, never been confronted by the power of the David, never allowed any conversation with John that night at the bar in the Bel Air, never lied about her meeting with Mrs. Hamilton and her daughters, never gone away with John, she would not be here now, bereft, alone without a past or a future.

Had her life before John Champion been of so little consequence that it begged for destruction? Wasn't it commonplace for people to live perfectly acceptable lives through dissimulation, dishonesty, and hypocrisy, without passion or love? Certainly creature comforts, luxury, possessions, pampering, and wealth could insulate people from pain, anxiety, and hardship. Banality, as she had learned in that other life, was safe.

Hadn't she attained a kind of contentment, through the exercise of compromise, toleration, and denial? Even the false devotion she had received from Tom had a tangible reality she could live with. Lies, after all, were a matter of perception. People survived securely with blandness. Too much emotion was dangerous. What was wrong with tranquility?

Had the attainment of grand passion, sexual ecstasy, and the transforming power of love been worth the astounding price she had paid for it? The question, like an aura, hung in the air around her.

But before she could venture an answer, her glance was

suddenly arrested by the outline of a man among the spectators viewing the David. His back was turned toward her, but his head was raised as if he were inspecting the statue's face. Yes, the man was vaguely familiar.

Perhaps he sensed that he was being scrutinized. He began to turn. His image came to her like a film in slow motion. Was it really John this time?

He turned full face toward her. She stood up and watched him approach her, slowly, as if taking steps were difficult. He was thin, his skin pale, almost as white as the statue. As he drew nearer, she stepped forward moving to meet him. Was she merely imagining him, allowing herself the last brief flicker of hope, like the final gasp of flame from a dying candle?

But when he touched her, she knew the truth of it. She fell into his embrace and, despite his sickly look, she felt the old strength of him. They kissed deeply and without shame, ignoring the curiosity of the crowd that surged around them.

She moved to study his face. Her hands stroked his cheek as if she needed to validate her presence with her touch, like a blind person.

"Is it really you?" she whispered, fearful that she might be imagining him.

"I was about to ask you the same question. For a moment there I thought I was still hallucinating."

"It must have been awful."

"Nobody gets born without pain, my love."

"Yes," she nodded. "I know."

He took one of her hands and put it over his heart. "As

you can feel, my heart remains where you left it."

She felt the pumping, the sense of life in him. For the first time in months, she laughed with joy and watched his face through a crystal mist, as she moved his hand to her lips and kissed his palm.

"We're home safe now," he said.

"Home?"

"Wherever you are, darling? That's home."

"Limbo wasn't much fun, John Champion," she said.

"I know what you mean. I spent a lifetime there."

"Half," she said, feeling girlish again. "Half a lifetime. The other half belongs to me."

Arms around each other, they moved toward the gallery's exit.

But before they went through the exit door, she turned, looked toward the David again. For a brief moment, his eyes seemed to come to life, the lips of his mouth turned upward in a smile, and his head moved. She turned away, determined to retain the image forever.

For complete catalogue including novels, plays, and short stories visit: *www.warrenadler.com*

If you enjoyed this title, do leave a review on *Goodreads*.

Connect with Warren Adler on:

Facebook—*www.facebook.com/warrenadler*
Twitter—*www.twitter.com/warrenadler*

Also by Warren Adler

FICTION

Banquet Before Dawn
Blood Ties
Cult
Empty Treasures
Flanagan's Dolls
Funny Boys
Madeline's Miracles
Mourning Glory
Natural Enemies
Private Lies
Random Hearts
Residue
Target Churchill
The Casanova Embrace
The David Embrace
The Henderson Equation
The Housewife Blues
The Serpent's Bite
The War of the Roses
The Children of the Roses
The Womanizer
Torture Man
Trans-Siberian Express
Treadmill
Twilight Child
Undertow
We are Holding the President Hostage

THE FIONA FITZGERALD MYSTERY SERIES

American Quartet
American Sextet
Death of a Washington Madame
Immaculate Deception
Red Herring
Senator Love
The Ties that Bind
The Witch of Watergate
Washington Masquerade

SHORT STORY COLLECTIONS

Jackson Hole: Uneasy Eden
Never Too Late for Love
New York Echoes 1
New York Echoes 2
The Sunset Gang
The Washington Dossier Diaries

PLAYS

Dead in the Water
Libido
The Sunset Gang: The Musical
The War of the Roses
Windmills

About the Author

Acclaimed author, playwright, poet, and essayist **Warren Adler** is best known for *The War of the Roses*, his masterpiece fictionalization of a macabre divorce adapted into the BAFTA- and Golden Globe–nominated hit film starring Danny DeVito, Michael Douglas, and Kathleen Turner.

Adler has also optioned and sold film rights for a number of his works, including **Random Hearts** (starring Harrison Ford and Kristen Scott Thomas) and **The Sunset Gang** (produced by Linda Lavin for PBS's American Playhouse series starring Jerry Stiller, Uta Hagen, Harold Gould, and Doris Roberts), which garnered Doris Roberts an Emmy nomination for Best Supporting Actress in a Miniseries. In recent development is the Broadway production of *The War of the Roses* as well as a number of film adaptations in development with Grey Eagle Films including **The Children of the Roses, Target Churchill, Residue, Mourning Glory,** and **Capitol Crimes,** a television series based on his Fiona Fitzgerald mystery series. Find out more details about all film/TV developments at www.Greyeaglefilms.com

Adler's works have been translated into more than 25 languages, including his staged version of *The War of the Roses*, which has opened to spectacular reviews worldwide. Adler has taught creative writing seminars at New York University, and has lectured on creative writing, film and television adaptation, and electronic publishing. He lives with his wife, Sunny, a former magazine editor, in Manhattan.

Printed in Great Britain
by Amazon

39986186R00219